Siamak Herawi

# Tali Girls

Translated from the Farsi by
Sara Khalili

*archipelago books*

ISBN 9781953861665
Library of Congress Cataloging-in-Publication Data available upon request.

Archipelago Books
232 3rd Street #A111
Brooklyn, NY 11215
www.archipelagobooks.org

Distributed by Penguin Random House
www.penguinrandomhouse.com

This work is made possible by the New York State Council on the Arts with the support of
the Office of the Governor and the New York State Legislature. Funding for the translation
of this book was provided by a grant from the Carl Lesnor Family Foundation.

This publication was made possible with support from Jan Michalski Foundation,
Lannan Foundation, the National Endowment for the Arts, the Nimick Forbesway
Foundation and the New York City Department of Cultural Affairs.

PRINTED IN CANADA

# TALI GIRLS

This story is based on the lives of Kowsar and Simin. *Tali Girls* is dedicated to the girls and women of Afghanistan.

# 1

I WILL START with my childhood. From the time I was three years old. I will speak of my earliest memories, of ants that crawl up the wall in columns and now and then stop to lock horns. They frighten me, I scream, I break into a fever, and everything fades into gray. It is difficult to describe how the world around me turns hazy and gray. Visualize a girl struck with such fright that she breaks into a burning fever, convulses, and loses consciousness. At times, she hallucinates. Perhaps of horrors beyond her young imagination. As a small child, dogs, cats, even people sometimes frighten me.

One day, the old man of the neighborhood stops when he sees me with Mother and smiles. He walks across the way and kneels in front of me. "Kowsar," he says, "you are so sweet. I could eat you!" I scream and hide under Mother's chador. I start to shake and my gray world sets in. I again see the old man. He is wearing a grimy lungee and his coarse beard is sticking out in every direction. His eyes are sunken and bloodshot. He kneels in front of me and grins. "Kowsar, I could eat you," he whispers. Then he opens his foul-smelling mouth, licks my face and digs his sharp yellow teeth into my cheek. With no resistance, I surrender to him. When all that remains are my bones, the old man licks his moustache and walks away laughing.

Mother picks me up and cradles me in her arms. "Oh, my girl!" she says, feeling my forehead. "It's the fainting spell again." And she hurries home.

"Mobin Khan, Kowsar fainted again. One of these days she'll stop breathing. When are you going to take her to a mullah or a doctor?"

Father, busy mixing hay and weeds near the sheep hold, stops, glances at her, and goes back to mixing his hay and weeds.

"Wife, it's nothing new. She's had it since she was little. They say it's epilepsy. Leave her be. We were seven brothers, disease killed until only two of us remained. Lucky the ones who died. We're only fooling ourselves that we are grateful being alive."

"Husband! She's helpless. It doesn't please God to let her suffer. Back then children died because there were no doctors, no medicine. These days people don't die that easily."

"Wife! Doctors and medicine cost money. Where's the money? If I start selling the sheep, how would I make a living?"

"Then take her to a mullah. They say there's a new one in Jawand who has healing powers. Take her to him. He can cure her with prayers and incantations."

"Mullahs don't heal for free! But, fine, I'll take her. I'll have the

2

man chant and do whatever he does to cure your daughter. Happy now? . . . It's almost time to harvest and thresh the wheat. When that's done, I'll take a sack of grain and sell it, so I can buy some tea and candied sugar. Now stop pestering me. Go brew a pot of tea, I'm vexed and exhausted."

Mother sighs and turns back. She feels my forehead again. The fever is gone. There's cold sweat on my brow.

After the wheat is harvested and threshed, Father ties a burlap sack of grain on our donkey and takes me by the hand to bring me to the mullah. We live in Tali, a village in a deep valley surrounded by mountains with tall peaks and massive boulders that in the morning and afternoon act as barriers against the sun. Our valley is green and lush, drunk with springs, waterfalls, and streams that intricately weave their way to where they meet and create a roaring mountain river. You can see schools of red- and cream-colored fish playfully swimming between the azure rocks, relishing their togetherness. The birds of our region are colorful and sweet singing. At dawn, they wake each other by chirping and with sunrise they fly off, going in flocks from one orchard to another, from one field to another.

The girls of Tali are beautiful. They have long wavy hair, large almond shaped eyes, and skin the color of wheat. They grow up learning to cook and sew. At seven, some are taught to embroider, as well. They stitch and seam and sing together. And when they reach puberty, they fall in love with the sunburned boys who wear their skullcaps cocked to the side and play their reed flute as they scale the mountains shepherding goats and sheep and stealing young girls' hearts.

Father takes me to the bazaar in Jawand. It's a two-hour walk from Tali. Rows of shops and stalls flank the dirt road crowded by shoppers and traders. Father sells his wheat, shakes the burlap sack, and throws it over the donkey, and we go to leave it at the stables behind the bazaar. Then Father asks around about the mullah. A man shows him the way.

Two rooms with a small, crooked door connecting them. In the first room, a dozen or so men and women are sitting along the walls on a threadbare rug. Some are moaning, grunting, others look so sulky and surly that it seems misery and pain have robbed them of the air to breathe. We sit in a corner, and I keep my head down to avoid looking anyone in the eye. There are strange sounds coming from the other room. A man is talking in a nasal voice that constantly fluctuates in pitch and volume. Now and then he shouts and loudly puffs, "*Choof!*" I shrink closer to Father and sneak under his jacket to not hear him, but I do.

We wait a long time for our turn. The adjacent room is dimly lit. At first, I see nothing. Father says hello and the nasal voice returns his greeting and tells us to sit. As my eyes grow accustomed to the light, I see the mullah. He's wearing a white lungee and his bushy beard is salt and pepper. He is sitting cross-legged behind a small low table with a few old books, white and yellow sheets of paper, and a pen arranged on it.

"Tell me," he says.

"Mullah Sahib," Father replies, "I've brought my daughter for you to heal her."

"What's wrong with her?"

"She has these spells. She breaks into a fever, shakes, and faints."

"Five hundred afghanis."

Father swallows hard and stammers, "Five hundred? That's a lot! Mullah Sahib, we're villagers, not from around here. Have some consideration."

"Very well," the mullah grouses. "Four hundred will do. Put it on the table."

Father fidgets and mumbles, "A hundred afghanis, praise God the merciful."

The mullah, impatient and in a hurry, glares at him and puts an end to the haggling.

"Put it on the table."

Father takes his money from of his pocket and in between the old bills finds a new one hundred afghani and lays it on the table.

"Name?"

"Whose name?"

"The girl's!"

"Kowsar."

"Bring her closer."

Father picks me up and sits me down next to the mullah. There's a dagger with a curved blade sitting on the floor between us. He takes it and holds it up in front of him.

"I seek refuge with God from the accursed Satan," he shouts, slashing through the air with the dagger. "In the name of God the Almighty. . . . *Choof!*"

His voice sinks deep inside me, his words seep into my veins. I stare at the blade gleaming in the air and feel the drops of spit flying onto my face. I start to tremble and I fall on my side. All is quiet in my gray world. I float from my body and watch as the mullah severs my limbs and arranges them on the table. Drops of blood splash on his beard and stain his white shirt.

"Her arms and legs are yours," he says to Father. "Take them and leave. I'll keep the rest of her."

Father holds up the front of his long tunic shirt like a cradle, piles my limbs in it, and hurries out.

Outside, I find myself in his arms. I squint against the sun beating down over the town and feel cold sweat trickling down behind my ears.

"Father's dearest," he says. "Can you hear me?"

I nod.

"The mullah chanted an incantation and wrote a prayer on a piece of paper. He said your mother should soak it in a glass of water and you need to drink it morning and night for seven days. And you'll be cured, sound and strong."

I don't understand what he said about the mullah, but I do understand seven days and seven nights and being cured. Father walks along the row of shops, stopping now and then to look at their wares. The clamor and commotion are unnerving to me. The crush of people looks like a jumble of lines moving every which way. I long for the comfort of Mother's hand stroking my hair as I laze on her lap.

Father walks into a shop and puts me down, and after a lengthy and at times heated bargaining, he buys a pair of shoes and a coat for Farrokh and some tea and candied sugar. Before packing them in the saddlebag slung over his shoulder, he opens the bag of candied sugar and gives one to me.

Overjoyed, I ask, "May I eat it now?"

"Yes, my girl," he says, smiling at me. "And I have a little money left, let's go and buy a new dress for you."

As the candy melts in my mouth, its sweetness intensifies. I remember the last time I had one. It was three months ago. A few women from the village up north had come to visit Mother. She had put on her nice purple dress with embroidery around the collar and sleeves and on the cuff of the matching loose pants that gather at her ankles. She was happy, fluttering around to please her guests. She quickly brewed tea and rinsed and dried the china tea bowls she keeps on the top shelf in the alcove. Then she went to her trunk and took out a bag of white and yellow candied sugar she had hidden under her clothes. She put some on a plate and brought it in on the tea tray.

"You have honored us and brought us joy with your visit," she said as she put the tray on the floor in front of her guests.

I could not tear my eyes away from the candied sugar. I desperately wanted one of each color. When Mother noticed me staring, she took a white one and put it in my hand. "Now go and play," she said, walking me to our second room. "I'll call you when they have left."

I paid no attention to her. All I could think of was the taste of the stale candy crumbling into powder between my teeth.

Father picks out a red dress with flowers on it.

"Do you like it?"

I don't want to think about anything other than the candy, but Father is persistent.

"My girl, do you like this one?"

I don't like red, it's the color of blood. I shake my head and he returns it to the shopkeeper.

"Show me another color."

The shopkeeper gives him a green dress and Father holds it up against me for size.

"How about this one?"

I nod.

He pays the shopkeeper and opens his arms wide for me.

"You're still a bit pale," he says as I leap into his arms. "But I can't carry you all the way home. With the wheat sold, we can ride the donkey." I cling to his neck, and he tenderly kisses me on the cheek. "You're going to get well, my girl. The mullah was imposing and practiced."

I don't want to think about that man and his dagger, though, when I'm with Father, which isn't often, I am brave and rarely suffer attacks. At home, I'm mostly alone. Father spends his days tending to the sheep and his small farmland, and Mother is busy baking at the kiln, cooking at the stove, or sweeping the rooms. Farrokh, who is two years older than me, is out every day playing with his friends. Their feet are always callused and chapped, and their pockets are always full of glass and stone marbles or sheep ankle bones they use to play a game.

Father takes the donkey out of the stable, tosses the saddlebag over it, and holding me tight, he steps up on a rock and carefully mounts. The chaos slowly fades into silence as we ride away. I desperately want another candied sugar, but Father is sitting on the saddlebag.

"My girl," he says. "When we're down in the valley, I will sit you in front of me and you can hold on to the saddlebag. All right?"

"No!"

"Don't be scared!" he chuckles. "I'll hold you."

I smile. He beams with joy. It has been a long time since he has seen me smile.

"God be praised, the mullah is a healer. There's already some color in your face."

From the cliff above the valley, we take the steep and rocky trail down to the village. Soon, I can hear the long-tailed black nightingales singing in the poplar trees. I remember the day Farrokh brought home one of their chicks. Like all of them, it had a patch of white on its breast and large, round eyes. It had yet to turn jet black and could hardly fly.

"You shouldn't have taken it from its mother," I said. "Take it back to its home!"

"That's none of your business!" he snapped. "I like it. And it will get used to it here."

For a few days, Farrokh had time for nothing but his nightingale and catching grasshoppers for it to eat. Until one morning when I woke up to him screaming. The bird's feathers were scattered all over the carpet. The neighbor's cat had caught it and run off.

His face pale, Farrokh shouted, "It's all your fault, Mother! You left the porch door open. . . . My poor little chick. If I get my hands on that cat, I'll kill it!"

Mother, knowing no words would calm him, said nothing. She went to the kitchen, came back with a bowl of dough, and went out on the porch to make noodles.

Our mud house, though small and humble like all the others in the village, can be seen from the middle of the valley. Father built it on top of a hill below a towering boulder and above a cluster of homes. No one lives on the wide stretch of verdant land bordering the river. The villagers farm there. But on the cream and gray slopes at the foot of the mountains, wherever there is a stream, there are mud houses. Every morning, girls and women go to fill their buckets and haul back the day's supply of water.

I see Mother on the stoop outside the front door.

"Father, look!" I say excitedly. "It's Mother."

"Yes, it's her," he says *heying* the donkey up the hill. "You have sharp eyes, Kowsar."

"And there's the black cat! Over there, on the neighbor's wall."

"May God save it from Farrokh's wrath," he chuckles. "This cat is doomed."

As we ride up to the house, Mother comes and holds the donkey as Father hops down with me in his arms.

"Kowsar was a very good girl today," he says. "She told me stories all the way home. From the moment the mullah said his prayers, she changed. You'd never believe she's the same girl."

"Praise to God!" Mother sighs with relief, covering me with kisses. "When my girl is well again, I'll sacrifice a lamb as alms for the poor. What good would a wretch see in her life, if even her childhood is nothing but pain and suffering."

"Wife, I'm so hungry, my innards are going at each other," Father says, leading the donkey into the yard. "Get me a bite to eat."

❧

I am well for only a day. No fever, convulsions, or hallucinations. The following morning, I see the black cat again, and for hours I cannot stop visualizing how it must have snatched the nightingale chick and torn into it with its claws and fangs, until I start to convulse, and I collapse.

When I open my eyes, Mother and Father are kneeling next to me, one looking more despairing than the other.

Incantations and water in which the mullah's prayer has soaked don't cure me, and four years pass. My life changes when I turn eight. I'm no longer lonely. I now have a friend who lives next door. Geesu has curly, light chestnut hair and bright hazel eyes. She is good at making dolls with pieces of scrap fabric and draws faces for them with a pen. She teaches me how to make them, too. Sometimes we make boy dolls and have wedding ceremonies.

My episodes of what Mother still believes are fainting spells and Father assumes are epilepsy seizures decrease. I feel healthier, happier.

There is great commotion in Tali one morning. Word quickly spreads that several representatives of the provincial government have come. They gather the villagers around and explain that Badghis's Department of Education has plans for a school in the village. They will fund and build it if the men approve.

The men are divided. Some agree, others don't. A fierce debate follows.

Nadim Khan, one of the handful of educated men in Tali, is adamant that the school should be built.

"This is the twenty-first century!" he shouts out to the crowd. "The year 2006! Villages and towns in this province still have no electricity, no plumbing for water, no paved roads. We have no doctors, no medicine! At least let our children go to school and grow up literate and educated."

"No!" Mullah Sikhdad cries flushed with anger. "Our children will be corrupted. They will grow up faithless sinners!"

The battle of words between the two sides continues for several days, until Mullah Sikhdad is offered a salary and the position of school principal. With his blessing, the villagers select a parcel of land in the middle of the valley and construction begins. It takes a year for the school to be built and for tables and benches, books and blackboards to arrive.

And on an unforgettable sunny morning, Geesu and I walk to school.

# 2

"Teacher Sahib, may I?" Kowsar asks, standing in the doorway with a broad smile across her lips.

"No you may not, Kowsar! Why are you late?"

"My turkey chick ran away, Teacher Sahib. I had to find it and take it back home."

She has hardly finished her sentence when a turkey starts gobbling in the schoolyard, and the class erupts in laughter.

"You idiot!" Kowsar grumbles under her breath.

"What did you say!?"

"Nothing, Teacher Sahib."

"Kowsar!" he snaps, getting up from behind his desk. "Why did you bring it to school?"

"Teacher Sahib, my turkey chick has no mother," she says, walking to her seat and shoving her bundle of books under the table. "A wolf got to it. At home, it gobbles all day. I thought if I bring it to school, it won't be sad and lonely."

"This is a school, Kowsar, not a barn for your animals!"

"Then why don't you scold Farhad? He brought his goats to school."

"What is this I'm hearing?" Teacher Sadeq says, rushing to the window.

Seeing Farhad's goats up in the schoolyard tree, already stripped of leaves and bark, he slaps his forehead and shouts, "Farhad! Get out there and do something!"

As the teacher stands at the window, watching Farhad clamber up the tree and coax his goats to climb down, the students sit in silence, not daring to provoke him even more by laughing and whispering to each other.

When Farhad returns, sweating and flushed with anger, Kowsar looks back at him and grins.

"I'm not done with you," he hisses, stroking his chin.

Kowsar giggles and turns away.

"This school belongs to all of us," Teacher Sadeq says, still looking out the window. "We have to take care of it with heart and soul. That young tree cast a shadow, year after year it would grow, and on hot days we could sit in its shade. But alas, what a terrible thing has happened."

Kowsar peeks back at Farhad. He is wallowing in shame.

"Teacher Sahib," she says. "It's not Farhad's fault. His mother went to the mountains for firewood and there was no one to take his goats to pasture."

"So he had to bring them here to eat the school's young tree?"

"That tree has nothing to do with the school," Farhad says with newfound courage. "It belongs to Village Chief Abed. Our school doesn't have any trees of its own."

"Even worse! If Abed Khan finds out one of my student's goats stripped his tree, he will blame me. He will say, what kind of education are you giving these children if they have no respect and show no pity for other people's property!"

"Teacher Sahib, in God's truth, I left them by the river. They followed me here."

"You should have brought them to class to learn the alphabet!" Zolfaghar cracks from the back row.

The students titter and quickly stop, seeing the teacher's frown grow deeper.

"Thank God Mullah Sikhdad didn't see them," Teacher Sadeq says. "Otherwise, he would have gone after them with a knife."

"Oh, no! My turkey stopped gobbling!" Kowsar screams, tearing out of the classroom. "What if Mullah cut off its head!?"

"You snitch!" Farhad growls running after her and grabbing her arm in the hallway. "Are you happy you got me into trouble?"

Don't be afraid, don't go gray, he won't hurt you, Kowsar repeats to herself. Don't be afraid, don't go gray, he won't hurt you . . .

"Yes, I am! I am happy I did it," she says defiantly, yanking her arm out of his grip. "You don't scare me!"

Farhad looks at her for a moment, then mumbling under his breath, shoves her aside and walks away. Shaken but relieved, Kowsar finds her turkey chick wandering behind the schoolhouse. She runs home with it and returns to school. Farhad doesn't.

"Kowsar!" her mother calls out at night. "Kowsar! Come to the door, Farhad is here."

"What does he want?" she shouts, looking up from her homework. "To get back at me?"

"Kowsar! Did you hear me?"

"Yes, Mother, I heard you," she says, running across the yard.

"What do you want?" she snaps at Farhad, standing out on the road.

"What did the teacher assign for homework?"

"For you or your goats?"

"For your turkey!"

Kowsar giggles, "I'm almost finished. Wait here. I'll bring it for you."

"Hurry up, Snitch!"

"Wait, Sponger!"

❦

Teacher Sadeq is a good-natured young man with a short, neatly trimmed beard, thick wavy hair, and gentle eyes. He is from Qala-e-

Naw and Chief Abed has provided him with lodging in the village. It doesn't take long for everyone to grow to like and respect the teacher. And soon, Chief Abed invites him to join the group of elders and learned men who regularly come together in his guestroom for a few hours of talk among friends.

At the end of each month, Teacher Sadeq goes home to see his family and comes back with stories for his students about the town, its people, and his six-year-old son Assem. And for the men, he brings news of the war between the Taliban and American forces in the eastern provinces of Helmand, Kandahar, Ghazni, and Kunar. He talks of the increasing number of suicide bombings that leave hundreds of Afghans and their children dead and wounded and worries that the Taliban might make their way to the western provinces and bring their ideologies and the war with them.

The men gathered in Chief Abed's guestroom know this would extinguish the small glimmer of hope people have for a better life. They contemplate the Taliban's extremist view of Sharia law and their practice of barbaric punishments. At night, they quietly share the news and their apprehensions with their wives.

The women worry and whisper to each other. They fear losing the freedom to work outside their homes and on their farms. They fear losing the freedom to leave their house unaccompanied, and the freedom to dress as they wish. They fear for their daughters. They have only now started to learn to read and write.

Kowsar has incredible aptitude. Teacher Sadeq and her classmates are astounded by how quickly she learns. In three months, she can read and write, and soon she has learned and memorized her arithmetic, Persian, and geography schoolbooks. In awe of her mind and photographic memory, Teacher Sadeq often calls on her in class and asks her impossible questions.

"What is the lesson on page eleven of the geography book?"

Kowsar closes her eyes, is silent for a moment, then word for word recites the text.

Convinced that she is an exceptional child, the teacher concludes that this far-flung valley is no place for her.

"May God reward you with goodness," Mullah Sikhdad says indifferently when the teacher tells him about Kowsar.

"Well, what can we do for her? We cannot allow her genius to be wasted here."

"Give her more difficult books."

The next day, Teacher Sadeq gives Kowsar the second grade's schoolbooks.

"Take these and read them, Kowsar."

Scarcely two weeks later, she returns the books.

"I read them, Teacher Sahib."

No longer astonished, he tests her on each subject, and true to his expectation, she answers every question correctly.

"You must have educated parents," he says. "Do they help you study?"

"No, Teacher Sahib. Mother and Father can't read and write."

The teacher is silent for a while, then says, "Kowsar, when you go home, tell your father I will come to see him tonight."

"Really!?"

"Yes, really."

"I will ask Mother to cook *eshkeneh* soup," Kowsar says excitedly.

"No, my dear, I won't stay for dinner. I will just come for tea. It's important that I talk to your father."

"So I'll tell her to brew tea. But I don't think we have any candied sugar."

"That's alright."

"We don't have any green tea either."

"That's fine. I prefer black tea."

After school, Kowsar runs all the way home and bursts into the kitchen.

"Good thing you came home quickly, my girl," Golrokh says. "Go put your books away and come start the cookstove. Your father has a cold. His chest is congested. I'm making *khalwak* for him."

"But Mother—"

"There's no *but*. Hurry up!"

Worried that her father might turn away the teacher, Kowsar hurries across the yard to the house and finds him in his bedding with the blanket pulled over his head.

"Go, my girl," he says, pushing the blanket away. "Go, or you'll catch it, too."

"Father, my teacher is coming to see you tonight."

"Why?"

"He said he wants to talk to you."

"He's welcome," Mobin Khan says, sniffling. "Hopefully your mother's hearty noodle soup will have me back on my feet. And it's only right that we invite him for dinner one night. He's away from home, and a generous well-intentioned man. Now go, Kowsar," he says, burying his head under the blanket again.

In the soot-covered kitchen across the yard, Kowsar quickly grabs an armful of the dry twigs and branches piled in a corner and puts it in the cookstove's furnace. The sooner Father has his bowl of soup, the sooner he will feel well enough to see the teacher.

"Wait, Kowsar," Golrokh says. "Wait until I'm done with the dough before you start the fire."

"Which pot do you want?"

"The one that has a lid."

Kowsar takes the copper pot from the cupboard and puts it on the cookstove, then squats down next to her mother and watches as the heels of her hands rhythmically knead the dough on the white flour-dusted cloth. Golrokh looks at Kowsar and her mind drifts to a bitter winter day when she sat and watched her mother cook. The snow had started the night before. Everyone was sitting around the *sandali*, cozy and warm under the heavy blanket spread over a low table with a brazier of hot coals underneath it.

"Wife," her father said. "Make some *mashawa*. It's good on a day as cold as this."

Golrokh remembers how her mother flushed with anger but said nothing. She only sighed and said, "Golrokh, go put on your warm coat."

Together they plowed a path across the yard, and in the cold kitchen she huddled down, tucked her head in her coat collar, and prayed that her mother would quickly prepare the ingredients and start the fire in the cookstove.

"My girl, I'll grind, you slowly pour in the wheat," her mother said as she brought the hand mill and took a bowl of wheat from the clay grain vessel.

Golrokh nodded, filled her small fist with wheat, and from the crook of her hand slowly poured it into the mill's opening as her mother turned the crank. The millstones crushed the grains with a piercing sound, spat out the chaff, and released the flour unto the white cloth spread under the mill.

"Mother, what's *mashawa* made with?"

"Meat, wheat, peas, mung beans, turmeric, onions . . . And when it's done, you garnish it with *qurut*, the whey curd I make."

She paused for a moment, then said, "Golrokh, watch me and learn for the day your husband tells you to get up and go cook *mashawa*."

Golrokh tucked her head deeper in her collar and said nothing.

Feeding grains to the mill, she stared at her mother's work-worn hands shivering from the cold as they turn the crank. They didn't look like they belonged to her young, angular face with bright hazel eyes and delicate eyebrows that met on the bridge of her nose. There was a tattoo of a crescent moon slightly above them on her forehead and another one of a star on her chin.

"Mother," Golrokh said. "You have a moon on your forehead and a star on your chin. Where's your sun?"

"My girl," she said, without taking her eyes away from the mill. "My sun set the day they gave me to a husband."

Golrokh stared at the mill, and somewhere in the rasps and shrieks of the stones was her mother's voice.

"I was a child. I knew nothing of keeping house and husband when they put my hand in Mohammad Khan's hand. He brought me to this house, and this kitchen became my place."

Golrokh looks at Kowsar and digs her hands deeper into the dough. She remembers how her mother's words instilled in her a sense of foreboding that gnawed at her soul until the day her father

24

came home and announced, "Wife, I have pledged Golrokh's hand in marriage."

"When was the last time you cooked *khalwak*, Mother?"

Golrokh knits her eyebrows, narrows her eyes, and thinks.

"It was a few years ago. I think that time, too, your father had a cold. . . . Pay attention and learn for when you're a wife. Start the stove and put half a ladle of oil in the pot."

"I think I remember," Koswar says as she strikes a match and tosses it in the cookstove's furnace. "You put a green bowl in front of me, and said, 'Eat this. You sound hoarse, too.'"

"May God forgive our sins!" Golrokh says, shaking her head. "You hear things that make you feel dumb. I can't even remember my morning tea."

The twigs and branches crackle in the furnace and the oil sizzles in the pot. Under Golrokh's watchful eye, Kowsar peels and chops an onion and a few cloves of garlic. All the while worried that her mother is teaching her to cook because Father has decided to give her to a husband.

"Mother, I don't want to go to a husband," she says quietly. "I want to go to school."

"Scared?" Golrokh teases. "Don't worry, the minute a man finds out about your fainting spells, he has two legs, he'll borrow two more, and run off as fast as he can!"

Stirring the onion and garlic that have turned a pale gold, she says, "Listen, Kowsar, a wretch has no voice of her own. No one will ask for her consent. She marries when the man of the house says so. And then she breeds and cooks and cleans. It is life, my dear."

"Mother, stop saying these things! I don't like it."

"I didn't like it either. But before I knew it, they married me to Mobin Khan."

"Well, thank God they didn't marry you to someone else. Father is a good man. I love him."

"Bring the turmeric and put just a pinch in the pot. Then we can add the water."

Kowsar sprinkles the turmeric in the pot and goes to fill a metal bowl from the water bucket next to the drain. The aroma of the seasoned fried onion and garlic fills the air. She slowly adds the water and listens as the sizzle of the oil gives way to the hiss of steam and the pop of vapor bubbles. With the other ingredients added, mother and daughter sit waiting by the stove on upside down buckets. Golrokh thinks, I hope Farrokh will come home by the time the *khalwak* is ready, and Kowsar frets over her teacher's visit.

"Mother, do we have any candied sugar?"

"Candied sugar!?"

"For the tea tray. My teacher is coming tonight."

"For dinner?" Golrokh asks in a panic.

"No, just for tea. He said he wants to talk to Father."

"We could have invited him to stay for dinner if we had a decent meal to offer."

"Do you have any candied sugar stashed away?"

"No. Your Father hasn't gone to Jawand in a while," Golrokh says, then suddenly sits up and exclaims, "There's the turkey! Tell your father to invite the teacher for dinner Friday night."

"No, Mother! I won't let you! I won't let you kill my turkey chick. Cook something else, cook *eshkeneh* soup for him."

"No one cooks *eshkeneh* for a guest! It's not proper."

"Why?"

"There is no *why*! We eat *eshkeneh* when all we have is onions, eggs, and flour. It's food for the poor."

Feeling low, Kowsar unfolds the napkin the dough has been resting in and holds it up as her mother pinches off small lumps, rolls them between the palm of her hands, and tosses them in the pot.

"Some people like larger noodles with a hole in the middle. Others, like me, make short rolls. I'll make a few large ones for you and Farrokh."

"It doesn't matter what shape they are, they all taste the same," Kowsar mutters. "May I ask Geesu's mother for some candied sugar?"

"No, my girl, she doesn't have any either," Golrokh says, making a hole in the last chunk of dough with her index finger. "I was there yesterday. Akbar Khan's wife had come to visit. Geesu's mother served tea with nothing sweet. If she had candied sugar, she would have brought it."

Koswar quietly folds the napkin in four and puts it away.

"So now you know how to make *khalwak*," Golrokh says, tasting the soup and stirring it one last time.

"Take a bowl for Father, and pour some for us, Mother. Farrokh is coming."

"There's still no sign of him. That boy doesn't come quietly. The entire neighborhood hears him."

"Mother!? Where are you?" Farrokh shouts as the front door crashes against the mud wall. "Give me a bite to eat before I faint from hunger!"

"In the name of God!" Golrokh prays, staring at Kowsar. "There is no power greater than that of the Almighty."

"Farrokh," Kowsar screams, running into the yard. "My teacher is coming here tonight. He wants to talk to Father about me."

Driving the sheep into the hold, he shrugs and says, "So what. Bring the watering can. I'm covered with dust, climbing up and down the hills with these damn sheep."

―◆―

In early autumn, the evenings are brisk and the air rejuvenating. When the sun sets behind the mountains, a breeze cooled by Ab-e

28

Pudah lake weaves its way through the peaks and valleys and drifts into Tali. It brushes through the poplar, willow, and ash trees, blows in through open windows, and carries away the lingering heat of the day.

Teacher Sadeq arrives after evening prayers. Having enjoyed his walk to the song of the frogs and crickets along the riverbank, he beams, "Mobin Khan, what a location you picked for your house, the entire village is at your feet!"

Mobin Khan, somewhat restored after a steaming bowl of *khalwak* and a pot of hollyhock and jujube tea, holds up the kerosene lamp and squints.

"Yes, it's me, Sadeq!"

"Welcome, man of God! Come in. This student of yours is driving me mad. She won't sit still, constantly asking, 'Where is Teacher Sadeq? Why hasn't Teacher Sadeq come?'"

"It seems she likes her teacher!"

"You make a friend; you're stuck for life!" Mobin Khan says, lighting their way across the yard. "As soon as Mullah Sikhdad chants morning *azan*, she leaps out of bed, goes through her lessons, gulps down her tea and counts the minutes until Geesu comes for them to walk to school. As early as it may be, she still thinks it's too late."

Standing politely on the porch, Kowsar and Farrokh watch the yellow glow sway on the ground, growing longer, then shorter.

"Salaam!" they say in unison.

"Salaam, Kowsar. Are you well?"

She timidly looks down.

"Say, I'm well, and I hope you are well, too," her father says.

Kowsar only giggles.

"And who is this young man?"

"My son, Farrokh. He is two years older than Kowsar," Mobin Khan says as he opens the door and holds the curtain aside. Teacher Sadeq takes off his shoes and walks in with Kowsar and Farrokh quietly following him.

"Please," Mobin Khan says, motioning to the floor cushion at the head of the room. "You are most welcome in our home."

Sitting by the door with Farrokh, Kowsar worries how bare the copper tea tray will look without a bowl of candied sugar. What if Teacher Sadeq doesn't like his tea unsweetened? Her father, sitting farther away from the teacher than is customary, apologizes and, still sounding congested, explains that he is suffering from a cold. Kowsar anxiously looks at him. Every time he wheezes, she imagines the germs rising from his throat and floating in the air. What if Father is not able to sit with the teacher long enough for her to learn what he has come to say?

"What did you say your son's name is?"

"Farrokh."

"A lovely name. May God make him an honorable man. . . . Well, Farrokh Khan, what do you do?"

Not allowing his son a moment to speak, Mobin Khan says, "With your blessing, we have a few sheep that he shepherds and takes to pasture every day. He's my crutch, my right hand, that's why I didn't send him to school with Kowsar."

"If only you would, Mobin Khan. In this day and age, it's a shame for such a fine young prince to remain illiterate."

"Yes, I know, Teacher Sahib. If anyone were to get anywhere and gain anything from raising sheep and plowing the land, I would have gotten somewhere and gained something. I have spent my life toiling in these mountains, but my one loaf of bread has not become two."

The teacher looks squarely at him and shakes his head.

"Raising livestock is not easy, Teacher Sahib. There's disease and loss. If the herd survive infection, they are prey for wolves and—"

Mobin Khan wrinkles his nose, quickly turns away, and sneezes several times. Kowsar smiles, picturing colorful specks of blue, green, and purple flying into the air and twirling around each other before fading away.

"Forgive me, it's this god-forsaken cold. . . . It was only a few years ago when no more than six of my goats outlived disease. The others, their stomachs swelled, their eyes turned white, and they choked to death before our eyes. . . . My girl, go tell your mother to prepare tea."

Kowsar darts out of the room and finds her mother in the kitchen with the fire already blazing in the cookstove and the kettle steaming.

"Father said to prepare tea."

"I know, I know! Tell him it's brewing."

"This is a beautiful village," Teacher Sadeq is saying when Kowsar returns and quietly takes her place. "I had heard of Tali being a green and verdant valley, but when has hearing ever been better than seeing? I was amazed when I first arrived. And such a pleasant climate. . . . But, Farrokh Khan, tell me, would you like to go to school?"

Farrokh nervously looks at his father.

"I didn't ask Mobin Khan," the teacher says, laughing lightly. "I asked you."

Farrokh looks down and remains silent.

"Have you ever been to Qala-e Naw?"

"Who? Me?"

"Yes, *you*, Farrokh Khan!"

"No, I've only been to Jawand with Father. And twice to Wuluswali."

"I love traveling," Teacher Sadeq says. "I would like to see all of Afghanistan. I have heard a lot about the beauty of Salang Pass,

Bamyan province, and Band-e Amir National Park. I pray God will one day bless me with the opportunity to see them."

"Teacher Sahib, how about Herat?" Kowsar asks. "Have you been there?"

"Herat? But Herat is only next door! I studied there at Teachers Academy. In school you will learn that we have an amazing country, Kowsar. We have people of every creed and color. Tajiks, Uzbeks, Turkmans, and Pashtuns. One is famed for carpet weaving, another for horticulture or farming, cattle breeding or architecture and fine arts. . . . Alas, Mobin Khan, if outsiders and inciters leave us be, if we have some measure of safety and security, our country could flourish into a blooming orchard."

"We have been hoping for more than fifty years," Mobin Khan says somberly. "But the news is more dire every year and every day."

Teacher Sadeq looks around the barren room, at the barely perceptible design of the timeworn carpet, at the lower end of the room where the floor remains bare. In the darkest corner, he can make out the silhouette of two sacks of grain with a salt block on top of one. In the opposite corner, a stack of mattresses and blankets are draped with a brown bedding cover. He knows that in this village, as in all others, this is the life of the majority.

Kowsar wishes he would say what he has come to say, but Teacher Sadeq is silent.

"Son," her mother calls from the porch. "Come take the tea."

Farrokh hurries out and she cautions, "The teapot is hot. Let your father serve."

Kowsar's eyes are fixed on the tray as Farrokh walks in and sets it down in front of Mobin Khan. A teapot, two tea bowls, and a plate of black raisins. She smiles and thinks, I knew you had something hidden away in your trunk, Mother!

"It would be wonderful if Farrokh's mother could come sit with us," Teacher Sadeq says. "I would like her to hear what I have come to discuss with you. Of course, if she observes hijab, it will be fine if she listens at the door."

"We don't have such constraints in Tali, Teacher Sahib. We all know each other. And you are our daughter's teacher. An intimate and a brother," Mobin Khan says, before shouting, "Golrokh! Come! Teacher Sahib has something to tell us."

"Of course, pour the tea, I'll be right there."

Mobin Khan fills the tea bowls in between stifled coughs and apologetically says, "Teacher Sahib, we don't have any candied sugar. Please sweeten your pallet with raisins."

Moments later, Golrokh, her long hair loosely covered with a scarf, walks in and greets the teacher before sitting with her children by the door.

"Forgive me for disturbing your evening, Sister," Teacher Sadeq says.

"A guest is a friend of God. You honor us. Kowsar has been in a tizzy since noon."

Teacher Sadeq looks at Kowsar, sitting with her arms wrapped around her legs and her chin perched on her knees, staring at him.

"Sister," he says, "your Kowsar is not an average child, and not an average student. God has blessed her with astonishing aptitude and acumen."

"May God keep her healthy," Golrokh says, having only understood that he is praising her daughter. "I wish you long life, Teacher Sahib."

"Mobin Khan, your daughter has very quickly learned to read and write, and in a short time, she has finished studying the first and second grade schoolbooks. She has passed every test I have given her. Everything she reads is stored in her memory. Kowsar is a genius child, a prodigy. . . . At the end of the month when I go home to Qala-e Naw, I will arrange to see the chief director of the province's Department of Education. Everyone should know about Kowsar. Your daughter should be supported and allowed to achieve what God has meant for her. And the education she deserves and needs when she is older, is beyond what she can receive in Tali."

Kowsar revels in her teacher's praise. Mobin Khan sits wide-eyed, though unmistakably pleased. Golrokh remains puzzled.

"Our Kowsar is clever," Mobin Khan says. "Sometimes she's a

mischief as all children are, other times she is as wise as a sixty-year-old. But what's the use? Even if she could swallow flames, what good would it do a small-time farmer and shepherd, a mountain dweller like me?"

"Mobin Khan, you should be thrilled and proud of being father to such a child. She is a gift from God! You have lived a decent and honest life to have been blessed with her."

"If only God had given her brain to Farrokh," Golrokh says. "What use are school and books to a helpless wretch? Which one of her troubles and pains will they heal? Soon she will marry and go with her husband to some distant place, to the far side of dark mountains. And her place will be at the cookstove, the washbasin, and the kiln."

A torrent of fears drowns Kowsar's joy. She imagines her Mother's words as bats flying from her lips and ripping through the air in the dim room. What Golrokh had said in the kitchen thunders in her ears. "A wretch has no voice of her own."

"If Kowsar's education is of no use to her and of no importance to you," Teacher Sadeq says sharply, "then why did you send her to school?"

Kowsar watches her mother's mouth open, and more bats fly out.

"Our girl has fainting spells. God only knows who put a curse on her. Prayers and cures were useless. They said burn hair from a horse's mane, feather from a crow, tail of a fox. Even the healing Mullah's incantations did no good. When the school opened, we sent her there with Geesu, thinking it would distract her, break her habit."

The bats tear in every direction. The air is stifling. Short of breath and convulsing, Kowsar loses consciousness. Now, everything is quiet, light, and fluid. All that occupies the air is the glow of the lamp.

"Son!" Mobin Khan says, jumping to his feet. "A bowl of water!"

Farrokh runs out and Teacher Sadeq, pale and panicked, rushes to Kowsar's side and feels her forehead. Golrokh quickly brings a pillow and Mobin Khan pulls Kowsar's skirt down over her knees.

"Don't worry, Teacher Sahib," Mobin Khan says, stroking Kowsar's hand. "She will come to in a minute."

Sadeq Khan, moves back and slumps against the wall.

"How could you say such things to your daughter?" he says, his voice shaking with anger. "Why do you tell her Farrokh deserves her brain? Why doesn't she deserve it herself? Why do you tell her she is cursed? Why do you frighten her, saying some man will take her to the far side of dark mountains!? Kowsar is a *child*. She thinks of you as her shelter, her protector. And yet, you traumatize her. She is not a *wretch*! She is a genius. She needs to be embraced and encouraged by you. I beg you, stop! Don't demoralize an innocent child!"

37

Golrokh and Mobin Khan, too occupied with Kowsar, pay no mind.

Farrokh comes with a bowl of water and Golrokh sprinkles some on Kowsar's face, wets her earlobes, and rubs them as she recites prayers.

Kowsar has no desire to wake. She floats out to the porch. The night sky is sprinkled with stars and the moon is showering the mountain river with its creamy glow. The poplars' leaves sway like dangling earrings, the frogs serenade one another, and the crickets sing an anthem to life, at times solo, at times in chorus.

The mountains each carry other peaks on their back, all dark, all menacing. Beyond them, Kowsar thinks, there are no rivers, no poplars, no frogs, no crickets. There is only silence as colossal as these mountains. I won't go. I won't go anywhere away from Mother and Father.

Inside, her parents are still tending to her, rubbing her hands, stroking her forehead. Farrokh's eyes are at times on her, at times on her teacher, who is staring at the moths circling the lamp.

"Teacher Sahib," Mobin Khan says. "Please, drink your tea, it's getting cold. We are used to Kowsar's bouts."

Teacher Sadeq says nothing. Mobin Khan goes to the tray, pours a fresh bowl, and sets it down next to him.

"Please," he says, holding out the plate of raisins. "Sweeten your pallet."

"Thank you, I have no appetite for sweets."

Teacher Sadeq takes a sip of tea and wonders if the doctors in Qala-e Naw can diagnose and cure Kowsar. He thinks, I must convince her parents not to allow her to waste away. She herself should become a doctor and heal thousands of others.

Kowsar softly slips back into her body, draws a sharp breath, and slowly opens her eyes.

"Are you all right, my girl?" Golrokh asks.

"Come, Kowsar, come sit on my lap," Mobin Khan says, bending down to pick her up.

"Don't, Mobin Khan," Golrokh warns, gripping his arm. "Your cold is catching, she'll get sick."

Sitting Kowsar on her knee, she says, "Teacher Sahib, now you see the state of our life. . . . Please, take a few raisins. Don't drink your tea unsweetened."

From under her drooping eyelids Kowsar watches Teacher Sadeq reluctantly take a few raisins and put them in his mouth.

"Tell us about yourself," Mobin Khan says, hoping to change the mood and atmosphere. "Where are you from, how many children do you have?"

"As I said, I'm from Qala-e Naw," he says flatly and halfheartedly. "I have a son, Assem. My father is in the pistachio trade and has a shop in the bazaar. I worked with him when I finished school, but the pistachio market suffered badly. The farms lost their owners and villagers repeatedly raided and pillaged them. The old saying goes: Though waiting is bitter, its fruit is sweet. But people stripped the trees before harvest time. We hoped the government would step in, but it was their own officials holding the bag. It's still the same plight and plunder."

"Yes, Teacher Sahib, I know. That's why the likes of me stopped going for pistachios."

"Well, I changed my path and became a teacher."

"Truth is the way of God, Teacher Sahib. As for me and my live-lihood, I have seven acres of land down the mountain, near Ab-e Pudah Lake. I sometimes plant rice, other times wheat or mung beans. If I can afford to buy more seeds, I plant peas and other beans on the mountainside. That's God's land. If it's a good year with plenty of rain, the mountain crop is not bad. But some years, what I pay for seeds is a loss."

Mobin Khan stops to cough and take a deep breath. "Golrokh, brew some more hollyhock and jujube tea," he says and turns to the teacher again. "You are from Badghis. You know how difficult life is in these mountains. Especially in the winter when heavy snows make getting around impossible. To make it to spring without suf-fering, we need to have two well-fed sheep and our grain vessels filled to the brim."

Kowsar watches the men, desperately hoping the teacher will go back to talking about her education. But he doesn't.

"Well, that's life in the mountains. . . . By the way, Farrokh Khan, until what time do you pasture the sheep?"

"What?!" Farrokh half shouts, jolting out of his daze.

Kowsar bursts into laughter but quickly covers her mouth.

"I asked, until what time do you pasture the sheep."

"Until noon, Teacher Sahib. Until Mullah's mid-day *azan*. That's when the weather starts to get hot, and I bring the sheep back to the hold."

"Well, come to school after lunch, and I'll be your teacher, too. You can learn to read and write."

Farrokh looks warily at his father. The only sound in the room is the drone of the moth, its wings now singed, struggling to fly away from the lamp.

"Nutcase! Say, *yes*!" Kowsar blurts out, and immediately lowers her head, knowing she has spoken against her father's wishes.

Despite the displeasure etched on his face, Mobin Khan remains silent.

"Farrokh Khan, you have an intelligent and educated sister," Teacher Sadeq goes on. "It's a shame for you to remain illiterate and not advance in life."

"You say it," Farrokh whispers, nudging Kowsar with his elbow. "Say I will go."

"Farrokh will come to school!" Kowsar announces, her eyes still fixed on the carpet.

"In fact," Teacher Sadeq quickly adds, "there are several other girls and boys who, like you, can't come to school in the morning, but they can come in the afternoon. I have free time then, so I'm organizing afternoon classes as well."

"Teacher Sadeq, I will not—"

"It's between you and God, Mobin Khan," the teacher interrupts. "Put your excuses aside. Your son wants to go to school. Let him! You'll see, he will make a man of himself, he will become an engineer, build bridges, dams, and roads for you."

With all eyes on him, Mobin Khan weighs his thoughts and words.

"Teacher Sahib," he finally says in a measured tone. "What is there for me to say. Now that Farrokh himself is eager, we will do as you see fit. But at home, he—"

"Excellent! It's a done deal. And, Mobin Khan, stop being so stern!"

"And you, so stubborn!"

Farrokh beams with excitement and Kowsar leaps up and cheers.

"Mother! Mother!" she screams as Golrokh walks in with the herbal brew. "Farrokh will come to school, too. Father said, yes!"

Golrokh smiles, sets the tea down in front of her husband, and says, "Mobin Khan, if Teacher Sahib's tea has cooled, I'll bring a fresh pot."

"Bless you, Sister, it's late. I should be on my way."

"Teacher Sahib!" Kowsar says anxiously. "You forgot to talk about that other thing."

"What other thing, Kowsar?!"

"About the doctors."

"Yes, of course. I did forget, but—How did you know?"

"I . . . you said . . . um . . . I can't remember," she stammers.

"I will speak to the chief director of the Department of Education, as I'm obliged to do," the teacher says, looking perplexed. "How he and others respond and what they decide, I cannot say. And yes, I will find a good doctor in town, and you and I, Mobin Khan, will take Kowsar to him."

Mobin Khan smiles and takes the lamp to see the teacher to the door.

"You are always most welcome here, Teacher Sahib. May you be blessed for your care and kindness. May God reward you and protect your son."

# 3

I GO TO SEE Nadim Khan one day. He is an educated, well-read man. A book collector with a flair for poetry. He is wise and forward-thinking, and many in Tali often don't quite understand his remarks and observations. Word is that some years back, he was Secretary of the Province, but unexpectedly left his position and took to seclusion in Tali. He volunteers as a teacher at the school and has given me permission to borrow books from him.

"I have a small library with doors that are always open to you, Kowsar," he said one day at school. "Among the volumes there are storybooks, fairytales, and fables. Come, take them and read."

The treasure trove in his house lays open a new universe for me. The more I read, the more I understand that there is a different world out there, different people living different lives. And the more I read, the more curious I become, the more questions I have.

When Nadim Khan learns that I am the visitor, he comes to the door and greets me with a smile.

"Remember," he says, sitting in his library, "the more your eyes open to the world, the more you are likely to suffer. But better that you learn and understand. You are a flower blossoming in a desert. Your life will not be an easy one."

I nod and think to myself, my life has not been easy from the start.

"There are few literate people in Tali. And outside of this village, there are now many who are quick to issue a fatwa proclaiming you a sinner the moment you talk of books, knowledge, and progress. They will make you so loathed that people will even refuse to eat at the same dining cloth as you. Ignore them. Build your own life. Show the world who you are. Let everyone see that you are different, that you are unlike anyone else. Fly away from this beautiful valley. Take wing and go out to the boundless world where life is not summarized into a sack of mung beans and a few sheep. Profit from your God-given talent and spit at ignorance and stupidity."

I cannot decipher all of what he is trying to tell me, but I can sense that coloring his words is an old and unfinished war he has fought. He picks out *Animal Farm* from among his books and hands it to me.

"It is a great book, a brilliant story," he says. "It was written around the time of World War II—it was a bloody war between many countries, long before you were born. In the book, the animals in a farm rebel against the owner and take control of the farm, because they want to live free and be happy. In the end, they are worse off than before. It's the story of our country today. Wolves and jackals, cloaked as humans, have made their way to positions of power. Our world is now full of them.

"I, too, was slowly falling into the cycle that creates the wolves and jackals, but I wasn't of the same cloth as them. No matter when you catch a mistake, it's a gain. The day I realized I was surrounded by creatures with fangs and claws, I changed course and took refuge in these mountains to not bear witness to the mauling and pillaging. I wanted to live and die with a clear conscience. Kowsar, to survive out there, you must learn how to live among them, you must learn to tell man from beast. That is where intellect and intelligence find meaning. Read, Kowsar, read to understand the world around you."

Nadim Khan continues loaning me his books and talking to me about life. Geesu sometimes comes with me to his house, but she doesn't like some of the books Nadim Khan gives me to read. She chooses fables and fairytales.

Farrokh is gradually learning to read and write, too.

❦

One morning, Mother tells me to put on my green floral dress. Then she carefully combs and braids my hair, puts cream on my face and kohl on my eyes, and puts my hand in Father's hand.

"Go with God," she says to him. "And don't forget tea and candied sugar, and clothes for Farrokh and me."

Near the school, Teacher Sadeq joins us, and we set off on foot for Jawand. When we arrive, we go to a teahouse for some tea and a brief rest before boarding a minibus traveling to Qala-e Naw.

There is a sad song playing on the minibus radio. The other seven passengers are all silent and withdrawn. It's my first time ridding in a car or bus. Lurching along the rugged dirt road, I grip the armrest, frightened that any moment now the minibus will fall into a ditch or gully and roll over, killing us all. But the driver expertly maneuvers his way around the worst of them.

As we leave Jawand, a parched desert of dust and dirt spreads before us. Uninhabited and host to a nomadic wind that whips up dry thorn bushes and whirls them in the air before abandoning them for another cluster of desiccated wilds.

The air inside the minibus is stifling. Every time someone rolls down a window, the wind gusts in, bringing with it heat and dust. I look at the men. Their cheerless faces are thin and weather-beaten. Among them, only Teacher Sadeq has lively eyes, some flesh on his face, and lighter skin. We travel far until we reach a fertile region.

"We will soon be in Qala-e Naw, and you will meet my son," Teacher Sadeq says, smiling at me.

Square mudbrick houses surrounded by tall walls line the streets like matchboxes. The town bazaar is much larger and more contemporary than the one in Jawand. Countless shops and stands and a crush of people coming and going. Music blares out of restaurants and teahouses. They all have generators. Cars of every color blow their horns and maneuver their way around the potholes. I am absorbed by all the signs and occasional flyers. Teacher Sadeq says eight kilometers of the town's main avenue is paved with asphalt. He says he will show it to me.

"Mobin Khan, have you ever been to Qala-e Naw?" Teacher Sadeq turns and asks Father, who is sitting one row behind us.

"Yes, several times, when I was young. Back then, the town was no bigger than Jawand. Now, in the name of God, it is sprawling."

"Then everything is new and worth seeing for you."

"Very much so."

I look back at Father. He, too, is wide-eyed and mesmerized by the scene outside the minibus.

"Kowsar, do you like the bustle of the bazaar?" Teacher Sadeq asks.

"Yes!" I say, and imitating Father, I add, "Very much so."

He laughs and pats me on the shoulder.

"Teacher Sahib!" I exclaim, as we pass a building with a large sign above its door. "A school! Hanzaleh Badghisi School!"

"I went to this school. I have many memories of it. Do you know who Hanzaleh Badghisi is?"

"Yes. He wrote poetry. In Persian."

49

"Kowsar! Where did you learn this?"

"Nadim Khan's books. He asked me to read one of the poems to him. I memorized it, but I don't understand it:

*If his Lordship in a lion's jaws should hang*
*Go, run the risk and seize it by its fangs*
*Yours shall be greatness, glory, rank and place*
*Or else, like heroes, there will be death to face."*

"So you've made your way to his library," he says, smiling approvingly. "I borrow books from him, too. Some evenings, I go there, and we sit with a pot of tea and talk for hours."

The minibus stops on the side of a street, and everyone climbs out. Standing on solid ground, I suddenly feel lightheaded, and I fall. Father quickly picks me up and shakes the dust off my dress and pants.

"Are you all right?"

"I got dizzy."

"To be honest, I'm a bit unsteady, too," Teacher Sadeq says. "These roads take a toll. We'll go to my house, wash up, and have some tea. The fatigue will be gone in no time."

Father picks me up and carries me in his arms. The scent of his skin is pleasant, a scent I have grown up with. It is often said that girls have a deep love for their father. That is not true. The feeling is closer to worship.

We turn onto a straight and even road.

"Father, I'm not dizzy anymore."

He gently puts me down and holds my hand as we follow Teacher Sadeq. Up ahead, I see two girls about my age walking together. Both are wearing black knee-length dresses, matching loose pants, and long white headscarves tied under their chin. Following my gaze, Teacher Sadeq says, "They are students, just like you. In Qala-e Naw schoolgirls wear black uniforms and white headcovers. They don't go to school in colorful clothes the way you do in Tali." Then he snickers, "I'm glad Mullah Sikhdad doesn't know about uniforms. What havoc he would cause with the students' families!"

I pay no attention to him. The girls each have a bag they carry on their back. I've never seen anything like them. One is light blue with the picture of a kitten on it, the other is violet, with the image of a beautiful girl. We don't have schoolbags in Tali. We carry our books and notebooks in fabric bundles or cotton sacks. Some time ago, Mullah Sikhdad told us a place called UNICEF will send schoolbags for us. We are still waiting. I stare at the violet bag until the girls turn onto a road and I lose sight of them. Now, all I can think of is how I wish I had one just like it.

Soon, we leave the crowds behind. Teacher Sadeq points to a pair of minarets visible behind the buildings and says, "My home is on the other side of that mosque."

We continue turning from one road onto another, until Teacher Sadeq stops in front of a gray metal door, sounds the knocker, and says, "We've arrived! By the way, did I mention that my parents live with us? Without them here, I wouldn't be able to leave my wife and son and come to work in Tali."

A minute later, the door grates open and reveals a handsome elderly man.

"Hello, Father!" Teacher Sadeq says, bending down to kiss his hands.

"Welcome home, Sadeq Khan!" his father says, patting him on the head.

"Father, this is Mobin Khan, Kowsar's father. And this is Kowsar herself. Mobin Khan, please meet my father, Enayatollah Khan."

The two men shake hands and exchange greetings. Then Enayatollah Khan squats down in front of me, strokes my hair, and says, "The last time Sadeq was home, he told me all about you, my girl. I very much hoped I would one day meet you."

He kisses me on the cheeks and is about to invite us in when a boy races out the door and throws himself in the teacher's arms, screaming, "Father!"

"Assem Khan, look who's here! This is Kowsar. I told you about how smart and special she is, and all the books she has read."

Assem eyes me with curiosity.

"Mobin Khan," Teacher Sadeq says, "please wait in the yard for a moment while I go and open the guestroom."

He hurries away with Assem and moments later returns to usher us to the small and simple house and the porch that the guestroom door opens to.

"*Ya Allah*," Father says as we take off our shoes and walk in.

"I must say hello to my mother and wife," Teacher Sadeq says. "Please make yourselves at home."

The guestroom is furnished with a red carpet, dark green floor cushions and bolsters, and white floral curtains over the two alcoves. Enayatollah Khan sits across from us, and with his right hand on his chest, he says to Father, "I welcome you to our home. We are honored by your visit." Then he turns to me and welcomes me in the same manner.

I don't know how to respond, but I do know that I should not leave his courtesies unanswered.

"May God keep you," Father says. "May you live long."

"May God keep you," I repeat after him. "May you live long."

He smiles at me and nods.

The two men quickly warm up to each other and carry on about farming, work, and life, until the door opens and Teacher Sadeq walks in with a tea tray.

"By the time we have some tea, lunch will be ready," he says. "Are you hungry, Kowsar?"

Contrary to what my stomach tells me, I shake my head.

"You are!" he laughs as he puts down the tray and sits to pour the tea.

There are four Minoo chocolates with red and green wrappers sitting on top of the candied sugar. I know how delicious they are. I had one two years ago at Akbar Khan's New Year celebration. And now I have neither the courage to ask Father if I may have one, nor the daring to just reach out and take one.

Enayatollah Khan takes one with a red wrapper, holds it out to me, and says, "Have this, my dear. You're tired, a little sugar will do you good."

I look at Father, he nods. I take the chocolate, slowly unwrap it, and put it on my tongue. I take a small sip of tea and it starts to melt. I am euphoric.

A few minutes later, Assem walks in cradling toys in the length of his tunic and empties them on the floor next to me. Small toy figures and plastic cars, most of them broken or damaged.

"Let's play!" he says.

"What game?"

He hands me a car missing three tires and takes one with all four tires intact for himself.

"Let's have a car race. Whoever gets to the door first."

"Son!" his grandfather says, bursting into laughter. "Who are you fooling? Obviously, she will lose with that dilapidated car."

"Well, I don't have another good one," Assem giggles.

"Then don't have a car race!"

Assem frowns, gathers up his toys, and tosses them behind the curtain of the alcove on the right.

"Did you know your father is my teacher?" I ask him when he comes back.

"Yes, I know."

"He tells our class all about your funny pranks."

Assem purses his lips and glares at his father.

"What grade are you in?" I ask him some minutes later.

"First."

"I'm in first grade, too. Have you gotten to the duckling story yet?" I say, chuckling.

"What's so funny?"

"I was thinking of how it got lost in the big town."

"You're in a big town," he says impishly. "Be careful *you* don't get lost."

The next day Teacher Sadeq takes me to the doctor. A kind man with eyeglasses and wearing a white frock.

"Bibi Kowsar," he says after he has finished my physical examination. "Do you have pain anywhere? Does anything hurt?"

I shake my head.

Father, sitting to the side with Teacher Sadeq, says, "Doctor Sahib, she has epilepsy."

Ignoring him, the doctor asks, "My dear, do you ever get headaches?"

"No, Doctor Sahib."

"When and how often do you experience these attacks?"

I don't know. I have never thought about it. I turn to Father.

"There is no particular time," Father says. "Sometimes it happens two or three times a week, sometimes once a month."

The doctor takes notes on a sheet of paper, and asks, "Bibi Kowsar, what happens, what do you feel right before an attack?"

"I get scared."

"It happens only when you are very scared?"

"No. It happens when I'm really upset, too. Then everything turns gray."

"Gray? Explain it to me?"

"I suddenly feel hot and start to shake. I fall and everything goes gray. Sometimes I think I see things."

The doctor asks more questions and takes more notes. Then he looks at me pensively, takes off his glasses, wipes them with a small cloth and puts them back on.

He asks me to tell him about a few times when I've had attacks. Where I was, what I was doing, what was happening.

"How long does it take for her to regain consciousness?" he asks Father.

"Doctor Sahib, sometimes a couple of minutes, other times a little longer."

"You are her teacher," he says, turning to Teacher Sadeq. "How is she academically? I mean her learning ability."

"She is far above average. She is a special child, a prodigy," Teacher Sadeq says proudly. "She learned to read and write in three months, and she finished studying the first and second grade schoolbooks in no time at all. Everything she reads, she memorizes without effort. Just yesterday, she recited a poem by Hanzaleh Badghisi."

"Has she had any episodes at school?"

"No. But I saw her experience one when I was visiting Mobin Khan one night."

The doctor asks Teacher Sadeq about that night. Then he adjusts his glasses on his nose and thinks for a while. I silently watch him with turmoil inside me. Can he cure me?

The doctor finally gets up and goes to the bookshelf in the corner and takes an apple from the fruit bowl sitting between the volumes.

"Bibi Kowsar, have an apple and enjoy it," he says, offering it to me. "You don't have a serious illness."

I smile and take the apple from him.

"Kowsar doesn't have epilepsy, fainting fits, falling sickness, or whatever you want to call it," he tells Father and Teacher Sadeq. "What she has is a form of convulsive syncope. To explain it simply, she is highly sensitive, and her body overreacts to certain triggers, predominantly extreme emotional distress—intense fear, angst, grief. On occasion, she also hallucinates, which is not uncommon. For her to suffer less and live a better life, people around her must be cautious of their behavior toward her. Teacher Sahib, please explain this in simple terms to her family members."

Then he smiles at me and, says, "And you, Bibi Kowsar, must be stronger. Don't let the words and actions of others frighten or upset you too much. Don't let any old wind shake you. The stronger you become, the fewer attacks you will experience."

Outside the doctor's office, Teacher Sadeq turns to Father and with his voice shaking with excitement he says, "Mobin Khan! What a relief! It's nothing terribly serious. Kowsar is just very sensitive. The older she grows, the stronger she will become. And the day will come when she will no longer suffer these attacks."

I cannot read my father's heart and mind, but from the gleam in his eyes and the smile on his lips, I know the doctor's words and the teacher's confirmation have brought him a measure of peace and relief.

"May God never deprive us of your kindness," he says, patting

58

Teacher Sadeq on the shoulder. Then he holds me tight and kisses me on the forehead.

"Kowsar, did you understand everything the doctor said?" Teacher Sadeq asks. "Thank God! I am so happy for you. Laugh, Kowsar, laugh!"

I smile at him, but I have a peculiar feeling. I'm happy that I don't have a grave illness, but I had hoped the doctor would give me some medicine that would stop the attacks altogether. Yet, all he said is I must become stronger.

"Kowsar! Did you hear what I said?"

"Yes, Teacher Sadeq. I am happy!"

"Then let's go for a walk and see the town."

The streets are crowded and noisy. The pulse of life beats faster in Qala-e Naw. Father hasn't forgotten Mother's request and looks at the clothing store windows. I am again absorbed in reading the signs on the shops and buildings. I see a bookstore across the street, and I'm automatically drawn to it.

"Mobin Khan," Teacher Sadeq says. "Let's go in so Kowsar can take a look at the books."

We climb the two steps in front of Haji Zaman's Bookstore and walk in. There are rows of shelves crammed with more books than I could have imagined. In one corner all sorts of school supplies are on display.

"Kowsar, Mobin Khan and I will wait over here," Teacher Sadeq says. "Go and choose three books. They will be a gift from me to you."

Ecstatic, I look around and run to where I see the children's books. I lose myself among them. All are wonderful, all appeal to me, but Teacher Sadeq said he will buy three, and I know Father has only enough money to buy the things Mother has asked for. I spend a long time looking at the books and leafing through them. I finally choose *The Lost Prince*, *Alice in Wonderland*, and *Cinderella*. I tuck them under my arm to take them to Teacher Sadeq when I catch sight of the schoolbags. They are similar to those the two girls were carrying. I hurry over to them. There is a lily-white one with a picture of a beautiful girl with large green eyes and long golden hair. I take it from the rack and run my hand over it.

"Do you like it, dear girl?" the shopkeeper asks, walking over to me.

I nod.

"The bag or the picture?"

"Both."

"The girl's name is Cinderella. We have the storybook, too."

"This one?" I say, showing him the book.

"Yes! Excellent!"

He goes back to the front of the store, and I look at the bag. I desperately want it. How I wish Father could buy it for me. Cinderella's dress is warm and soft. I feel it move under my fingertips. Suddenly, Cinderella blinks and smiles at me.

"You are so pretty," I whisper.

"I am grateful. You are pretty, too, Kowsar," she quietly says.

"I have a friend in Tali that looks like you. Except her eyes and hair are dark, not green and gold like yours."

"Do you like it, Kowsar?"

The teacher's voice jolts me and my bond with Cinderella breaks.

"Yes, a lot," I say, handing him the books.

"You chose very well. Shall we go?"

I put the bag back in its place and follow him.

At the front counter he pays the shopkeeper, who puts the books in a paper bag and gives it to me.

"Thank you, Teacher Sadeq."

As we walk to where Father is waiting, I imagine Cinderella calling me.

"Kowsar!" she cries. "Take me with you. You and I love each other! Don't leave me here."

I race back to the schoolbags and stroke her golden hair.

"I have to go. I live far away."

"I come from faraway, too," she says. "Take me with you. I'm so lonely here."

I look back. Father and Teacher Sadeq are standing at the door.

"I can't take you," I say, breaking into tears. "My father doesn't have the money to buy you."

"Kowsar," I hear Father calling. "Come, we have to go now."

Tears rolling down my face, I clutch Cinderella to my chest. I know the gray is setting in. As I fall, I see Father and Teacher Sadeq running to me.

"Water! Bring some water!" Father shouts to the shopkeeper. "She has epilepsy."

Father, I want to say, stop saying that.

I feel Teacher Sadeq loosen my grip on the bag and pick me up.

When I open my eyes, I am still in his arms and Father is caressing my face.

"Was it because of the schoolbag?" Teacher Sadeq asks.

I look at him. He knows.

He hands me to Father and takes the Cinderella bag to the shopkeeper. I hear the man say, "Seven hundred afghanis." Teacher Sadeq leaves the bag on the counter.

"Forgive me, Kowsar. I don't have that much money."

~

The next day is ill-omened. Looking back, I wish we had never gone to Qala-e Naw. That hateful day tore me from the seventh heaven of childhood and hurled me into earthly reality.

"Last month, I managed to meet with the chief director of the Department of Education," Teacher Sadeq tells his father over breakfast. "I spoke to him about Kowsar. He was very pleased and agreed that the department must recognize and support her as an exceptional student. We are going to see him this morning."

The Department of Education is noisy and chaotic. People come and go, walk in and out of offices. Everyone looks busy. We wait several hours for our turn to meet with the chief director. At the far end of a spacious office, he is sitting behind a large desk piled with folders and papers. He is a heavyset man with thick glasses that exaggerate his eyes. Without getting up from his chair, he shakes hands with Teacher Sadeq, nods to Father, and invites us to sit on a long, cushioned bench facing his desk.

"Chief Director Sahib, excellency," Teacher Sadeq says. "If you recall, I came to see you last month, and I spoke to you about a genius student we have at the school in Tali, a village in Jawand district."

"Yes, I remember."

"Chief Director Sahib, excellency, this young girl is that student. Her name is Kowsar."

Without looking at me, the chief director starts leafing through a folder of papers, and says, "Sadeq Khan, truth be told, I am

63

extremely busy this time of year. I hardly have time to scratch my head. On the one hand salary reviews have come in, on the other, budgets for a hundred schools have to be determined. Which school is she in?"

"Tali, Chief Director Sahib."

"Right, of course, Tali. Which district?"

"Jawand, Chief Director Sahib."

"Right, right, Jawand. Isn't this one of the schools the Director of Religious Education manages? The learned Mawlawi Khodadad."

"Yes, it is."

"Aha. So, you should go see him. Tell him I sent you. He'll take care of this. I have bigger worries these days. The Minister is on television every night saying we have the greatest number of schools among all the countries in the region. I worry about that noble gentleman's reputation suffering if someone comes and actually counts. Yet, what to do? What to do?"

Teacher Sadeq hesitates, but given the chief director's obvious lack of interest, he turns to Father and nods toward the door. Outside the office, he stops and thinks, wondering whether we should go to Mawlawi Khodadad or not. We should, he concludes. At the end of the corridor, we walk out the back door of the building that opens to a planted courtyard. There is a small building on the opposite side with the sign: Department of Religious Education.

We walk in and Teacher Sadeq tells the man at the reception

desk that the chief director has sent us to see Mawlawi Khodadad. He directs us to the last of the five doors along the hallway.

"Come!" a gruff voice calls out when Teacher Sadeq knocks.

Inside, a middle-aged man wearing a white lungee of fine fabric and a black robe is sitting behind a desk sipping green tea. His beard, which is dyed red, seems familiar to me. I quickly remember seeing him in Tali. He had come to inspect the construction of the school. We walk up to his desk and after offering his salutations, Teacher Sadeq explains the reason for our visit.

"Mawlawi Sahib," he says in conclusion. "The chief director has requested your special attention to this case. We hope this young girl will reap the rewards of what she has achieved and will be encouraged and supported by the department."

Mawlawi Khodadad half-rises from his chair, leans over his desk, and looks at me more closely.

"Take a seat," he says, pointing to a bumpy wood bench.

"What is your name?" he asks me.

"Kowsar, Sahib."

"Come, Kowsar. Come closer."

I feel uneasy. I look at Father.

"Go," he says quietly, pressing his hand on my back.

I get up and reluctantly walk over to his desk, but he waves for me to go closer. I circle the desk and stop one step away from him.

He again scrutinizes me head to toe and stares at my face. His eyes are dark and fierce and now and then restlessly dart back and forth.

"Have you studied the Holy Quran?"

I look down to avoid his eyes.

"Mawlawi Sahib," Teacher Sadeq says. "Alongside her lessons, she has read and knows by heart part one of the *Sipareh*. She will gradually study the rest as well. She has also studied the schoolbooks for first, second, and third grades, and read many other books."

"No! No!" Mawlawi Khodadad shouts. "The *Sipareh* takes priority! She must finish studying it before all else. Who knows who's alive and who's dead a year from now? There's no time to waste. And if a husband takes her, she won't have time to sit, much less study."

I take a few steps back, run to Father, and bury my face in his jacket. Mawlawi Khodadad bursts into laughter.

"The word *husband* had her run as though from sudden death! . . . But jokes aside, she has great beauty indeed, and of course virtue. May God protect her."

I hide my face deeper in Father's jacket.

"Where did you say she's from?"

"From Tali, Mawlawi Sahib," Teacher Sadeq says, his voice slightly shaking.

66

"Well, then! It's a good thing you came. The administrative director has been telling me for some days now that it's time for me to inspect that school. I'm quite busy these days, but I will come as soon as I can. Mullah Sikhdad and Village Chief Abed are friends of mine. It's a good excuse for me to visit them as well. . . . And frankly, I've been looking for a wife. One with a pretty face and gentle temperament. I've heard a lot about the beauty of Tali girls. . . . And what a houri your Kowsar will be in a year or so! Take her home and safeguard her."

Teacher Sadeq remains silent.

"I have two wives," the mawlawi says, getting up and strolling toward us. "One is ailing and the other idle. Neither one is worth a grain. This time, I've decided to take a young one and train her myself."

He laughs again and stops in front of Father.

"Why has she crawled under your jacket?"

"My girl . . . my little girl is a bit shy," Father says nervously.

The man takes my arm and pulls me away from him.

"Come, let me show you to Bibi Maryam," he says, dragging me away. "You two wait here. I'll show her to the old custodian and bring her right back. I want Bibi Maryam to see what smart and suitable girls you have in Tali. She will be proud."

Not allowing a moment for either man to intervene, he opens

the door and steps out. I turn and desperately look at Father. I can tell from his expression that fear is coursing through his veins. I think he is afraid I will panic and faint.

Mawlawi Khodadad pulls me down the hallway and into a dim office. He grabs me under the arms, lifts me up, and stands me on the desk. I don't understand what he wants, but the look in his eyes frighten me. I imagine flames licking out of them. All I want is to run back to Father.

"Have you sprouted hair?"

I stare at him. I don't understand his question.

"I asked you, has hair started growing on your thing?"

I'm trembling. I want to leap off the desk and escape. But he holds me tight with one hand and with the other pulls down my pants.

"Don't be afraid," he says, lifting up my skirt. "I just want to look."

I can no longer hear him. My vision blurs. I float away from my body. Standing in the middle of the room, I see myself sprawled out on the desk. He doesn't care that I have lost consciousness. He looks at my thighs and vagina with greed in his eyes. He runs the palm of his hand between my legs, smiles, and pulls up my pants.

"Get up, it's all right," he says.

He grabs my arms and tries to sit me up, but I am limp. He picks me up and walks back to his office.

"She fainted before we got to Bibi Maryam," he says. "Take her."

Father runs and takes me from him and remains standing in the middle of the office, waiting for Teacher Sadeq to get up and leave with him.

"On my life, she's good!" Mawlawi Khodadad says, sitting back in his chair. "She will soon step into puberty. It's time for a husband."

"Director!" Teacher Sadeq flares, incensed and guilt-ridden. "I brought this girl from far away so that the Department of Education would recognize and laud her genius, so that you would support and further her education. I expected you to guide her, to encourage her. Instead, you are talking about matters that should be of no concern to you, matters that she knows nothing about."

"Don't lecture me, teacher!" he sharply retorts. "I told you to take her back and safeguard her. I will come to Tali myself and bring her to town and take her around to girls' schools for the students to learn from a destitute mountain girl. . . . How old is she?"

"Nine, and too young!" Teacher Sadeq snaps, joining Father at the door.

"Do you know how old the good and honorable Aisha was when Prophet Muhammad married her?" the mawlawi shouts. "She was nine! Aisha was nine when she became a bride. And shame on you for calling yourself Sadeq when you don't even know the words of Imam Sadeq! That holy man proclaimed that a man's felicity is for his daughter not to reach menstruation under his roof. He declared that God's Prophet went to the pulpit one day and announced,

'Gabriel brought me word from Holy God that girls are like fruits on a tree. If not picked in time, the sun will ruin them, the wind will drop them.' And this girl has started to ripen."

He wishes me to be his third wife. I cannot bear it. I float out into the courtyard. I sit under a tree and watch through the window as men hurry up and down the corridor of the Department of Education. I don't like the world outside of Tali. It is full of cunning and dishonesty. I feel sorry for Father and Teacher Sadeq who have been slapped in the face by that man.

They walk out into the courtyard. I'm still limp in Father's arms, my head resting on his shoulder, my eyes closed.

～

It is a somber evening. The kerosene lamp sits on the floor in the middle of the room, its flame gently swaying. Steam rises from the teapot in the tray and dissipates in the air, but no one has appetite for tea. The bowl of candied sugar and Minoo chocolates is there, but I have no desire for sweets. Father is leaning against the wall, staring at the carpet. He looks weary and lost. Teacher Sadeq's high spirits have died away, and Enayatollah Khan sits quietly rolling his prayer beads.

I wonder if I should tell Father and Teacher Sadeq about Maw-lawi Khodadad's hideous act. No, I'm afraid Father will be dishonored and distraught, and he might no longer allow me to go to school. I wish Assem would come with his toy cars so that I can stop thinking about that man and his kohled eyes. But Teacher Sadeq has sent him to his mother's room.

At last, Enayatollah Khan breaks the silence.

"What education!? In my day, there were manners and morality, honor and respect. Alas! The cows lay it all to waste, leaving no blessings behind. The man who is now the province's chief director of education, was in the same school and cycle as me. He failed every grade two or three years in a row. Even now, if the first letter of the alphabet were as tall as a shepherd's stick, he would struggle to read it. He was a thief, too. He stole from the students' bags. If he found nothing of value, he would take notebooks and pens. And this is who God has handed the reins to! He cares nothing about children's education. His only concern is fattening his pockets.

"And Khodadad is just as much a charlatan. At the time of the raids on the pistachio farms, he used to hold up and rob the poor people of Deh Yek. He lived in Khalishkak, a parched desert village where snakes shed skin, but it's near the pistachio farms and an ideal hideout for thieves. In the winter they burn pistachio trees to keep themselves warm and in the summer, they pilfer raw pistachios from the farms or steal what the poor villagers have picked. . . . That's the Talib the chief director sent you to see. Damn their fathers!"

He is silent for a moment, then shaking his head he says, "Sadeq Khan, I'm glad you saw for yourself who these people are. All your hard work and struggles will lead nowhere. Kowsar is the example."

He takes a few sips of tea and asks, "Have you heard of Hassan Khan Shirin Sokhan?"

"Yes, Father," Teacher Sadeq says bleakly. "The forester, poet, and man of letters. God rest his soul."

"How about you Mobin Khan? Have you heard of Shirin Sokhan?"

"No, Enayatollah Khan. This is the first time I'm hearing his name."

"He has an interesting story. When I was young and going to school, Shirin Sokhan was a forester and guarded several pistachio farms. He was a learned, God-loving man. He tried to convince the villagers not to cut down the trees for firewood and to respect the farms, because they were the source of their daily bread. He would recite poems from the Persian poet Saadi's *Bustan*, tell them about Avicenna, who considered pistachios curative and medicinal. But who would listen? Khodadad's father was the least God-fearing of them all. He would have trees chopped down in broad daylight, knowing that the governor and even the King were powerless before him!

"Well, it is said that one day Shirin Sokhan carried a coffin to Khalishkak and said, 'My child has died.' The villagers gathered to share his grief. They dug a grave and recited the prayer for the dead. When they opened the coffin, they found a branch from a pistachio tree inside. But what do fools know about irony and symbolism? They continued to cut down the trees, and they still do. That's where Khodadad's wealth came from. The lowlife Talib has no need for a government salary, he just snared the position so that he can also plunder public money."

Silence returns to the room until sometime later when Teacher Sadeq says, "It came to nothing, Mobin Kan. Take care of your business tomorrow, and we'll return to Tali the morning after."

"It was God's will, Sadeq Khan. You wanted to do a good deed. You did your duty. May God bless you and your son."

It is still dark when Father wakes me.

"Kowsar, get up and wash your face. We'll eat and head for home."

I rub my eyes and sit up. The dining cloth is already spread and tea and breakfast laid out. Enayatollah Khan and Teacher Sadeq are dressed and ready, waiting to eat.

"Wake up, Bibi Kowsar," Enayatollah Khan says cheerfully. "Freshen up so we can eat. You have a long journey ahead."

I want to say *salaam*, but I remember Teacher Sadeq telling the class one day, "When you wake up in the morning, you must first wash, then say salaam to your parents and elders." I hurry out to the corner of the yard where the bucks of water and the watering can are and return fresh and clean.

"Salaam, Uncle Enayat. Salaam, Teacher Sahib. Salaam, Father."

As we sit down to breakfast, Enayatollah Khan gives me a package and says, "Bibi Kowsar, please accept this as a gift from me. It isn't worthy of you, but—"

I take it from him and turn to Father. He is as puzzled as I am.

"Open it my girl," Enayatollah Khan says. "Open it!"

I slowly open the package and peek inside. It's the lily-white Cinderella bag. I shriek. I have been given the world.

"Father, look!" I say, running to him.

"Enayatollah Khan!" he says gratefully. "May God bless and keep you."

# 4

Kowsar doesn't waste a moment. As soon as they arrive home, she runs off with her new treasures to find Geesu.

"I have never seen a bag like this," she says rapt in awe. "What a beautiful color, what a pretty girl!"

"Her name is Cinderella. There is a storybook about her. I have that, too. It's in the bag."

"She looks like you."

"No, she doesn't. She looks like Simin. Her hair and eyes are a different color, but she is as beautiful as her," Kowsar says.

"It must have cost a lot of money."

"Enayatollah Khan gave it to me. He said it's a gift. And Teacher Sadeq bought the books."

Not caring who Enayatollah Khan is, Geesu carefully opens the bag and looks inside.

"All your books can fit in here. Are you going to bring it to school?"

"I don't know. What if the boys scratch it or scribble on it? I love it so much. When I saw it in the shop and I knew Father couldn't buy it for me, I went gray."

"Didn't Teacher Sadeq take you to the doctor?"

"He did. The doctor said, 'Bibi Kowsar, you don't have epilepsy, you're just very sensitive.' He said it was syncope-something. I can't remember. Then he said I must be strong and not let things frighten or upset me so much. But I wanted the bag so badly."

"Did Teacher Sadeq take you to see that director, too?"

"Geesu, he was horrible. He was rude to Teacher Sadeq and sent us to see another director. This one was even more horrible. He was ugly, and he looked at me like a hyena. Then he told Father it's time for him to give me to a husband. When we left, Father said he is a Talib."

"Did he like you?" Geesu giggles.

"Don't say that! He pulled — Come on, let's read Cinderella."

"You read it to me."

"You're so lazy!" Kowsar says, wiping her hands on her dress before opening the book. "Once upon a time, in a faraway land, a gentleman lived in a grand house with his young daughter. One day, the man thought his daughter needs a mother and decided to get married again. He married a woman who had two daughters of her own."

"She's here!" Geesu cries. "Our Cinderella!"

Kowsar looks up from the book and watches Simin walk into

the yard. She looks at her and Geesu with her bright eyes and smiles.

⌒

Two weeks later, on a sunny afternoon when the village is alive with the racket of children playing, a car stops on the cliff above the valley and a messenger hurries down the trail to inform Chief Abed that his guest has arrived. The chief quickly has two spirited horses saddled, and riding one and leading the other, he goes to greet his visitor.

Dressed in cornsilk tunic and pants, with a fine wool robe draped over his shoulders, Mawlawi Khodadad has come to inspect the school and pay a visit to Mobin Khan. He intends to tell the man, before your daughter begins menstruating, set your bride price, and I will take her as my wife. We both stand to gain. Me, a child bride of great beauty, and you, freedom from poverty.

Chief Abed bows and kisses the mawlawi's hand.

"Abed Khan, your women are not fair and rosy-cheeked for no reason," Khodadad says as they ride down to the village. "If this valley and this climate didn't breed houris, where in the world would?"

"Mawlawi Sahib, indeed our women are beautiful. They are wise and hardworking, too."

Khodadad gazes up at the mountains and breathes in the cool air. "This gorge of yours has many merits. Even your ugly crows give birth to sweet nightingales," he says, bursting into a laughter that shakes his beard and brings tears to his eyes.

Not wishing to counter his formidable guest, Chief Abed forces a grin and changes the subject.

"Mawlawi Sahib, would you like to first come to my house and rest, or shall we go directly to the school?"

"The school, of course. The school."

Some minutes later, they dismount their horses in the school-yard to the boisterous sound of students repeating after Teacher Sadeq, "The sky! The sky!"

Sitting at his desk, sipping tea, and cracking pumpkin seeds, the school principal jumps to his feet when he sees the mawlawi standing in the doorway, glaring at him. He quickly wipes his mouth with his sleeve and rushes to kiss his superior's hand.

"Director Sahib, the sight of your face has brightened my eyes," he stammers, taken aback by the unexpected visit. "Welcome, Sahib! Welcome! You bring us joy."

Ignoring him, Khodadad silently surveys the room, walks over to the desk and sits in the principal's chair.

"Sikhdad Khan," he says dryly, looking at the plate of pumpkin seeds. "You live in luxury, while the rest of us run around breathing dust in that damn town, trying to earn a bite of bread."

Alarmed by Khodadad's tone, Mullah Sikhdad finds it wiser to remain silent. The two have always taken each other's rank and position into consideration and helped each other along.

"Did you hear the children screaming, the sky, the sky?" Khodadad says, looking at him standing there with his hands on his chest as though in prayer or servitude. "That's where you fell from. You fell from the sky, with no name, no title, no nothing, and became principal of this school. It is thanks to me and my benevolence that you sit behind this desk. Even with a magnifying glass no one would have ever noticed your existence, much less given you a job."

Fears and speculations crowd Sikhdad's mind as he tries to figure out what could have made the mawlawi this cantankerous. Perhaps it's a ploy, he thinks. Perhaps the school budget and his salary have been cut and Khodadad is setting the stage, taking the upper hand before breaking the news to him.

"Are you a learned man, Mullah? Do you qualify for the position you hold? Students who studied religion under your tutelage have all ended up unemployed loafers!"

"But Director Sahib—"

"Shut your donkey-sack mouth!" Khodadad shouts and breaks into a cough.

Flustered, Mullah Sikhdad looks around for the water pitcher. Giving up, he runs out and returns with one.

"Please, Director Sahib, remain calm."

Khodadad grabs the pitcher, drains it in one breath and clears his throat.

"A girl in this school has read and committed to memory all the schoolbooks. And yet, she has not read even a fraction of the Quran! Woe is me! You would have done better taking your own life than sending her to *me*, the Director of Religious Education!"

Damn you, Sadeq, Mullah Sikhdad thinks to himself, I told you a hundred times not to take that cursed girl to Qala-e Naw. You didn't listen. You argued that you have spoken to the chief director. So confident, so convincing. Now, *I* am to blame! *I* have to pay the price. I knew no good would come of it. I will skin you alive if it's the last thing I do.

"And you call yourself a *mullah*!" Khodadad carries on. "How true that old saying: What befalls us is fallout of our own doing."

Sikhdad tries but fails to find the courage to tell the mawlawi that Teacher Sadeq was to take the girl to the chief director, not to him. Instead, he stands quietly as Khodadad gazes out the window at the trees and the narrow stream that feeds them.

"To the classroom!" he barks, abruptly standing up and marching out the door.

Hurrying after him, Mullah Sikhdad waves to Chief Abed, who has been pacing the hallway, to join them. As Khodadad opens the door to the only occupied classroom, children's clamor blares out and instantly dies down.

Teacher Sadeq is stunned to see the mawlawi.

"Stand at attention!" he quickly orders the class.

The students jump to their feet. Kowsar, panicked at the sight of the man, holds her head down and prays he will not notice her.

"Sit, sit. That's enough," Khodadad says, waving his hands up and down.

All eyes turn to Teacher Sadeq for permission. He nods.

"Teacher Sahib, how are the lessons coming along?"

"God be praised, Mawlawi Sahib, they're coming along well enough. Some students come to school in the morning, others in the afternoon. All are eager learners."

With her eyes pinned to the desk, Kowsar follows the sound of Khodadad's footsteps as he randomly moves around the classroom and calls on a few students to read from their book or answer a question. Her heart pounds wildly as she hears him move closer and closer to her and stop.

"You, cowering down like that, stand up!"

Frozen with fear, she cannot.

"Kowsar," Teacher Sadeq says, walking over to them. "The director asked you to stand."

Geesu nudges her. Still, Kowsar doesn't move.

"I said, stand up, girl!" Khodadad barks.

Geesu takes her arm and pulls her to her feet. Suddenly the classroom spins around, breath freezes in her lungs, and shaking violently, Kowsar falls.

Khodadad swings around and gapes at Mullah Sikhdad standing by the door, as Teacher Sadeq quickly lifts Kowsar off the floor and walks away from him.

"Director Sahib, the girl has fainting spells," Mullah Sikhdad says. "Nothing to worry about."

"I see, I see," Khodadad says, quickly walking out of the classroom.

Back in the principal's office, he drops down in the chair and looks out the window. Listening to the black nightingale in a poplar tree, he tells himself, the child is indeed beautiful and desirable, but an epileptic girl will soon become a nuisance.

"Malawi Sahib," Teacher Sadeq says, walking in with Mullah Sikhdad. "You are a compassionate man. You will surely forgive her. Anxiety is the cause. But as I mentioned the day I brought her to you, God has blessed her with unrivaled genius."

"Yes, she fainted that day, too. But never mind," he says, sitting up straight. "Teacher Sadeq, to be blunt, I do not approve of the way you conduct your class. And Mullah Sikhdad, I'm disappointed at how you're running this school."

He raises his hand, silencing Mullah Sikhdad who is instantly stiff and on the defensive.

"With thirty boys and girls crammed in one classroom, what sort of teaching and discussions could you possibly have? What values will these children learn?"

"Mawlawi Sahib, we have only recently opened the school," Mullah Sikhdad argues. "We started with one class in the morning and then added a second one in the afternoon. To have more classes, we need more teachers. Even now, Nadim Khan helps as a volunteer. And we will need more students. Many families don't want to send their children to school. They need them to work and help earn the daily bread. There have even been instances when the boys have had to bring their goats and sheep to school with them."

"You misunderstand, Sikhdad. My indignation is at seeing girls and boys sitting together. What were you thinking!? Separate them! *Immediately*. And may God forgive you. . . . As of tomorrow, one class will be girls only, the other boys only. And Sikhdad, instead of sitting here cracking pumpkin seeds, start teaching Islam, the Quran, the Prophet's teachings. And he who fails to comply will pay dearly. Do you understand?"

"Certainly, Mawlawi Sahib. Certainly," the mullah says, bowing his way out of the office.

"And you, Teacher Sadeq, don't just stand there. Go and see to your students."

With both teacher and principal gone, Khodadad turns and grins with satisfaction at his silent host, sitting quietly across the room.

"Now, Abed Khan, let you and I go for a walk and some fresh air. And send word to your servant to prepare mutton stew."

"Upon my eyes, Mawlawi Sahib," Chief Abed says, touching his fingertips to his eyes.

Effervescent water ripples and weaves its way among the rocks. The canopy of willow and ash trees casts shade a sanctuary from the sun. The two men stroll in silence until Mawlawi Khodadad sighs deeply and muses, "People say mullahs think of nothing but their stomach and women. But to my faith I swear, this divine nature has me as excited as a greyhound. That damned Qala-e Naw has nothing. You spend all day worrying about louts and lowlifes who think the Americans have come to save them, and soon their world will be a field of flowers... They have lost their religion, their honor. They watch whores dancing on television. Their mouths water and their hands stay in their pants all night. Faithless imbeciles run the media, incite people with music and debauchery. Believe me, Abed Khan, if this bedlam continues, even the faith of the mullahs will go to the wind."

Chief Abed, his fingers laced behind him, continues in silence. Prudence, he knows, is in neither agreeing nor countering his guest.

"You should thank God, you have no electricity, hence no television, in your corner of heaven," Khodadad goes on. "Only a few days ago, some fool with a foot-long beard was lecturing that a girl's consent must be a precondition to marriage! Well, damn your father, you degenerate letch! The day you ask a girl if she likes so-and-so for a husband, it's all over. Decency lost!

"And you should see the schools in Qala-e Naw. Lessons and learning are done with. Hijab, lost! Black chadors have shrunk into headscarves the size of your hand. With their faces and hair showing, girls strut around swinging their asses. They all have a mobile telephone and send each other hearts, flowers, and butterflies! . . . The cows ate all purity. May God save and absolve us."

A tight cluster of wild pennyroyals has bloomed on the edge of the stream. Water washes over those that have bowed their heads and releases their perfume into the air.

"Abed Khan, do you understand what these flowers are telling us? . . . They're saying, If you don't like us, don't sit with us." He bursts into loud laughter and slaps his host on the shoulder.

Later, as they head back, Khodadad says, "I swear, Abed Khan, I will not leave you and Sikhdad in peace until I have one of these Tali nymphs. I will have my foot on your neck day and night." He chuckles amicably and adds, "And you know, my sting is far worse than what you imagine."

"Mawlawi Sahib," the village chief says, forcing a smile. "Pick any girl you like. I wish you would take a wife from our people so that we will always be blessed with your care and protection."

"Who would you propose?"

Chief Abed looks at Khodadad, trying to muster the courage to ask his age.

"Speak up, man! What are you wringing your hands about?"

"Well, I'm considering matters of suitability."

"You want to know my age? Well, I might be fifty-eight. But don't concern yourself with age, I'm as virile as ever. A hundred of your little chicks couldn't keep up with me."

"And, well, should I assume you desire a virgin?" Chief Abed asks apprehensively.

"Of course! Don't you think I deserve one? And I'll be generous with the bride price. Two hundred sheep. . . . To be honest, when the teacher brought Kowsar to Qala-e Naw last week, I said to myself, I will not let this one go. But I've changed my mind. Her fainting will be too much of a headache."

Chief Abed, needing time to quiet his mind and temper, goes to the stream and drinks a handful of cool water.

"Yes, Mobin Khan's girl will be a headache," he says, walking back. "It's best you choose someone else."

"I will, I will. . . . By the way, what do your people plant in their farms?"

"Wheat, peas, mung beans, sometimes potatoes, eggplant, zucchini and the like."

"These will fill neither their pockets nor their stomach. How about opium? Does anyone plant it around here?"

"Thank God, no," Abed Khan says warily. "That seed has not made its way here."

"Don't get me started on how much the damn crops yield in valleys with a good climate."

~

Mawlawi Khodadad spends the night at Chief Abed's house, enjoys two hearty servings of mutton stew and carries on about any and all subjects. The next morning, he returns to the school and interrupts Teacher Sadeq's class.

Standing with his back to the blackboard, Mawlawi Khodadad lectures the students about heaven, hell, and Judgement Day. He urges them to embrace abstinence, honesty, and morality, and frightens them of sin and depravity. All the while his restless eyes appraise the girls.

Kowsar again holds her head down and prays he doesn't approach her. Her prayers are answered, but now and then, the mawlawi peeks at her, worried that she might faint and ruin his search and sermon, which is now meandering through the hereafter. And when his eyes land on Simin, his voice cracks.

"May God bless you, girl. What is your name?"

"Simin," she says, rising to her feet.

"Excellent. Simin, dear, whose daughter are you?"

"Abdul Ghafoor's, Sahib."

Khodadad walks to the window and looks out. The child is indeed a delicate and delectable beauty, he thinks to himself. He takes a deep breath and collects himself. He mustn't let his excitement show.

"And Simin," he asks, turning back, "can you read and write?"

"Yes, Mawlawi Sahib," Teacher Sadeq says. "She can read and write."

"May God bless this child. Take your seat girl. . . . Well, where was I? Yes, hijab. Hijab is a woman's shield. Concealed in a burqa, a woman is safe."

He goes on to counsel that pubescent girls and those whose breasts have started to grow must wear a burqa, or at least a black chador, so that men who are not kin do not cast eyes on them.

"God," he prays in conclusion. "Save this land from the infidels and protect the poor and innocent from tyranny, oppression, and evil. Amen."

Before leaving the village, Khodadad pulls a sulking Mullah

Sikhdad aside and instructs him to prepare a roster of five teachers and enrollment documents for a hundred students, and to send monthly reports to the Administration Office, so that salaries for the teachers and expenses for school supplies and maintenance are sent in a timely manner.

"Mawlawi Sahib, you are asking for the impossible!" Mullah Sikhdad objects. "Where am I going to find that many students and teachers in this nowhere land?"

"You don't have a grain's worth of brain!" Khodadad snickers. "On paper, Sikhdad. On paper! That's all! Send it at the end of every month so that funding can be arranged. Or do you not favor my herd to graze around Tali!?"

Color returns to Mullah Sikhdad's face and the fear that had festered in him dissipates. "May God bless your forefathers, Mawlawi Sahib," he says, his hands again on his chest. "You've had me in knots since yesterday."

"Don't play coy! You are lucky that the lottery produced your name, and we built a school here, and even more fortunate that there is someone in the chief director's seat who has filled the villages and valleys of this province with schools, teachers, and students, and now has more money than banks can handle. You and I adding a few teachers and students to the books is no great heist, we are simply getting what is due to us. . . . Now, go. And don't think too much, it will age you."

"Yes, Mawlawi, upon my eyes."

"Also, I have asked Abed Khan to make certain arrangements for me. Help him out and make sure it is taken care of."

"Of course, Mawlawi," he says with a deep bow.

As Mawlawi Khodadad leaves for Qala-e Naw, Chief Abed sends his servant to summon Abdul Ghafoor. An hour later, the anxious man is standing in front of his desk.

"Please, take a seat, Ghafoor Khan. I want to talk to you about a blessed and beneficial matter."

"Chief, I don't have much time. I left my four sheep in Asb-e Khuni pasture. If the wolves get to them, I'll be done for. I have seven hungry mouths to feed."

"Yes, I know. That's why I wanted to see you. If you agree to a certain proposal, you will never have to worry about those seven hungry mouths again. Mawlawi Khodadad, director of religious education in the province, was here to inspect the school. He is a man of power and position in Badghis. While at the school, he saw your Simin and took a liking to her. He has asked me to request her hand in marriage. Talk it over with your wife and bring me your answer. And you should know that the mawlawi is a wealthy and generous man."

"Marriage? To whom? His son?"

"No," Chief Abed says as casually as he can manage. "To himself."

"Himself! But how old is he?"

"I believe around fifty, perhaps fifty-five."

Pain stabs between Abdul Ghafoor's shoulder blades and the blood drains from his face.

"But he must already have a wife!"

"I believe he has two," Chief Abed says, shuffling though the papers on his desk. "Go, Ghafoor Khan, go before the wolves get to your sheep. There are three girls held up in every house, waiting for a suitor. If you don't give him your daughter, someone else will. What man wouldn't want a herd of two hundred sheep? What man wouldn't want his children's stomachs to be full? Come back when you've had time to think."

"But, Abed Khan, my girl is only nine! A sapling!"

"Well, Ghafoor Khan, that's what he wants, a sapling. Otherwise, there are plenty of old maids around. Believe me, I told him Simin is very young. But he said, 'What good fortune for a father to have his girl start menstruating in her husband's house.' He's a mawlawi, if you open your mouth, he will close it with a hundred hadiths and verses of Quran."

Abdul Ghafoor drifts out to the vestibule, puts on his patched-up shoes, and goes to find his sheep.

A thousand thoughts rage in his mind as he hurries back along the river trail. The waves break against the rocks, the nightingales sing, the doves coo, and someone is playing a reed flute up in the mountains. Now and then, a passerby greets him. But Abdul Ghafoor is deaf and blind to it all.

Yes, he thinks to himself, I am penniless, I am helpless, I hardly have bread to feed my family, but I have honor and decency. Damn your father, you pig, for going after my daughter. Simin is young enough to be your grandchild. You are rich. Good for you! Go to your own village and find yourself a new wife. Don't come sniffing around my house. And in ten years' time you will drop dead and make a young widow of any girl you marry. No, Mawlawi Khodadad, even if you were to offer me the world, I would not give you my daughter."

Abdul Ghafoor is restless. At night he lies down to sleep, but sleep does not come. He is thinking of Simin, thinking that if he turns away this suitor, the man can have his pick of a thousand other girls. Chief Abed's words echo in his mind. "There are three girls held up in every home, if you don't give him your daughter, some-one else will. Who wouldn't want a herd of two hundred sheep?"

Abdul Ghafoor tosses and turns in battle with himself.

"Ghafoor, are you alright?" Homeira asks, sitting up.

"Wife, I'm robbed of sleep. And don't ask me why."

"Do you want me to rub your back?" she asks, sliding her hands under his nightshirt. "Did you have a nightmare?"

"No."

"Then what's wrong?"

"Let me be. Life and misery are what's wrong."

Homeira asks nothing more, but her hands massaging his back confuse Abdul Ghafoor's thoughts. He pushes her away, takes his pillow, and goes up to the roof. The night is clear and the sky full of stars. He stares at them. Some blink, some move around, now and then one shoots across the sky and disappears.

Long ago, when he was a boy, his father told him everyone has a star in the sky. "The large bright stars belong to the wealthy, the medium stars belong to those of mediocre means, the small fading stars belong to the poor. And those that rip through the sky and burst belong to the dying."

"Where is my star, Father?" Abdul Ghafoor grieves. "Am I so destitute that I don't have one at all? Father, if there is a heaven, complain to God. Tell him Ghafoor has fallen to his knees. For two years the seeds he has sown have reaped nothing. His milk cow yelped in the middle of the night and died. All he has left are a few sheep. One by one he sells them for wheat and rice. And when the last one is gone, his world will crumble.

"God! My father was a good man, honest and hardworking, never missed a prayer. You gave him nothing. You gave his son nothing. But you gave and you gave to the likes of Khodadad, so that he can set his eyes on a little girl who doesn't even have a pair of plastic slippers to wear and goes barefoot even in the dead of winter. And now, what a crossroads you have set before me!"

Floundering and wallowing in his thoughts, it suddenly occurs to Abdul Ghafoor that Mawlawi Khodadad's intent might in fact be God's benevolence. After all, Badghis is full of girls, but the man came knocking on his door. Uncertainty stirs inside him. Perhaps this is God showing him mercy.

Abdul Ghafoor pictures himself in a long sheepskin coat, standing on a boulder, looking out at a sprawling field crowded with his herd. He sees the ewes pregnant and the rams robust. He sees a slaughtered lamb hanging from a hook in the kitchen. Ghafoor, Homeira asks, what cut of meat should I roast for you tonight?

Abdul Ghafoor leaps to his feet and hurries down the stairs. He grabs his shepherd's stick and races out of the house. I will not let this godsend go the way of someone else, he says to himself. I'd be a fool to say no. And Simin will live in comfort. Who knows, the man might live another fifty years and my daughter can happily settle beside him. I must not deny God's gift.

He beats the knocker on Chief Abed's door until the startled man comes to the window and shouts, "Who is it? What has happened?"

"It's me, Ghafoor. I agree. I agree to two hundred sheep and two milk cows."

"You oaf! Couldn't you have come in the morning?"

"No, by God, no! I thought, what if you change your mind and ask someone else."

"Go, you fool, go home and sleep."

❦

"Wife! Wake up and make me some tea. I betrothed Simin to a wealthy suitor!"

"What did you say?" Homeira asks half asleep.

"I said I betrothed Simin to a wealthy suitor."

Homeira jolts up and gapes at him. "What have you done!?"

"We are free of misery," Abdul Ghafoor says, leaning against the wall. "We own two hundred sheep and a pair of milk cows. Our life has finally come together, and for good. I promised Simin to a rich and powerful mawlawi. He is in the government and well established. Everyone in Badghis knows him."

"Ghafoor, you are *sick*!" Homeira screams. "You've gone mad!"

"Shut your mouth, wretch! Your father and forefathers were sick and mad. Your gypsy clan were sick and mad. Another word and I'll give you a beating like the last time! You won't be able to hold your head up for a month."

Remembering his stick coming down on her, Homeira instinctively recoils and wraps her arms around her head.

"Now, open your ears and listen," Abdul Ghafoor growls. "Abed Khan had me go see him yesterday. He said Mawali Khodadad has asked for Simin's hand in marriage, he'll give two hundred sheep. And I'll haggle for a pair of milk cows out of him, too. Abed Khan said every father dreams of a groom like the mawlawi. He said if you say no, someone else will say yes. I thought about it. At first, I said Simin is too young. But in the middle of the night I realized this may be God taking pity on me, that if I say no to this rich and powerful soon-to-be son-in-law, I will be poor for the rest of my life. So I went to Chief Abed and said, yes. I gave him my word and that's the end of it."

Homeira is silent, buried in sorrow as colossal as the mountains of Tali.

The next day, Chief Abed, Mullah Sikhdad, and three village elders arrive at Abdul Ghafoor's house. Given the man's circumstances, Chief Abed has brought a bag of candied almonds, and discreetly gives it to him at the door.

"Do you have an embroidered napkin?" he whispers.

"No, we just have a plain rose-colored one."

"That's good enough. Put the almonds on the napkin in a plate and offer it to Mullah Sikhdad after we have given our blessing."

"Please come in," Abdul Ghafoor says, quickly tucking the bag under his jacket. "Welcome. Our humble home is graced by your visit."

Leading the men to the small guestroom on the rooftop, with every step he climbs he slightly bows and awkwardly repeats, "Welcome, you have brought us joy."

Up on the roof, he unlocks the weather-beaten door and stands aside as the men take off their shoes and walk in. Abdul Ghafoor follows them and sits quietly by the door.

"Ghafoor Khan," Chief Abed says. "Go tell your children's mother to prepare tea, and hurry back."

Abdul Ghafoor leaps to his feet and the forgotten bag of almonds falls out from under his jacket. Embarrassed and at a loss for what to do, he stands there blankly looking at Chief Abed.

"It's all right, man. Pick it up," the village chief says lightly. "We don't stand on ceremony among friends."

With the bag snatched off the floor and their host out of the room, Mullah Sikhdad snickers, "He would have died of shame if only he had a shroud to be buried in."

"Don't compare yourself with others," Chief Abed retorts. "You know very well that the majority of the villagers have no more than he does. Alas! What is one to do with you mullahs?"

"As long as a mullah and a mufti remain on this land, we have yet to suffer more!" Yar-Mohammad Khan quips.

Everyone laughs, with the exception of Mullah Sikhdad who shifts on his cushion and warns, "For the good of the people of Tali, I would suggest you refrain from such comments in front of the new groom. Or else, may God protect you."

The men look at each other and grin in silence.

As soon as Abdul Ghafoor returns, Chief Abed, clears his throat and says, "Mullah Sahib, although I spoke with Ghafoor Khan yesterday, for everything to be rightfully sanctioned, with witnesses, assurances, and agreements in place, I declare that we are here today on behalf of Mawlawi Khodadad to ask Ghafoor Khan for the hand of his daughter Simin in marriage."

"Ghafoor Khan," he continues. "God be praised, have you consulted with your family and given the request enough thought?"

"Yes, Chief Abed, I have," Abdul Ghafoor says, his eyes cast down.

"And what have you decided?"

"I have decided to give my daughter to Mawlawi Khodadad."

"How many children do you have?"

"God be praised, five."

"May God the benevolent give you more. And, how old is the eldest?"

"Twelve, Chief Abed."

"And Simin is . . ."

"Nine, soon to be ten."

"Do you expect a bride price for Simin?"

"Yes, Chief Abed. I am a man without means and I cannot enter this kinship without an offering."

"What are your expectations?"

"Two hundred sheep — a hundred mish and a hundred chaari breeds," Abdul Ghafoor says in keeping with the chief's promise. Then he pauses, fidgets, and mumbles, "And two milk-cows. Also, I have no money for the wedding celebration and can't provide a dowry."

"There is no power greater than that of God. Man, you might as well ask the mawlawi for his life!" Mullah Sikhdad grumbles, unable to hold his tongue. "Where is your shame, your modesty? You are a man of faith, do not be covetous!"

"Ghafoor Khan," Chief Abed says. "Perhaps you would forego the cows."

"I cannot, Sahib. I won't accept anything less than two hundred sheep and two milk-cows."

"Well then, given the mawlawi's eagerness, bring the tea and sweets and let us celebrate the union."

"You were too hasty, Abed Khan," Mullah Sikhdad says as soon as Abdul Ghafoor is out of earshot. "You didn't give me a chance to bargain with the man. I could have brought it down by forty, fifty sheep!"

"You know as well as I do, the mawlawi has his eyes set on the girl. He is willing to give up two hundred sheep for her, and I will gladly wrestle two cows out of him for this poor man. Just don't do anything that would make Ghafoor change his mind. Otherwise, we will all pay dearly."

"Mullah Sahib," Chief Abed says when Abdul Ghafoor hurries in with the tea tray and the plate of candied almonds. "It's time for the prayer."

Mullah Sikhdad scowls, holds up his hands, and begins.

—

News of Simin's betrothal explodes like a bomb in Tali. Many envy Abdul Ghafoor his overnight wealth, many reproach him for the ill-suited and inappropriate match. Now a prosperous man, Abdul Ghafoor pays no mind to any of it.

At the school an unfamiliar air weighs in the classroom. The students are withdrawn, Teacher Sadeq sits by the window, deep in thought and drained of his enthusiasm to teach, and Kowsar looks at Simin's empty seat and imagines her in the clutches of a demon. Her mother's words echo in her mind, "A wretch has no voice of her own. No one will ask for her consent." Everyday there will be one less girl in class, she thinks to herself, and soon there will be none. Every day they will take one of us away, until it's Geesu's turn, my turn.

"No! I won't!" she screams.

Teacher Sadeq jumps out of his seat.

"What's the matter, Kowsar?"

Embarrassed, Kowsar stammers, "Nothing, Teacher Sahib. Do you read storybooks?"

"When I have time," he says, puzzled by her outburst. "Why do you ask?"

"It's just that when Geesu and I were reading Cinderella, Simin kept popping into our mind. She looks like her. Cinderella has almond-shaped eyes, arched eyebrows, and beautiful hair, and she is funny and smart. Just like Simin. So I gave Simin the book to read. She read it in one night. She really liked it, she said she loved the happy ending. But now I feel so sad."

Teacher Sadeq paces the classroom, knowing that if it was not for Kowsar fainting that day, it would be her seat that is now empty.

"Teacher Sahib, where is the Land of Fairytales? The place that has a town of toys and dolls."

"Kowsar, my dear, there is no Land of Fairytales. What many cities have are amusement parks with rides and games for children. They believe that children need to play, that it's healthy for them."

"Teacher Sahib, do their girls go to husbands, too?" Geesu asks.

"Well, yes, but only when they are old enough and if they want to. In many countries young people have to be eighteen to get married. We have a similar law in our country. Boys have to be eighteen, girls sixteen, but—"

The teacher stops himself and reluctantly goes to the blackboard to start the day's lesson. Minutes later the door opens, and Mullah Sikhdad walks in.

"Starting tomorrow, girls and boys will have separate classes," he announces. "Girls will come to school in the morning, boys in the afternoon."

❧

The day Simin is taken away, there is halfhearted celebration in Tali. The villagers sacrifice a cow and cook *shorba*. The men gather near the school, happy that after a long time they will feast on a bowl of beef stew. The women have congregated in the homes of Abdul Ghafoor and his neighbor, Samad Khan. They have adorned their hands and feet with henna and have donned colorful dresses with matching pants and vests, their sleeves, edges, and hems trimmed with sequins, beads, or embroideries. They play the *doyra*, sing, and dance with less vivacity than is their tradition and despite Mawlawi Khodadad's fatwa that music is haram and forbidden by Islam.

Simin's cheeks have been rouged, her eyes lined with kohl, and her lips caked with lipstick. In a bride's traditional green dress festooned with gold-colored sequins, she resembles Cinderella more than ever. Silently enduring the rituals, she still cannot understand why her father has given her to a husband, and wonders what that man will expect of her. The first time they told her Mawlawi Khodadad is to be her husband, the world spun around, she screamed and fainted. Now, seeing Kowsar and Geesu walk in, her lips tremble and she bursts into tears.

"Get out of here!" Homeira screams, running toward the two like a scorpion ready to sting. "Go home and stay there. Simin doesn't need to see your ill-omened faces! Go!"

Kowsar and Geesu, confused and frightened, run through the crowd of women and children and escape to the road. Homeira is plagued by an even greater fear, that her delicate child will not survive the conjugal night. Filled with trepidation, she has decided that when her husband puts her daughter's hand in Mawlawi Khodadad's hand, and before they are sent off with God's blessing, she will quietly plead with the mawlawi to be gentle with Simin. Yes, she thinks to herself, now that Ghafoor has devastated and destroyed my daughter and reduced her life to ashes, I fear nothing and no one. I will beg that man to not harm my child.

Abdul Ghafoor solemnly stares at the men as they stuff their mouths with beef and quickly chew and swallow, hungry for the next mouthful. And in between, they talk and laugh. But the owner of a large herd of sheep who now deems himself a prosperous man of dignity, secretly fears for his daughter, too. God, he prays, you heard my pleas and blessed me with a herd, freed me from poverty. Bless me once more and protect my child.

Later that afternoon, as the men return to work and the women sit talking, Mawlawi Khodadad arrives on horseback, escorted by a company of cheering and ululating men. Dressed in fine white tunic, pants, vest, and a handwoven robe, his beard freshly hennaed, and his eyes lined with kohl, he beams with joy in anticipation of the night he will spend with his beautiful nine-year-old bride.

Seeing the party arrive, Abdul Ghafoor hurries home and tells the women to quickly leave the guestroom and go to the room downstairs.

"Welcome, Mawlawi, welcome," he calls down from the edge of the roof. "Please, come in."

The men carefully help the groom dismount, and Mullah Sikhdad tidies his clothes and smooths his bushy eyebrows.

"Now go," he says. "I have said prayers to ward off evil."

"May you be rewarded," Khodadad says, smiling at him. "I hope soon I will see you become a groom again, too."

"Hush! My wife is here," Mullah Sikhdad whispers. "I won't live to see the sunrise if she hears you."

"What a henpecked husband you've turned out to be!" Khodadad snickers.

The guestroom is small for the number of Khodadad's men. Some stand in the doorway, others remain out on the rooftop. The groom takes his place at the head of the room, flanked by Chief Abed and Mullah Sikhdad.

"Go to your daughter and tell her to accept you as her lawful representative," Mawlawi Khodadad instructs Abdul Ghafoor. "And we need a second representative. Abed Khan, go with him and get the girl's approval."

Abdul Ghafoor is filled with trepidation, knowing he will be in grave trouble if Simin panics and creates a scene that proves embarrassing for the mawlawi. Outside the room downstairs, he announces himself and Abed Khan, and opens the door. Only a few women have stayed behind to console the bride. Simin, with streaks of kohl on her cheeks, looks desperately at her father and bursts into fresh tears.

"Don't cry, my life, don't cry!" he begs. "God will bless you and make you happy. My dear Simin, do you accept me and Chief Abed as your lawful representatives?"

Simin doesn't understand. All she knows is the pain in her heart that she felt the moment her father appeared in the doorway. Abdul Ghafoor signals to his wife to step in.

"Say, yes, my girl," Homeira says. "It is not proper to keep Father and Abed Khan waiting. Say that you accept them to represent you."

Confused and exhausted, Simin wishes everyone would leave so she could lie down and sleep.

"My girl," Abdul Ghafoor says gently as he walks in and kneels in front of her, "if you love Mother and Father and you want us to have honor and respect, you must say, yes."

"I do, I love you very much," Simin says, choking on her tears.

Seeing the situation take a turn for the worse, Chief Abed says, "Come, Ghafoor Khan. It's done. She said, 'I do.' Let's go."

The two hurry back to the guestroom, and to the men's delight attest to having the bride's permission to speak for her. Mullah Sikhdad recites the marriage sermon, says a prayer, and takes a handful of sugared almond slivers and sprinkles them over the groom.

"Felicitations! May God have you grow old together."

Khodadad stands up and the men one by one come to congratulate and embrace him.

"The day is near its end," he says cheerfully as the last man pays his respect. "I must take my bride back to town."

"Go with God," Chief Abed says. "Ghafoor Khan, bring Simin outside."

Rushing down the stairs, the nervous father trips and falls. He quickly gets up and shakes the dust off his pants.

"Homeira," he calls from behind the door. "They're ready to leave. Get Simin ready."

Wails rise inside the room as the women mourn.

"They're taking my little Simin!" Homeira screams. "They're taking Mother's heart, Mother's helping hand."

"I won't go!" Simin shrieks. "Mother, don't let them take me! Father, I don't want to go!"

Abdul Ghafoor sinks to the floor and cries.

Sounds of grieving travel outside the house. The men agree, it is a difficult moment, the women should be left alone to cry and unburden themselves. But Mawlawi Khodadad is impatient to return to Qala-e Naw before the call to evening prayers, and eager for a memorable night with his new wife.

"Abed Khan, go put an end to this," he says. "Otherwise, they will weep and whimper until morning."

"Wait, Abed Khan," Mullah Sikhdad intervenes as he heads back to the house. "If my wife is of any use for a single day in her life, that day is today."

At the door to the women's room, he coughs loudly and calls her. "Nematollah's Mother, my dear, step out for a moment."

His wife walks out and wipes away her tears.

"What a surprise," she snickers. "Today of all days you call me with affection!"

"Today of all days you shined like the moon among a thousand women. Who, other than you would I call with affection?"

"Out with it, man! This is no time to sweet-talk me. What do you want?"

"Bring the bride. Mawlawi Khodadad has far to travel. Left alone, there will be no end to you women sniveling."

Smiling, he returns to the men waiting outside.

"If I know my wife, she'll bring the bride right away."

Hardly a minute later, the sound of women bursting into sobs again echoes from the house.

"Didn't I tell you!" Mullah Sikhdad chuckles.

"Ghafoor Khan, come and take your daughter," Homeira says from the front door.

Simin, draped in a green chador, throws her arms around her father and weeps.

"My girl, don't cry. In a couple of days, I'll come to see you," he says, carrying her to Khodadad. "May you be happy, may God protect you."

Already on his horse, Khodadad reaches down and takes Simin by the arms, but she shrieks and tightens her grip around her father. Impatient and annoyed, Khodadad smacks her hands, pulls her up, and sits her in front of him on the saddle. Homeira runs to them, hoping to kiss her daughter one last time and have a word with the groom. But Khodadad quickly drives his horse into a gallop and leads his men away. Homeira can see or say nothing through the cloud of dust in the wake of the horses' hooves.

Kowsar and Geesu, standing in the distance, watch as the white horse carries Simin away.

It is the time of year when silver tarnishes, the mountain river no longer roars, the black nightingales grow quiet, and the partridges mourn. The sun wishes a cloud would cast a curtain between God and Earth. The horse speeds along the trail. One rider triumphant, the other paralyzed with fear.

Life resumes its course in Tali. The birds sing, the sheep bleat, and the shepherd boys play their flutes. Clouds bring rain and the farms turn green. Harvest time comes. The wheat is threshed and bread is baked for dinner spreads.

# 5

THE MOMENT WE ARRIVE at his house, Khodadad throws me in a room and locks the door. Sometime later, he comes and tries to undress me. I won't let him. I'm afraid. He is ugly and terrifying. His breath is foul, and his eyes are menacing.

"No!" I beg, cowering in a corner. "I want to go home, I want my mother!"

"If you behave," he says, coming toward me, "everything will be all right."

I run around the room to escape him, but he grabs me by the hair and pulls my face close.

"I am your husband," he growls. "Do you understand? I have taken you as my wife. Now, stop or I will break every bone in your body."

He throws me on the bedding, straddles me, and grabs me by the throat.

"Wretch," he says, tightening his grip. "Don't give me any trouble."

He tears off my clothes and throws them aside. Then he sits and leers at my body. I don't understand what it is he wants to do with me. He starts fondling, kissing, and licking me. Then he gets up and undresses. His hairy figure is grotesque. I cover my eyes with my hands. He throws himself on top of me. Buried under his bulk, I gasp for air. I pray for someone to save me, to get him off of me so I can breathe. But hard as I fight and scream, there is no savior, no defender. An excruciating pain stabs between my legs. I shriek and faint.

—

When I regain consciousness, pain still throbs in my abdomen and vagina. The sheet is wet with blood and a piece of cloth has been tucked between my legs. I don't have the energy to move, and I can't see clearly. I hear women whispering in the room. As my vision clears, I see them. An older woman with a small green tattoo on her chin and forehead. Her face has started to wrinkle. The other one is younger, with sunken eyes and pockmarked skin. Hearing me moan, they hurry to my side. The older woman holds up my head and the other one pours some bitter liquid in my mouth. When I have swallowed it, she lays my head down on the pillow and tells me I will be well by tomorrow.

But I am not. I suffer all night. The slightest movement is painful and causes blood to ooze between my legs. In the morning, the two come to change the cloth. Seeing my face, they are alarmed. The older woman, who has a kind face, runs out of the room.

"You brute!" I hear her shout a few minutes later. "Old world remedies will not keep this girl alive! She is bleeding an ocean and her face is as white as cotton. If you don't take her to a doctor, you might as well bring a corpse-washer when you come home tonight."

"May she suffer my pain, too!" Khodadad shouts back. "I will kill her with my own two hands before I take her to a doctor and allow a man to see her."

"Then take her to a woman doctor! There are now three or four of them in town. The girl is all alone, she has no kith and kin here."

"If you are so concerned, you be her kith and kin and take her to whatever hell hole you want. But don't ask me for anything! I have a thousand other headaches. And if she dies, she dies. I'll get another one."

The sound of his mocking laughter moves away and fades.

The older woman, who I later learn is named Zoleikha, wraps me in a blanket, hoists me up on a donkey, and takes me to a woman doctor. She tells her that I am her husband's new wife. The doctor shakes her head and says I am too young and not of marriage age.

"I know," Zoleikha says. "But what can I do?"

The doctor examines me and explains that there are severe internal and external lacerations. "She needs to have an operation," she says. "And I will need to call on another doctor to assist. It will cost around twenty thousand afghanis. You can take her to a public hospital, but they don't have women doctors there."

Zoleikha thinks for a while and says, "She is in a bad state. Do what you must. I will find the money."

An hour later, the doctor anesthetizes me.

~

A creature with sharp claws and fangs is tearing at my hair and slashing through my skin. I run, it chases after me and grabs me. I struggle for what seems an eternity, until I open my eyes and remember everything. I am distraught realizing I have not died. I am still alive. Zoleikha is sitting at my bedside. There's a serum attached to my arm. A yellow liquid drips down and makes its way into my vein.

"Are you all right, dear?"

My tears flow.

"You little girl," she says, caressing my hair. "I know what you're going through. I come from where your heart is now."

Hearing Zoleikha talking to me, the doctor comes over and examines me.

"Her blood pressure has improved," she says. "She is doing much better than yesterday. But I must tell you, she will not be able to bear a child."

"When can I take her home?" Zoleikha asks.

Khodadad's image appears in front of me. I moan.

"Even the mention of home frightens her," the doctor sighs. "You can take her tonight, but not on a donkey. You must get a car and not let her move too much, there is still a risk of hemorrhaging. I will write a prescription for you to take to the pharmacy. She needs to take the medication for fourteen days. Then bring her back for me to examine her. And tell the mawlawi not to touch her for three months. If anything similar happens again, no doctor will be able to save her."

Zoleikha takes me home that night. Looking out the car window, I remember how I used to dream of one day riding in a car, someday seeing the town where Teacher Sadeq lives and talks about. How I now loathe it all. I want to be in Tali, with my mother beside me. An impossible wish. Tali is far away, on the bright side of dark mountains.

﹌

At home, he comes and sits next to my bedding. I despise him. I close my eyes, but he barks at me to open them and look at him. I obey.

"Listen carefully, you are my wife, and if you hadn't misbehaved, this would not have happened," he says. "Zoleikha asked me for a lot of money to pay the doctor. From now on, you will be obedient and not make a fuss. If you turn your ass to me one more time and do not do as you're told, may God save your parents and those brothers of yours. I will make them pay for the doctor and medicine, I will take back everything I gave them, and I will bury Abdul Ghafoor in debt. Understood?"

He gets up and leaves. I forget my pain. I see my family drowning in misery. I see my father suffering like a bird caught over flames. Simin, I imagine him saying, don't do this, my girl. This jackal has mercy on no one. Don't be stubborn. He has taken you as wife, there is no way back. Bear with it! And I imagine myself saying, Father, see what he has done to your child! I cannot tolerate this cruelty, this violence. Father, it is still my time to play with dolls, give back the sheep and take me home.

Tears stream down my temples and wet my hair. I know Father cannot hear me, but I sense his angst. He stands on a boulder, watching his herd. At times he is content and at times he is not. My mind wanders to Teacher Sadeq and our classroom. I think of Kowsar, Geesu, and Zahra. I could hardly wait to run to school every morning and be with them. I believe I will not see them again. I believe I will not see the star-filled nights and the sweet-singing black nightingales of Tali again.

Zoleikha walks in with a bowl of soup and sits on the floor next to me.

"My girl, you have a fever," she says, feeling my forehead. "Try to sit up. I made the soup with plenty of chicken and turmeric, eat some so I can give you your medication. The louse has gone out."

She tucks another pillow under my head and props me up.

"You shouldn't be obstinate with him. He has a hand for hitting. He is capable of anything you can imagine. God willing, when you are well, I will tell you my story, and you will understand what a depraved, ungodly man you have fallen prey to."

She takes a spoonful of the soup and holds it up to my lips.

"Eat, my girl, eat."

I try to sit up a bit more, but I feel paralyzed from the waist down. She puts the spoon back in the bowl, holds me under the arms, and slides me up against the pillows. I look at her face. I imagine life in this house has been a leprosy eating away at her.

She picks up the spoon again. I eat, and I cry. She has the same scent as my mother.

⟁

A month later, Father comes to visit me. He has gained some weight and his face is less sunburned. The moment he walks in the door with his saddlebag, all that I have suffered erases from my memory. I swing my arms around his waist and cling to him. He kisses me on the head, holds me at arm's length and says, "You have turned into a handful of bones!"

"Oh, it's nothing, Father. The air here doesn't agree with me, but I'm getting used to it."

He isn't convinced and looks at me with concern.

"Father, how is Mother?" I ask, changing the subject. "And my brothers?"

"All are well and send their salaams. God be praised, life is good. Your brothers have milk and cream every morning and meat every night. And when a sheep is ready for slaughter, I sell it and spend the money on the family. We think of you morning and night, and every time we sit to eat. Your brothers always say, 'We wish Simin were here, too.' And your mother speaks your name all the time. But tell me about yourself. How are you? Have you seen the town?"

"I've only gone once, but I don't like it here. Tali is something else. Tell me about the village, about the school, about Kowsar, Geesu, and Zahra. About everyone and everything."

"My dear Simin, don't worry about Tali. If a flood washes away the world, Tali will still be there. As always, everyone is busy working. The only news is that they gave Zahra to a family in Qades. In fact, they made a trade, they gave a bride and took a bride. As for me, I'm very busy. Cattle raising is not easy. The herd needs care and watchful eyes, otherwise the shepherd will come to me once a week with four or five sheep skins and claim the wolves got to them, disease killed them, they fell off a boulder. And by the end of the year my income will be gone. Me and your brother Youssef shepherd the herd, too. . . . I'm already worried sick about him. In a couple of years, it will be time for him to take a wife, and these days no one will even talk to you if you offer anything less than a hundred sheep."

Father puts his saddlebag on the floor and takes out a yellow cloth bundle.

"Your mother baked some egg biscuits for you."

I open it and smell the biscuits. They smell of Mother's hands. I break off a piece and put it in my mouth. The taste of home fills my senses. Father digs into the saddlebag again and pulls out a plastic bag.

"Some homemade butter," he says. "Have it with your breakfast. Your mother couldn't bring herself to eat it if you didn't have some, too. Go and put it somewhere cool."

I take the plastic bag to the kitchen and put it in a bowl of cold water. By the time I return, Father has emptied the saddlebag on the floor. There was nothing that my mother had not sent. From *qurut* to tart pottage and milk porridge, dried apricots and black raisins, local melons and wild mountain garlic. I cannot hold back my tears.

Three months have hardly passed when Khodadad orders for his bedding to be moved to my room.

"Simin, are you healthy? Happy?" he asks as he caresses my hair. "I heard your father came to see you. What did he say of cattle raising? He is well-off now, his dinner spread is plentiful. Thanks to you, he is now a somebody, wears a sheepskin coat, and sits at the head of the room at gatherings. And he prays to you for it all."

He slides his hand under my nightshirt and gropes me as he talks.

"I waited three months. I told myself, I should allow my young wife to get used to her new home and new life. I couldn't tolerate it anymore. I would have exploded if I hadn't come to you tonight. It's not easy having a wife as beautiful as Simin and sleeping apart from her."

He runs his fingertips over my lips. His stench invades my nose. Mother used to say, so and so has rotten underarms. I never understood what she meant. Now I do. I feel nauseous. I pray for God to help me bear it. Khodadad is pleased to see me submissive. He kisses me, then sits me up, takes off my nightshirt, and lays me down on his mattress.

"Very gently," he whispers in my ear. "Don't be afraid. I won't do anything for you to have to go to the woman doctor again."

I'm trembling. I see his shadow on the wall. He looks like a ghoul ripping off his clothes. I can't watch. I close my eyes. The ghoul and his sickening smell sits beside me.

"Simin, if you make a fuss, I'll turn your father into the beggar he was. Do you understand?"

I nod and silently cry as he pulls me under him and kisses me.

"Gently, all right?"

Unbearable pain tears inside me. I scream. He ignores me and does as he pleases until his body goes limp and he slumps on his side. Pain ripples from my groin to my hips and lower back. I start to bleed.

～

That night is the start of a new season in my dismal life. His wives, who have so far ignored my presence in the house, quickly learn that I have endured him raping me. In the morning, his second wife, Mah Jabin, comes to me and sneers, "You didn't die, pretty little Simin! I thought that scream of yours would have you going to the lady doctor again."

She laughs insolently and says, "Your days of being the favored wife are over. As of next week, you have to take your turn—sweeping, washing, scrubbing pots and pans."

Contrary to her name that suggests a face as beautiful as the moon, Mah Jabin is not only unattractive, but has a perpetually harsh expression and coarse manner. She believes I have replaced her and Khodadad will no longer pay attention to her.

One night as Khodadad returns from evening prayers at the mosque, I see Mah Jabin out on the veranda.

"Wait a minute," she snaps, blocking his way. "How many nights has it been since you shared my bed? Religious law and the spirit of Islam!? I may not be a mullah, but I am a mullah's daughter. They say take a wife when you can be fair and just. Where is your fairness? You cannot go to her tonight."

"Move out of my way," Khodadad sneers through his grin. "Don't compare yourself to a beautiful young bride."

"Mawlawi master!" Mah Jabin persists. "Even if the world topples, tonight is my night."

Khodadad's grin vanishes, and he glowers at her. "For years, you robbed Zoleikha of her rights and what was due her, and she never breathed a word. Now you think yourself equal to my new wife? You never learned how to flirt and when to seduce. . . . Get out of my way!"

With no intention of giving up, Mah Jabin braces herself against the door.

"If you don't come to me tonight," she threatens, "I will raise such hell and mayhem that will leave you shamed and disgraced! And I won't leave a single strand of hair on that little girl's head!"

I suddenly realize the perilous swamp I am trapped in. Dragged into a battle not of my making. I want to run outside and scream, Mah Jabin, he is all yours! He is all yours for all eternity. I hate him, I hate this fetid silo of filth. Take him as yours and tell him to send me back to Tali. But I shudder imagining the consequences.

Khodadad shoves her aside and walks in. He comes to my room and before closing the door, he shouts, "Zoleikha! Heat some water for me to cleanse myself before morning prayers."

The instructions seem to be aimed at infuriating Mah Jabin even more. He is about to hang up his jacket when the sound of china plates shattering reverberates throughout the house. He tears out of the room and moments later I hear Mah Jabin screaming.

"Don't! Stop, you bastard! Stop!"

━━◆━━

Early the next morning, as soon as Khodadad leaves the house, Mah Jabin comes to my room. Her face is badly bruised. She grabs me by the hair and drags me out from under my blanket.

"Get up, you whore! Get up!"

My hair is tearing out and my scalp burns.

"No, Mah Jabin, don't!" I plead, grabbing her hands. "I am miserable, so miserable! I am more miserable than you!"

She clenches my throat and shakes me.

"You bitch!" she screams. "It was your ill omen that ruined my life. I died waiting for him, but he didn't come to my bed. And last night I asked for fairness, instead he beat me with his fists. If you let him into your room tonight, I swear, I will tear you to pieces!"

Gasping for air, I nod. She shakes me again and throws me against the wall.

"You little slut! Tell him Mah Jabin has rights, too. She's your wife, too. Tell him he is a mawlawi, a Muslim, he must show justice. Do you understand!?"

I sit in my room and cry for hours, until Zoleikha walks in and sits next to me.

"Little Simin," she says, stroking my hair. "What can I say? Who can I blame? Learn to be patient. You have yet to see Mah Jabin and Khodadad at their most evil. The two are alike. One viler and more venomous than the other."

She is quiet for a while, then softly says, "I gave birth to three boys and two girls for him. Before the girls could tell their right hand from the left, he married them off and made them fly from their nest. It's been years since I heard from them. Of my sons, measles killed one, dysentery another. The one who survived, Khodadad took out of school, gave him a wife, and sent him off to Khalishkak to oversee his lands and herds. Then he took Mah Jabin as wife. But she turned out to be infertile. After all the mullahs, sorcerers, and doctors, still no child. . . . My girl, it's not easy getting along with her. She has the spite of a camel. In the early days, she had it in for me, too. I told her, take the husband and the house. I told her, it's all yours, I don't need or want him or his wealth. Over time, she calmed down. But the arrival of a beautiful child bride has made her crazy again. May God shelter and protect you. The old saying is true. Fear a sordid woman and a dog with sunken eyes."

I don't know what to say to her. All I know is that I am caught between millstones.

"Your father married you off too young, and he gave you to a man with two other wives," Zoleikha says. "What should I pray for God to do to such fathers? The day yours came to see you, the devil tempted me to scream, Take your pastries and gifts and don't ever show your face to this innocent child again! If you were kind and caring, you would not have traded her for sheep, you would not have given her away to a man who has no fear of God. But I held my tongue. Why pour salt over your wounds? What's done is done. . . . And now, you are barren. Soon, he will start finding fault with you and think of taking another young wife who can bear him children. I know the seed of this perverted man."

My life grows darker with each passing day.

At night, when Khodadad returns from evening prayers, he finds my door locked.

"Open the door," he barks.

"Go to Mah Jabin tonight," I call out. "It's her turn."

"I see! So, she has shown you her rabid side."

I want to remain silent, but I fear Mah Jabin's rage.

"Khodadad Khan, go to Mah Jabin, she is your wife, too. She has a right to you."

He wildly kicks the door until it breaks open.

"You miserable wretch," he shouts. "You're still a filly chomping hay and you dare lock the door on me!"

He slaps me hard across the face. My eyes flash and my nose starts to bleed. He takes a silk handkerchief from his pocket and holds it out to me.

"Take it! All I have to do is look at you, and you start bleeding!"

I wipe away the blood. My only consolation is that Mah Jabin knows I obeyed her.

~

Over time, the kitchen becomes my place. Now and then, when Zoleikha is not busy at the kiln, she helps me, and once in a while I lend her a hand. She says I am too young and small to work the kiln alone.

"Mah Jabin says the heat harms her complexion," Zoleikha says, quickly covering her mouth with the tip of her headscarf before bursting into laughter. "God sees and God gives. A ton of powder and rouge will be lost on that face!" Wiping her eyes, she puts her finger on her lips and whispers, "If she hears me, she will tear herself apart."

From Zoleikha I learn to sometimes laugh, I learn to keep Mah Jabin subdued. Khodadad is traveling more often, and with every trip his power and business dealings increase. When he's home, the guestroom across the front yard is always filled with Talibs, mullahs, and merchants. Several times a day, we brew tea and cook. We set the trays outside the door and knock for Khodadad to have his disciples take them inside.

Days when I have no work, I go to the second-floor room that overlooks the road we live on. I open the curtains and watch the busy intersection. I listen to the cars honking their horns and the traffic police shouting into their megaphones. I can feel there is life outside, people coming and going about their business. Occasionally, street vendors and peddlers come to our road. They sell everything from plastic watering cans to nail polish, hairbrushes, clothes, and fabric. Some are on motorcycles and play loud music to attract women and girls to shop. But we are not allowed to leave the house. Khodadad has warned that any wife who dares step outside without his permission will be cut in half. I like music. Father had an old transistor radio that he sometimes turned on and we would listen to songs and folk melodies. Taliban consider music to be sinful. It is banned in Khodadad's house. He says it will soon be banned everywhere.

From the window, I can also see the front yard of the house next door. There's a beautiful garden filled with colorful flowers that radiate peace and spread their perfume. The neighbor's children are always clean and tidy. Sometimes they help their father in the garden or play with their fluffy white dog. Watching them reminds me of Youssef and our own dog. There are happy people living around us, and Khodadad hates them. He calls them faithless, detestable sinners with no fear of God.

My life grinds on. Nights go and days come, days go and nights come. I spend my days at the cookstove and my nights in the arms of a loathsome man.

—❦—

On a cold autumn morning when everything is still floating in a silvery fog and leaves are heavy with dew, Khodadad tells me to pack my things. I am to go to Khalishkak with him after midday prayers. I imagine it is a long trip to a distant place for him to have asked that I take my belongings. Questions whirl in my mind, but I lack the courage to voice them.

Zoleikha helps me pack. A little later, Mah Jabin shows up and asks me over and over again what Khodadad has said to me. I tell her what I know, but she remains restless and uneasy. She walks out and again comes back.

"He didn't say anything about the trip these past nights?"

"No," I answer.

The next time she comes in, Zoleikha dashes whatever hope Mah Jabin might have had.

"You still can't figure him out, can you?" she says. "It's obvious. He's taking a new wife to bear children for him, and he wants to hide Simin from her. So, don't get your hopes up. He had enough of you and me a long time ago."

Mah Jabin sinks to the floor and sags against the door.

"My son's grandmother lives in Khalishkak," Zoleikha says, turning to me. "I will ask her to keep an eye on you. I have other relatives, too. You won't be alone. Khalishkak is better than this prison."

---

Khalishkak is a small winter village. There are no blaring car horns, no shouting street peddlers, no crush of pedestrians weaving their way along sidewalks. A cluster of small mud houses lean against each other on the slopes of a sprawling gray hill with not a single tree for birds to perch on. There are no rivers and no streams. The villagers take their donkeys to bring water from a spring that is an hour's walk away.

To the east and south there is a vast desert where howling winds whip dirt and gravel into the air and shower them over the village. The sky is always hazy and overcast. To the north and west of the village, there are low hills with a few occasional tall ones that stretch all the way to the region's pistachio farms. Much later, I learn that the village is a lurking-place and a hideout for plunderers and pillagers of the farms.

Khodadad takes me to a house on the hillside facing the sun. His son Majid lives here.

"Clear out a room for Simin, and tell your wife to take care of her," Khodadad tells him. "Get her whatever she wants. She will be your guest, but leave her to cook for herself and eat whatever she wants. I will be visiting often, and God help you if I hear a single complaint from her."

***

Majid and his wife Halimeh are kind and amiable. They have a one-year-old son named Yassin. I quickly grow close to Halimeh and make friends with Yassin. I am happy that I don't have to lay eyes on Khodadad and don't have to wrangle with Mah Jabin. But

I do miss Zoleikha. I often tell her son and daughter-in-law about her kindnesses to me.

"I wish he would allow her to come live with us," Majid says longingly.

"Then who would bake at the kiln for Khodadad Khan?" Halimeh says sarcastically. "Who would cook for his Talibs and mullahs, prepare their tea and hookah, empty their spittoons?"

Halimeh and I regularly take the donkey to bring water from the spring. Like Tali, there are no social constraints here. Women work inside and outside the house. The men take their cattle to pasturelands away from the village and occasionally trespass into the pistachio farms to chop down trees for firewood.

Walking to the spring one day, I tell Halimeh about Tali, about how our valley is a green and lush paradise compared to Khalishkak. I tell her about the villagers, about my friends, about Kowsar and her genius. I tell Halimeh that I was going to school when Khodadad showed up and robbed me of my life. I tell her that I still miss my friends, that I still like making dolls out of rags. Halimeh is sixteen or seventeen years old. She tells me I am still very young.

"I wish he would let me go back to my family," I say. "He is keeping me here and away from Qala-e Naw because he is taking a new wife. I wish he would just divorce me and send me back."

"Men like Khodadad will kill a wife rather than divorce her,"

Halimeh says. "They believe divorce will bring them dishonor and shame, that it is an act of weakness and cowardice."

Halimeh is from the village of Mangan and dislikes Khalishkak as much as I do. She tells me the village was originally called Khoshlucheh, which means sister-in-law, and she bursts into laughter.

"That's what many believe," she says. "Perhaps a kind sister-in-law set up her tent here and people followed. Others say, Turkmens settled on these hills long ago, and Khalishkak means field of mud and dirt."

She giggles and asks, "You're not a sister-in-law, are you?"

I think of my oldest brother Youssef, who I suddenly feel I love more than the world.

"No, my brothers are still young."

We fill the water containers from the spring, load them on the donkey, and head back. When we arrive, Majid walks out into the yard.

"Simin, you were right," he says laughing. "My father has one more wife!"

"Your mother had figured out what he was up to," I say indifferently.

❧

It is a cold and snowy day. I have been here for almost a year. I am sitting at the window, watching the flakes dance their way to the ground when I see a car emerge from the white haze. It stops at the foot of the hill and Khodadad climbs out of the back seat and hurries up the path to the house. Panicked, I run out to go to Halimeh's room, but I change my mind and take refuge in the cold kitchen. I stand there for a minute, but I'm restless and edgy. I run back to my room and crawl under my blanket.

"Majid!" I hear him shout from the front yard.

A few seconds later, I hear the house door open.

"Father, is that you?"

"Who do you think it is? You can't even beat a dog into leaving its hole in this weather!"

"Salaam, Father!"

"Salaam to you, too. Go to the car and bring my things and tell Khairullah to give you the sack of goods in the trunk."

"Of course, Father."

"Where is Simin's room?"

"Upstairs, to the left."

I hear him stomping up the stairs and the door swinging on its hinges. I feel I have been struck by lightning.

"How are you, Simin?"

I stare at him. His beard is bushier, his paunch larger, and his neck thicker. But the smirk on his lips has not changed.

"A Muslim woman greets her husband when he arrives," he says.

I cannot find my voice. It's as though I have been mute all my life.

He gently pulls me out from under the blanket and holds me in his arms.

"Are you sulking?" he asks, kissing me.

That old smell churns my stomach.

"The moment the snow started, I thought of you," he says, caressing my temple with the back of his fingers. "I said to myself, I have a beloved out in the wilderness, I worry about her and miss her slender thighs. Simin, you have every right to sulk, but believe me, I've been in terribly poor spirits without you. A hundred times I wanted to come, and some obligation came up. Now go and bring some hot water so I can do my ablution. And brew some tea."

As I escape the room, he says, "It's cold outside. Put on your coat."

I pay no attention to him and run out of the house and across the yard in my thin dress. Halimeh has already started a fire in the cookstove and set a large pot of water on it.

"Congratulations!" she says.

Still unable to speak, I bring the watering can.

"Wait," she says. "The water isn't warm enough yet."

I squat down next to the cookstove, hoping its heat will stop me from trembling, but it doesn't. My teeth chatter.

"Go put something on!" Halimeh says. "You'll catch pneumonia."

I stare at her.

She takes off her shawl and wraps it around me.

"You're in shock," is all she says.

When the water starts to steam, she fills the can and trickles a few drops on the back of her hand.

"It's good. Lukewarm."

I take it from her and return to my room. Khodadad is busy putting wood in the heater. He has taken off his overcoat and hung it on a long nail in the wall. I think Halimeh had used it for Yassin's cradle.

"Come in and close the door," he says. "Why is the heater not on? If you're not concerned for yourself, you should be concerned for me! I don't want my beautiful wife to get sick."

I step in and close the door behind me. When flames start licking from the logs, he turns to me and says, "The heater is for heating. Why don't you use it? . . . And don't tell me you feel sorry for the pistachio trees! This cold will kill you."

I am still standing by the door, holding the watering can.

"My dear mute," he says, taking it from me. "Make the room nice and warm so we don't catch a cold tonight."

Some time passes until he comes back and takes his overcoat.

"I'm going to the village chief's house to tend to some matters. I will have dinner there and come back after prayers. I want the room to be warm. Now go to Halimeh and see to the food and staples I brought."

I am alone. That familiar horror that had forgotten me is back. I again live in fear. I have a feeling that the night he threw himself on me like an animal and tore my insides will repeat itself. Leaning against the wall, I stare at the blue flowers on the curtain over the alcove. Night comes and they darken and disappear.

"Don't you want to eat?"

Halimeh's voice outside the door brings me to myself.

"No, thank you. I'm not hungry."

My voice drowns in the night.

"No, thank you," I repeat a little louder. "I'm not hungry."

She leaves and I remain lost in the dark.

"Simin, where are you? Are you playing dead?"

He is back.

"Why haven't you lit a lamp? And there is no fire in the heater again. . . . Majid!" he shouts. "Bring a lamp."

A few minutes later, there's a flickering yellow flame in the room.

He takes my hand and says, "Are you all right, Simin? Why are you standing in the dark? Aren't you happy to see me?"

He is quiet for a while. Then, in a softer tone he says, "You're right to be upset. You've been here a long time, and I haven't come to see you. From now on, I promise to visit often and keep you warm in my arms."

He goes to the crate of firewood, takes a few logs and puts them in the heater. The hot coal left over from earlier quickly kindles the fire. He takes off his overcoat and jacket and hangs them on the nail. Then he brings a mattress and bedding from the alcove and arranges them next to mine. No longer caring about my silence, he takes a toothbrush from his jacket pocket and brushes his teeth for a long time.

"I don't want you to say my mouth smells of dipping tobacco," he chortles, tossing the toothbrush aside and pulling me to him.

He undresses me and lies me down on my bedding. As always, I close my eyes and tolerate his weight. He goes limp sooner than usual and rolls onto the mattress. I open my eyes. He is wiping the sweat off his forehead and neck with the edge of the sheet.

As he buries his head under the blanket, a voice deep inside me groans, "I want to talk to you."

He pushes the blanket away from his face.

"I want to talk to you," I say again.

"I'm listening."

"Let me go to Tali."

"Go where!?"

"To Tali."

"Why?"

"I'm lonely here. What difference would it make if I were here or there?"

"It makes a big difference. This is your husband's house, and there is your father's home. The day a girl marries, the door to her father's house closes to her forever."

His words crush me.

"You have a new wife," I plead. "What do you need me for? Just divorce me."

He leaps up and grabs my throat.

"Wretch, don't *ever* utter that word again," he snarls. "I paid for you. Two hundred sheep and two milk cows. And divorce is not in our custom. Only the coward and the depraved divorce a wife. I will kill you, but I will not divorce you. Who put this nonsense in your head? . . . *Who!?*"

He squeezes my throat so hard that I start to wheeze. I beat him with my fists, but hard as I struggle, he will not let go of me.

"So, bitch!" he growls. "You've learned to yap like a dog."

I kick him and ram my knee into his chest. His fingers tighten around my neck. Unable to breathe, I feel around for something to hit him with. There's only his toothbrush. I grab it and stab at his face as hard as I can. Its handle pierces his eye. I twist it. He lets out a terrifying scream, stumbles to his feet, falls, and writhes on the floor.

I gasp for air. I'm still clutching the toothbrush. His eyeball is on it. I shriek and hurl it across the room. I stare at my hand. I cannot believe that it tore out his eye. He is howling and thrashing about like an injured bull. I crawl backward into a corner.

Majid and Halimeh are pounding on the door, shouting, "What happened!? What's wrong! Open the door! . . . Simin! Father! Open the damn door!"

"*I'm burning! . . . My eye! . . . My eye!*" Khodadad screams.

Khairullah is now kicking the door. It breaks open and the three of them burst into the room. Seeing us naked, the driver and Halimeh swing around and hurry out. Majid grabs a blanket and covers me. Then he rushes to his father and lifts his head. Seeing his face, he turns and gapes at me.

"You gouged his eye!?"

I stare at him. He sees the toothbrush and races out shouting for Khairullah.

The two men throw a sheet over Khodadad and carry him and his screams down the stairs. Minutes later, I hear him in the guestroom. I look around the room. The crate of firewood on its side, the broken door flat on the floor, the rumpled rug and bedding stained with blood.

The wind stealing in through the gaps in the window brings the scent of snow. Shadows sway with the flame of the lamp. I don't know what will become of me.

Khodadad howls and groans for a long time. Then I hear him laboring up the stairs.

"If any of you come near me," he shouts, "you will pay dearly!"

He is holding a dagger. His eye is bandaged with a handkerchief and his beard is crusted with dry, darkened blood. The veins on his neck are bulging. Without a word, he walks over to me. Swift as a leopard, he grips my neck, lifts me up, and walks across the room. He drops the dagger and rips his coat and jacket off the nail. Grabbing me with both hands, he slams my back against it. Breath freezes in my lungs. Hoarse rasps burst from my throat.

He takes a step back, picks up the dagger, and looks at my frail body hanging on the wall.

"So, your cunt was this precious!?" he hisses.

He stabs the dagger between my legs and pulls up the blade, slicing my skin. It stops at the base of my throat. There is fire inside me. I see blood splattering on him. He stands back and observes his work. A look of satisfaction spreads across his face.

"Now, that's very nice."

Pain suffocates my screams. My teeth bite into my tongue. My body jerks and shudders. I feel the blade in my armpit.

God, for what sin am I being punished? For what crime am I being butchered?

"You dared raise your hand on me? You blinded me?"

He severs my arm.

My vision blurs. His blood-crusted face disappears. I float away from the body Mawlawi Khodadad is manically dismembering. Still growling, still cursing.

"Your father be damned, you whore! You wanted to go home? I *will* send you home!"

Part of me is still suspended from the nail. My eyes are open, looking at him. There is a smile on my lips, perhaps a sneer. I would have liked to spit at his repugnant face. My ribcage slips off the nail.

He steps back, looks at my remains, and wipes his face with the hem of his tunic. Then he squats down and separates my head from my torso. He grabs it by the hair and holds it up to his face.

"Wretch, now do you understand who you raised your hand on?"

His son is standing in the doorway with horror in his eyes.

I don't stay.

―――――

Three years of seasons come and go until one snowy afternoon, the people of Tali run out of their warm homes. Some crowd the hills, others stand on rooftops. All stare at the trail down to the village.

Men shouting, "*Allah o Akbar,*" are bringing Simin back in a coffin hoisted on their shoulders.

# 6

Majid grabs hold of the doorframe to steady himself. He looks at the nightmare before him, at his father's hands dripping with blood.

"What are you staring at?" Khodadad says, tossing the dagger aside. "*Move*! Bring a sack and clear her up. We must leave for town right away."

His face contorted with pain and rage, he shouts, "Wait! Take my hand."

Majid holds his arm and walks him back to the guestroom.

"Khairu, warm up the car," Khodadad groans. "We're going back."

Seeing the mawlawi splattered with fresh blood, Khairullah jumps to his feet, but hesitates at the door. It is lunacy to drive at night in the middle of a heavy snowstorm, but he dares not utter a word. Out in the vestibule, he pulls on his boots and walks out.

"That whore," Khodadad grunts as he sits down and leans back against a bolster.

Some time passes before Majid returns to the guestroom, trembling and ashen, holding a bloodstained burlap sack by its neck.

"Father, it would be better if you changed into clean clothes."

"Your forefathers be damned, we're not going to a feast of benefaction!" Khodadad barks. "And you are coming with us. After you've dropped me off at the hospital, get a coffin, throw the sack in it, and deliver it to the bitch's father. Tell that ungodly louse, Mawlawi Khodadad has sent her back. And tell him, the mawlawi himself will come in a few days to take back his herd."

Halimeh, cowering in the dark end of the hallway, whispers, "Majid, no! Don't go! I will die of fright."

"Can't you see the mess we're in!" Majid whispers, walking over to her. "Ask Abdulsami's mother to come and stay with you tonight."

"Majid, where did you go?" Khodadad yells. "Bring my overcoat."

Majid hurries up the stairs and moments later returns.

"Father, it's covered with blood."

"There is no power greater than that of God," he says, struggling to his feet. "And I repeat, we are not going to a feast of benefaction."

Majid silently helps him on with his coat, fetches his own, and holds his father by the arm as they walk out and trudge through the snow. Khodadad crawls into the back seat of the car while Majid puts the sack in the trunk and takes the passenger seat. Khairullah, shaken and dreading the rugged road buried under snow, turns and looks at him. There is fear written on Majid's face, too.

The headlights pierce the dark and show the way. Now and then, the wind whips up the snow and blows it at the windshield, leaving the passengers blind. Khodadad moans and Khairullah mumbles prayers of penitence.

"I'm not afraid of the rocky road. Praise God, the car is strong," he says. "What I'm afraid of is the engine or the battery failing. This freezing weather will show no mercy. It will kill us."

"We haven't come far," Majid says. "Turn back. We will set out after sunrise."

"Majid Khan, you are not the one in agony!" Khodadad says. "Khairu, pay no attention to this cow. Drive on."

Khairullah remains silent. Leaning over the steering wheel, he peers through the snow and struggles to maneuver the car along a dirt road he can no longer see. The only thought on his mind is to deliver Mawlawi Khodadad to the hospital without incident. For five years he has been his attendant, and of Mawlawi's overt and covert gains, a decent sum has always fallen on his lap.

Majid buries his head in his collar. There is chaos inside him. Just when he forgets the hazard that lies ahead, just when he pushes away the sight of his father's gouged eye, the image of Simin floats before him. He cannot believe that innocent and gentle child's butchered body is in the trunk of the car. They had grown to like each other, and his wife had found a friend and a confidante. Even though Simin had lost faith, hope, and heart, Halimeh did not allow sorrow to become the core of her life. Yet, as quickly as a smile appeared on her lips, it always disappeared.

I knew she was unhappy, Majid thinks to himself, I knew she hated Father. But I never imagined this would be her fate. What drove her to such violence? Gathering her limbs, I thought I saw joy in her eyes. . . . Simin, were you so disgusted with life that you laughed as he cut you? What were you laughing at, your death or his blind eye? . . . And now, I am to deliver your flesh and bones to your parents. . . . Father, how many young girls do you intend to destroy? You are a learned mawlawi, what are your Talibs to learn from you? Father, the helpless suffer and their pain is contagious. Anguish comes suddenly.

Late into the night, they arrive in Qala-e Naw. As Khairullah turns in the direction of the hospital, Khodadad says, "No, don't go there. There is nothing they can do for me now. Drive home."

He calls for Zoleikha the moment he arrives.

"Wife, ask no questions. You have always been my healer. Boil some water and wash and bandage the wound. And bring me some potion or poison to ease the pain."

Shaken by the sight of his eye and his bloody clothes, Zoleikha dares not speak and does as he has asked. A small piece of opium quickly tempers his pain and allows him to sleep.

~

Early the next day, Majid buys a coffin and with Khairullah at the wheel, he leaves for Tali. At the end of the passable road above the valley, he sends Khairullah to the village to find Chief Abed and have him come to the car with a few of his men.

As Khairullah makes his way down the snow-covered trail, Majid buttons up his coat, puts on his sheepskin hat, and climbs out of the car. It's after midday and the sun is shining bright, but the valley breathes a bone-piercing wind.

Majid looks at the mountain peaks and thinks, the sun will soon leave them in the hands of the night and howling wolves. He walks to the edge of the cliff and looks at the village below. It is blanketed with snow that has the trees bowing under its weight. Only the poplars remain standing tall. The mountain river is frozen along its banks, but a narrow course at its center has still not surrendered to the ice. It slithers and snakes its way to Ab-e Pudah Lake.

Khairullah is a black spot moving on a white canvas. Majid knows that the news this black spot bears will devastate the village. He knows that soon men will arrive, and on their face will be an unanswerable *why?* He sees Simin's beautiful face, her large hazel eyes looking at him. They, too, ask, *why?* The question choking him becomes a scream that bursts from his lungs and reverberates among the boulders.

Tears stream down his face. If only Khodadad had not mutilated her. If only he had left her whole. What am I to say to her parents?

What crime did she commit to deserve this death? How am I to introduce myself to these people? As whom, as what? No, it is best that I take the village chief aside, tell him to take Simin's remains and wait for Father to come and answer their questions. Perhaps when they see his blind eye . . .

The cold has him shivering. He climbs back into the car, wraps his arms around his knees and buries his face in them.

God, I do not have the strength to face the men who come for Simin's coffin.

Bitter winter days are short. By the time Khairullah finds Chief Abed, delivers his message, and returns to the car with him and a few men, the sun is pale and means to leave.

As Majid climbs out of the car, Chief Abed looks at him with disdain, and without speaking a word, reluctantly shakes his hand. Disregarding his scorn, Majid takes Chief Abed's arm and leads him away from the car.

"Abed Khan," he says in hushed voice. "You need to know that it was my father who took Simin's life. And you need to know that she was mutilated."

"No!" Chief Abed gasps, his face suddenly drained white. "But why? For what reason?"

"I don't know. The mawlawi will come in a few days and tell you himself."

Khairullah opens the trunk, stands aside, and prays, "May God forgive and absolve us of our sins."

Chanting "*Allah o Akbar*," the men lift the coffin, rest it on their shoulders, and head down to the valley. In the fading colors of the day, they appear as phantoms drifting on snow.

"Let us leave," Khairullah says to Majid. "Mawlawi's orders have been carried out."

By the time the pallbearers arrive in the village, news of Simin's death has reached every ear.

Kowsar, wearing a heavy black headscarf, stands on the rooftop with Geesu and watches. People who had climbed up to their rooftops and gathered on the hills are coming together behind the pallbearers and adding their voice to their cries of "*Allah o Akbar*." Every few steps, a bearer gives his place to another man, so all can shoulder the burden of the dead.

Kowsar's heart heaves with pain, and Geesu stares at the coffin, her eyes brimming with tears. Neither can accept their Cinderella's death.

Haunting wails of a mother rise from Abdul Ghafoor's house as he and his sons run toward the coffin like figures stripped of their soul. Seeing them, the procession stops.

"Move on," Chief Abed orders. "Move on. Don't stop."

He walks ahead and takes Abdul Ghafoor in his arms.

"May God forgive and absolve your dead and ours."

The grieving father's lips tremble. He wants the chief to stop and tell him why his child has suddenly died. But Chief Abed, with his arm around him, continues to lead the villagers through the ice and snow. Outside Abdul Ghafoor's house, he holds up his hand for the crowd to stop and instructs the pallbearers to follow him inside and leave the coffin in the hallway.

"We will let her mother see the deceased. Then we will take the coffin to the mosque and hold the funeral tomorrow."

The screams and sobs of Homeira and the women keeping her company peaks.

"Light a lamp and bring a bedsheet," Abed Khan tells Abdul Ghafoor before going outside to call for Mullah Sikhdad to join him.

Swallowing his sobs, Abdul Ghafoor disappears down the dark hallway and returns with the sheet and lamp.

"Ghafoor Khan, now go and wait in the yard," Chief Abed says firmly. "I will call you when we are ready. I will ask the women to leave, too. Stay with your wife."

Waiting for the house to empty, Chief Abed quietly explains the

148

circumstances to Mullah Sikhdad. "But, *why?*" the mullah hoarsely whispers, his eyes wide with disbelief.

"This is no time for questions, and I have no answers to offer. Now come and give me a hand."

"Penance! Penance!" the mullah repeats as he helps Chief Abed open the coffin.

"Hold up the lamp," Abed Khan says as he kneels and pauses to gather his will and courage. Then, he takes a deep breath, holds it in, and unties the sack. Mullah Sikhdad closes his eyes and turns away as the chief feels inside and takes out Simin's head. He shudders and grips the edge of the coffin. Then he takes a fresh breath, quickly closes the sack and carefully places Simin's head over the tied end.

"Alas!" he sighs, carefully covering the sack with the sheet and wrapping the top edge around Simin's head, leaving only part of her face uncovered. "We have no choice. We will say only what we know. That she was killed. Nothing more. We will leave the rest to come to light when Khodadad comes."

Chief Abed places the lid on the coffin at an angle to allow only Simin's face to show, takes the lamp from Mullah Sikhdad, and calls Abdul Ghafoor.

"Bring your wife to see her daughter before we take her to the mosque," he says. "And you must not allow her to touch the corpse."

Moments later, Abdul Ghafoor returns with his arm tight

around his wife. She is no longer crying. Drained and exhausted, she herself seems bereft of life. Abdul Ghafoor sits her down next to the coffin and Chief Abed brings the lamp closer.

"Simin!" Homeira screams. "You have come back to me! You have come back to Mother! The light in my heart dimmed the day you left. This house has been dark ever since.... You have come for me to cook *kichiri* for you. I will. Wake up, my girl. Wake up, my life. But ... but why is there blood on her face?"

She fights to free herself from her husband's grip and reach into the coffin.

"Ghafoor, take her away," Chief Abed orders. "*Now!*"

Abdul Ghafoor drags Homeira out of the house as the chief quickly closes the coffin and calls for pallbearers to carry it to the mosque.

Escorting the coffin, Chief Abed remains silent until they are some distance away from the house. Then he takes Abdul Ghafoor's arm and gently says, "With God's will and blessing, we will bury your child tomorrow and hold the ceremony of prayer for the dead. May God keep her soul. It was not her time to go."

Abdul Ghafoor is desperate to ask why his daughter's face is bruised and bloody, but he cannot bring himself to speak those words. "I beg of you, Abed Khan," is all he can manage.

"I said nothing in front of your wife to spare her even greater pain. But as Simin's father, it is your right to know," Chief Abed whispers. Then, carefully deliberating his words, he says, "It seems the mawlawi had a hand in the matter. She is no longer whole."

Abdul Ghafoor falls to his knees.

"I've been told he had some reason," Chief Abed says, squatting down next to him. "He will tell us in a few days. . . . Have courage, Ghafoor Khan. Have courage. What is done is done. Such things happen these days, and there is little the likes of you and me can do. We must tread with caution."

Abdul Ghafoor takes a handful of snow and cools his face. Chief Abed gives him a moment, then takes him under the arm and helps him to his feet.

"What wrong could she have committed?" he murmurs, as though to himself. "My Simin was a child. She could do no harm."

❦

Chants of "*Allah o Akbar*" once again reverberate in the valley. People who had gone indoors to warm themselves join the procession to the mosque. The descending dark has brought colder air. Shivering, Kowsar stands on the mound of snow Mobin Khan shoveled off the roof the day before. Simin's coffin is traveling the same route she ran barefoot every day, excited to go to school and see her friends.

"Wake up Simin," Kowsar hums. "It's too soon. Wake up so we

can play with our dolls. Wake up so we can play hide-and-seek under the trees."

"Kowsar, did you watch?" Farrokh shouts, running up to the house. "They brought Simin back in a coffin! Now they're taking her to the mosque. Abed Khan said they will bury her in the morning."

Kowsar nods as he races into the house. Reality washes over her, it burns into her veins and shakes her. She falls. The winter wind swallows her like a fog. She drifts above the pallbearers and slips into the coffin. If only she could put Simin together again. Her bruised lips are closed tight. As if they never spoke a word after she left Tali. Laugh, Simin! Laugh! Remember the day Geesu tried to leap over the river rocks and fell into the water with her books? We pulled her out, and you told her she would get home faster if she swam. She sighed and said she would end up in Ab-e Pudah lake instead! We laughed so hard."

Kowsar talks until the wind sweeps her away. With eyes barely open, she sees her mother kneeling beside her.

"Kowsar, you fell on the pile of snow. Thank God I saw you."

"Mother," she whispers. "She's in pieces."

Simin's coffin is locked in the small room next to where the men perform their ablutions before prayer. Chief Abed asks Abdul Ghafoor's friends to take him home, and in the tradition of consoling the bereaved, to stay with the family and see to their meals. Then he hurries home to the men who have gathered in his guestroom. He must share with them what he knows. His greatest concern is how best to tie up the loose ends and bring this tragic affair to a quiet close.

Nadim Khan, perhaps more so than others, is heartbroken over Simin's sudden death and anxious to learn why and how she left this world.

With the flames in the heater at a lively burn and the chill of the night having left the room, Chief Abed takes a sip of tea and says, "Simin's death has shaken me to the core. The innocent girl was too young. Perhaps my heart would not bleed so, had she died otherwise." He pauses, takes a deep breath, and adds, "Mawlawi Khodadad has dismembered her."

Eyes wide, the men stare at him.

"Only God and Mawlawi Khodadad know the reason why. His son Majid delivered the coffin and said the mawlawi will come in a few days."

"God have mercy on us!" Mullah Sikhdad sighs.

"Mullah, as long as you marry off young girls and make brides of

153

nine-year-old children, you will live to see greater horror than this," Nadim Khan says, his voice shaking with rage.

"Do not lecture me, Nadim Khan! It is said that it's best for a girl to begin menstr—"

"Mullah! Do not repeat this yet again! Do not pin this on God! So what if a girl reaches puberty under her father's roof? Would it upset the order of the world? If a girl is allowed to grow up at home, so that her mother can open her eyes to the world, she can perhaps better deal with what lies ahead. . . . And Sikhdad Khan, might I add that your own daughter is almost twelve, and I am certain you are in no hurry to make a bride of her now."

"Don't speak of this! You once locked horns with people in Qala-e Naw and you ended up here. If you do the same with the people of this village, where would you go then? Don't show your scorn. Every man has authority over his home, wife, and child. One weds his girl early, another does so later. What is it to you?"

"I mean no scorn, Sikhdad Khan! If you, a mullah, counsel them not to make wives of little girls, they will be more accepting of it."

"Nadim Khan, my decent man," Yar Mohamad Khan snickers. "Don't have such expectations of a mullah. Have you forgotten that Abdul Ghafoor's daughter was taken not only by a mullah, but a mawlawi. They like unripe fruit."

"Yar Mohammad Khan!" Mullah Sikhdad says, raising his voice.

"Do not mock the clergy. God will not look kindly upon you. Not in this day and age."

"Does God look kindly upon a clergyman, a so-called man of God, who butchers an innocent child?"

"There is no power greater than that of God! You were with us the day we went to Abdul Ghafoor's house to formalize the betrothal. You saw that he happily and willingly agreed."

"Yes, I was, and I remember. But when a destitute and desperate man is offered a wealth of two hundred sheep—"

"All this be damned!" Abed Khan interrupts. "What are we going to do when Khodadad shows up?"

～

Majid returns to Qala-e Naw and finds his father's guestroom crowded with powerful Talibs, friends, and ranking members of the provincial government. From the governor and head of council to the commandant of security, all are there.

"Father, I delivered the coffin," he whispers to Khodadad who is resting in his bedroom. "You should perhaps delay going to Tali right now. Perhaps wait until you are feeling better."

"I had no intention of going there now. Go take care of these people. They've been told that a divine light from heaven, a celestial beam, blinded my eye. Tell them to distribute their alms and offerings among the needy, and to pray for this helpless subject of God."

Dumbfounded, Majid stares at him.

"Go, you mule! And tell Khairu what I just told you. He has more brains than you."

———

A month after Simin's burial, late on a clear night, the people of Tali see flames licking up to the sky in the middle of the valley. They grab their buckets and shovels and run to put out the fire. Before long, they return fretful and distraught. A corps of armed Taliban has arrived by night. They have ransacked the school, piled the books, benches, tables, and blackboards in the schoolyard and set them on fire.

When the ill-starred night ends and the sun rises, an errand boy runs from house to house to tell the villagers that the Hamzeh militia have occupied the valley and established headquarters at the school. They have called for the man of each household to present himself there.

———

Men with weather-beaten faces and no gleam in their eyes move about like ghosts. They have detained Mullah Sikhdad, Teacher Sadeq, and Nadim Khan, and tied them to trees by the river. They are to be executed for the crime of corrupting and perverting children, and for bowing to the infidels and the infidel government.

Chief Abed pleads with their commander for hours, imploring him to pardon and forgive the three. Obeidullah, dressed head to toe in black, his lungee loose and tangled and his eyes lined with kohl, listens impatiently. In the end, he releases Mullah Sikhdad out of reverence for his rank as a man of God. And agrees to spare the lives of the two teachers, but he shames and disgraces them by ordering his men to parade the two around the village, sitting backwards on donkeys.

The children and their parents are devastated seeing Nadim Khan and Teacher Sadeq humiliated. They have grown to love and respect the two men. They have even forgotten that the school principal, Mullah Sikhdad, is a conniving and meanspirited man.

After the ride of shame, Nadim Khan is released, but Teacher Sadeq is taken to the school. Obeidullah shoves him to the floor and viciously flogs him before telling his men to throw him out of the village. After dark, Talibs take the teacher up the valley trail and abandon him on the cliff.

A few days later, Mawlawi Khodadad arrives in Tali with a demeanor stripped of its former bravado, and his blind eye carefully concealed with the length of his white lungee.

Chief Abed and Mullah Sikhdad speculate that he has come with a solution to the Taliban's hold on the village. They already have their foot firmly on the villagers' neck and extort money and their daily needs from them. But the two soon realize that Obeidullah is in fact a friend and associate of the mawlawi.

Going directly to the school, Khodadad sends two Talibs to bring Abdul Ghafoor to the classroom where his daughter used to sit.

"Mawlawi Sahib, forgive me!" Abdul Ghafoor pleads, sitting on his knees across from Khodadad and Obeidullah.

"Forgive you for what?" Khodadad sneers.

His eyes fixed on the floor, Abdul Ghafoor says nothing.

"Now, what should I do with you? Even if you were to give me the world, it is no longer worth a grain to me."

Obeidullah smirks at the sight of the miserable villager as fraught as a fish in a net.

"Well, what should I do with you? What is left of the herd and cattle I gave you?"

A cold shudder scales Abdul Ghafoor's spine. His fear has

become reality. I knew you would come to take back what you gave, he thinks to himself. You loathsome beast! You took my daughter and murdered her. Why? For what? Wasn't she God's creation? And now you come expecting restitution!?

"I asked you a question?"

Weary, Abdul Ghafoor leans back to rest against the wall, but it is too far to offer him support. He falls and hits his head on the floor. The two Talibs flanking him laugh and sit him up. Shaken, Abdul Ghafoor picks up his lungee lying unraveled on the floor and gathers it on his knee.

"I will not ask you again," Khodadad warns him.

Abdul Ghafoor closes his eyes and counts.

"One cow and eighty-something sheep."

"Eighty-what? Be precise."

He again closes his eyes, but this time he is not counting. He is imagining what will become of his life if he loses the sheep. Determined to not surrender easily, he goads himself, say your piece man, say your piece, even at the cost of your head.

"Why, Mawlawi Sahib? Why are you asking about the herd? Did you bring back my daughter healthy and alive?"

Khodadad leaps to his feet and grabs a rifle from the guard at the door.

"Your forefathers be damned!" he shouts. "You have a sharp tongue. It's too bad you don't have another daughter, you vermin. If you did, I would take her even if she were two years old and I would send you her carcass a week later. Be grateful that I'm not gouging your eye before I send you home to your whoring wife!"

Obeidullah takes the rifle from Khodadad and puts a firm hand on his shoulder for him to sit down. Then he walks over to Abdul Ghafoor and strikes him on the collar bone with the butt of the rifle.

"Now, stop your drivel and answer the question you're asked."

"Eighty-three sheep and one cow," Abdul Ghafoor stammers.

"And the rest?"

"The wolves got a few and some died of disease. Others, I sold or slaughtered for meat."

"I knew it! All laid to waste," Khodadad snarls. "Keep six sheep, so you don't claim that Mawlawi Khodadad snatched the bite of bread from your children's mouths. Now go and bring the rest. *Move!*"

As Abdul Ghafoor scurries out, Obeidullah turns to Khodadad and says, "I've been waiting for you, and I need to leave as soon as possible. I have work pending in Helmand and Ghor, and I'm needed at the front in the West. . . . Over the past few days, I have surveyed the valley. It is indeed fertile. We will do well here. I'll have the village chief and a few landowners come tonight for us to talk to them."

"Excellent," Khodadad says. "Excellent."

Before evening prayers, Chief Abed, Mullah Sikhdad, and several farm owners are told to join Obeidullah and Mawlawi Khodadad on the riverbank behind the school.

"I have been going up and down your valley for several days," Obeidullah says in a measured tone. "Your land is good, but what you grow is not. If you continue planting wheat, beans, melons, and the like for a hundred years, you will still not double your one loaf of bread. We, on the other hand, have been planting poppy in Ghormach and other regions, and the crop has been a success. Three acres of wheat produces no more than twenty thousand afghanis, but three acres of poppy will reap two or three hundred thousand afghanis. You may find it hard to believe, but Badakhshan province has greatly developed and progressed as a result. Your valley has an even better climate."

He pauses, giving the men time to absorb his words. "Here's what I would like to propose," he goes on. "We will provide you with the seed and supplies, as well as the manpower and security. All you need to do is plant and maintain the crops, and after harvest, refine the opium."

He stops and scrutinizes his audience. There is fear and dread in the eyes of a few.

"As long as we are here, no one will so much as look at you sideways," he says reassuringly. "We have friends and associates in the local and provincial government, powerful men such as Mawlawi Khodadad. There are others, too, but you need not worry about that."

Yar Mohammad Khan, who has more farmland than the others, and his cattle breeding has been profitable, is the most ill at ease.

"Obeidullah Khan," he says. "What about sin and the immorality of what you are proposing? Opium is not sanctioned by any judicial or Sharia law and authority."

"But it is!" Obeidullah says with a sly smile. "The opium is sold to the infidels and exported to their countries, to the land of the aggressors. Jihad is not just with guns and rifles. If you can't rid your land of the invader with arms, then do so with opium.

"Yar Mohammad Khan, if you don't wish to plant it, someone else will. Every year we have succeeded as the number one country in opium production. Do you think we achieved this status from the crops in Helmand alone? No, my good man. We are planting everywhere."

"This work requires backbone," Mawlawi Khodadad interjects. "It requires courage and ambition. It is not for the fainthearted."

Yar Mohammad Khan who was about to voice concern over their own children falling victim to addiction, bites his tongue and says no more.

"Soon, it will be time to plant the poppy," Obeidullah says. "I will partner with anyone who decides to do so. And I will pay fifty thousand afghanis per three acres. In cash."

The men are astonished. What he is proposing adds up to a considerable sum of money. Even Yar Mohammad Khan, starts to quietly calculate. His nine and half hectares would bring a million one hundred and fifty thousand afghanis. That is more money than he could make in a decade. One by one, the farm owners stand and declare their agreement to the terms.

"Obeidullah Khan," Yar Mohammad says, rising to his feet. "Jihad against the infidel is incumbent upon us all. Now that I see this endeavor as a moral, Godly deed, as well as financially beneficial, let us shake hands."

Obeidullah slaps his hand in a hearty handshake and laughs.

"You will be the first to receive the seed and your money," he says. "After all, you have more land than the others."

As the men leave, Khodadad takes Mullah Sikhdad's arm and says, "Come now, don't sulk because you have no farmland. A seasoned and astute mullah never falls behind."

Sikhdad, astounded by the wealth that could be gained and wretched that he will not have a share of it, pays no attention.

"Mullah!" Khodadad snaps. "You are agitated and upset. I lost an eye, what is your excuse? A bout of hemorrhoids!?"

"I wish it were that, Mawlawi Sahib. Your Talib friend has reduced my work and livelihood to dog shit! He might as well have paraded me around sitting backwards on a donkey. . . . You and I were doing well with the school. You got your share and I got mine. But Obeidullah shut it down and took away my only source of income. What is there to be happy about?"

"You simpleminded man of God!" Khodadad says, laughing. "Who says the school is closed? As far as the government is concerned, it is up and running. The students are studying, the teachers are teaching, and the school principal regularly sends progress reports and account ledgers of employees and expenses. If the government ever has the nerve to investigate, the investigator will either be me or one of my acquaintances. . . . When are you going to wise up?"

"Only God knows and you!" the mullah says, relieved and once again cheerful.

"As long as I breathe and walk this earth, you should not have a worry in the world," Khodadad assures him.

"May God give you a long and healthy life, Mawlawi!"

"Well, now that we're done with that, I must tell you, Sikhdad, even though I took my revenge on Ghafoor's girl, I'm still not consoled. Every night, I jolt awake to the sound of my own screams. Thank God, I took back the sheep, otherwise my heart would have burst. Are you certain that the man has no other daughter?"

"Yes, Khodadad Khan! How many times do I have to tell you?

The man is devastated, destroyed. Lost and done in. And he has no other daughter."

"Yet, my soul is not comforted..."

Sikhdad, shakes his head and pats the mawlawi on the back.

"Knowing you, your soul will not be comforted until you take another wife."

# 7

MY CHILDHOOD YEARS are difficult. Before I can tell my right hand from the left, my father dies.

The sun is fading when he comes home from the farm one day looking pale.

"Zubaideh, I have a terrible stomachache," he says to Mother. "Make some ginger and walnut tea, and don't forget the cardamom."

"Farhad, stay with your father," Mother says as she leaves for the kitchen to put a saucepan of water to boil and brings back a lump of barberry root extract. "It should ease the pain," she says. Father pinches off a small piece and swallows it.

I watch him lying there, suffering. I cannot believe that the man I always saw as invincible could ever be this helpless. The more he suffers, the more frightened I become.

"Mother, what's wrong with him?" I ask, running into the kitchen.

"Nothing, my boy. He ate four hardboiled eggs this morning. He is probably having trouble digesting. I kept telling him it's too much, but he's stubborn. He said, 'Wife let me eat. I'll be turning soil all day.'"

The water comes to a boil and Mother adds the ingredients to the saucepan. We can now hear Father's groans across the yard. I don't want to leave Mother's side. She lets the brew simmer for a few minutes and strains it into a tea bowl.

I hold onto her skirt and follow her back to the house. Father is keeled over and looking even paler.

"This pain is killing me," he moans. "I can't tolerate it."

"The barberry root didn't help?" Mother asks, caressing his head.

"No. Zubaideh, it's bad. . . . Getting worse by the minute."

"The tea should help, but it's still too hot."

A few minutes later, she holds the tea bowl up to his lips and helps him drink. But the tea doesn't relieve his pain either. He gets up and restlessly staggers around the room, lies down again and asks Mother to rub his stomach. It irritates him and he asks her to stop.

Late at night, his face has turned a pale yellow, he wails and cries. Watching him breaks my heart.

"Farhad, put on your slippers," Mother says. "We're going to Javad Khan."

Father must be in a critical state for her to turn to my uncle. Father and his brother have not been on speaking terms for several years.

Mother takes the kerosene lamp, and we step out into the dark. The dogs start barking. Now and then, I hear a jackal howl in the distance. Down by the river, the calves are mooing and the crickets singing. Haunted by Father's cries, every sound startles me as I run to keep up with Mother. I trip and fall several times, she pulls me up to my feet and snaps, "Are you blind!? Look where you're going!" I have scrapped my knee and it stings. I want to cry, but I grit my teeth. Let it sting, I tell myself, Mother is in no mood for me to start crying.

When we arrive at Uncle Javad's house, Mother takes a stone and bangs it on the door. Their dog runs over and growls. It quiets down when it picks up our scent and starts to whine and paw at the door. Before long, Uncle leans out a window.

"Your brother is unwell," Mother calls up nervously. "He has been screaming with pain since afternoon prayers. Extracts and brews haven't helped. Come see him, God forbid, he gets any worse."

"Hurry back, Bibi Zubaideh," he says. "I'll be there soon."

We retrace our steps back home. Father's moans are now slow and barely audible. Mother puts the lamp down and rushes to his side.

"Morad Khan, is the pain worse?"

Father nods. Mother feels his forehead and the color drains from her face.

"You're as cold as ice!" she says as she runs and brings a heavy quilt. She spreads it over him, and we sit there in silence. Minutes later Uncle Javad arrives and panics at the sight of his brother. Kneeling next to Father's bedding, he asks him a few questions and Father manages to mutter a few broken words. Uncle thinks for a moment then hurrying out the door, he tells Mother he will be back soon. I sit there for what seems like an eternity until Uncle Javad runs in with two boxes of medicine.

"Bibi Zubaideh, quickly, water," he pants.

Mother brings a bowl of water and holds up Father's head as Uncle Javad gives him two tablets. Father gags a few times but manages to swallow them. A few minutes later, he breaks into a sweat, and waves me to his side.

"Come Farhad," Mother says. "Don't be afraid."

Father raises his head and kisses me on the cheek with trembling lips and falls back on his pillow.

"Morad! Morad!" Uncle shouts, clutching his shoulders and shaking him.

I run and huddle in a corner and watch as Mother sprinkles water on his face and Uncle grabs his chin and pours a little in his mouth, but it streams out the corner of his lips. Uncle takes Father's pulse and again races to the door.

"Prayers . . ." he says, pulling on his shoes. "Mullah Sikhdad . . ."

I crawl over to Mother, she wraps her arm around me. Her body is hot, and I can feel her heart racing. I look up at her face. Tears are rolling down her cheeks. I don't quite understand what is happening, but I don't dare ask. My eyes shift back and forth from her face to Father lying motionless. The lamp is still burning in the middle of the room and the moths are as usual circling above it. Tonight, the hum of their wings grates on my nerves.

By the time Uncle Javad returns with Mullah Sikhdad and Mobin Khan, the night is fading. Gray dawn pours in when the door opens and Mullah Sikhdad runs to Father's side, drops to his knees, and puts his ear against his chest.

"His heart is beating. Slowly, but beating."

He sits there cross-legged and starts to pray. He pauses every few minutes and blows in Father's direction, and each time, I expect Father to open his eyes, but he doesn't.

"May God protect him," Mullah Sikhdad says when he is finished. "Perhaps the prayer will help. . . . I must leave for the mosque now or I'll be late for morning prayers."

Mobin Khan and Uncle Javad remain by Father's side, quietly watching him. Mother is distraught but silent. I know my world is crumbling.

An hour later the sun rises. Uncle leans over and listens to Father's heart. "I'll take him to town," he says, getting up. "I can't just sit here and stare at him. Mobin Khan, come with me as far as Jawand and return once I have him on a minibus."

"Of course," Mobin Khan says, his hand on his chest.

Uncle Javad goes out and puts the packsaddle on the donkey and asks Mother for a mat to spread over it. With Mobin Khan's help, they carry Father outside and lay him facedown across the donkey. Mother watches them, all the while praying under her breath. As they leave, we stand outside the front door with our eyes fixed on the valley. It takes a few minutes before they appear from behind the houses and head down the hill. Seeing them, Mother bursts into sobs. I hope once we lose sight of them among the trees, she will stop crying, but she doesn't.

—

Uncle Javad returns the next day, with Father's corpse. He died before reaching the hospital. We bury him, and our life of hardship begins.

Mother's tears have yet to dry when one late afternoon Uncle Javad, Mullah Sikhdad, Chief Abed, and a few other men pay us a visit. Mother tells me I must sit with them in the guestroom, and she leaves the tea tray outside the door for Uncle Javad to bring in and serve. When he has finished filling the tea bowls, Uncle comes over to me, takes my hand, and walks me to the head of the room to sit with him.

The men reminisce about Father and talk until Mullah Sikhdad finally says, "Evening is approaching, let us get to the heart of the matter. Javad Khan, call the boy's mother to come sit at the door."

"Son," my uncle says. "Tell your mother to come. Mullah Sahib wishes to talk to her."

I find Mother in the courtyard, waiting in the dusk as though she has been waiting to be called.

"Tell them I'm coming," she says.

In the guestroom, Mullah Sikhdad waits a few minutes, then calls out, "Sister Zubaideh, can you hear me?"

"Yes, Mullah Sahib, I can."

"May God absolve the deceased. Sister Zubaideh, we have come tonight to lift the sorrow that has settled in your house. God be praised, you are young, and your boy is no more than five. You both need a guardian. It is not easy being a single mother. Life is pinned on cattle raising, farming, and hard labor. Until you have a man watching over you, your life will not come to order and your son will not prosper. As such, we have come to formalize wedlock between you and Javad Khan. As the saying goes, what falls from the mouth, falls onto the collar. . . . If there is nothing you would like to say, I will start the nuptials sermon."

Mullah Sikhdad looks at the door.

"Sister, if your silence means, *yes*, I will begin."

"No, Mullah," Mother says sternly. "I did not say, *yes*. I do not wish to remarry. May God bless you all for having taken the trouble to visit us. But should you come again with the same concern, I would have to excuse myself."

Chief Abed shifts on his cushion and clears his throat. "Bibi Zubaideh, if you were a man, we would not worry. We would say, live your life in any manner you wish. But you are a woman, vulnerable and helpless. Javad Khan is concerned about you. You were his brother's wife, and now his brother's widow. You will not find a better man than he."

"Chief Abed, why do you assume I cannot run my own life? I have done so ever since Morad Khan left us. So far, I have not found myself helpless, and I pray for God to not make me so in the future. Based on what have you determined that a woman is helpless and cannot work as well as a man? My mother singlehandedly raised six children, and her wheat vessel and tallow container were never empty. Nor did she ever hold out her hand to anyone. . . . If a woman has no children to raise, no man could compete with her. Bless you, Chief Abed, may God keep you. If the day comes when we hold a needy hand out to you or to Javad Khan, then you can tell me I was wrong."

She pauses for a moment, then adds, "And please rest assured about our safety. My deceased husband's rifle is loaded, and my aim is good. If a thief or a crook so much as looks at my home, I will put a hole in his forehead."

"Mullah Sahib, it's time to go," Chief Abed says as he gets up and throws his wool wrap over his shoulders.

Clearing away the tea tray after the men have left, Mother says, "Son, go wash your hands. We have bean stew for dinner."

～

With the first rays of morning sun, Mother wakes me. After breakfast, she tucks a loaf of bread under my belt and hands me a shepherd's stick. By the time I drive the sheep out of the hold, she is waiting at the door with her shovel and black kettle.

"Farhad, you are a shepherd to the core!" she says cheerfully.

At the farm, I watch over the sheep in the grazing area while Mother turns the soil for new seeds to be sown.

"Son, take the kettle to the river and fill it," she calls out a few hours later. "I'll make tea."

By the time I return, she has started the fire pit, a memento of Father. I set the kettle on it, she adds the tea leaves, and we wait for it to brew. A few minutes later, she fills our tea bowls and sits leaning against a tree.

"Son, you must understand," she says, cupping the bowl in her hands, "these men don't care about us. They care about your father's bequest, this six-acre riverside farm. God rest his soul, no one could ever replace him as a father to you. That uncle of yours has five children of all ages and a thousand worries. If I had said yes last night, we would have ended up with even more grief. He would get his hands on this land, you would become a stepson, and I a stepmother wrangling with his children. Even now, I am certain these men will not leave us be. But never worry, as long as your mother is alive, she will hold these rascals at bay."

She stops, and perhaps needing time to weigh the words she wishes to speak, she goes to the fire pit, stokes the fire, and refills our bowls.

"Up until your father died," she says, walking back, "Javad Khan who is now so kind to you and wants to be our protector and guardian, would have shot your father's shadow if he could. Sometimes I even wonder if he poi—"

She presses her lips together and says no more.

"Mother, what were you going to say?"

"Nothing, my dear. I will not speak *haram* words. Drink your tea, it's getting cold, and there's still work to be done."

---

Mother moves her bedding close to the window and sleeps there every night, with the rifle always by her side. At the slightest sound, she grabs it and peers out, ready to aim and shoot. And every night, she tells me stories. She knows many. The Wolf and the Lamb, The

176

Goose that Lay Golden Eggs, Aladdin. Often, she tells me stories about herself, her family, and her childhood. Mother's stories develop my mind and my imagination, they teach me how to tell apart good from bad, right from wrong.

"My father, too, died before his time," she says one night. "He only managed to go to Qala-e Naw once to see a doctor. He said my father had high blood pressure and gave him medication that he needed to take for the rest of his life. But we had little money and lived in Bom Valley, far from any town where we could buy medicine. The doctor had told Father to stop eating fatty foods and salt, but in wintertime it was impossible for a herd keeper's spread not to include tallow and salt-cured lamb. My mother would cook eggplant, squash, and other vegetables for him, but he wouldn't eat them. He would pinch food off our plates and laugh. 'No ill befalls the lowly,' he always said. But it did. On his way to the mosque early one morning, he fell in the snow and gave his life to the life-giver. He left behind eight kilos of seed, a farm with only the rain to irrigate it, twenty sheep, and a milk cow.

"And don't think suitors only come for your widowed mother, they came for mine, too. But she was wise. She said no to all of them. She told my uncle, who had two other wives, 'If you care so much about your brother's children, buy decent clothes and shoes for them, and now and then bring us a sack of rice and a sack of wheat.' Still, my uncle managed to swindle her. Pretending he wanted to register the farm under her name with the government office, he took her fingerprint and forged a document giving him four of our eight kilos of seed.

"We grew up and soon had families of our own. My brothers went their separate ways. I ended up in Tali and your aunt went to a husband in Keshk. My dream is to one day see her. . . She won't need to tell me if she has been fortunate in life or not. I will look at her hands and know.

"Farhad," she sighs, "this is life. No one will be a pillar for you to lean on. You must stand on your own and be a man. These rugged mountains pity no one. We who live among them must be harder than rock."

Mobin Khan and his family are the only people Mother truly trusts, and any give and take is with them. If she needs a donkey for a day, or a shovel or pickaxe, she borrows from them. When she has wheat or beans or potatoes to trade, Mobin Khan sells them for her in Jawand and buys tea, sugar, salt, and kerosene for us. And his son Farrokh is the only boy in the village I'm really allowed to play with. When Mother has free time, she takes me with her to Mobin Khan's house. Farrokh and I play, while she and Auntie Golrokh sit and talk for hours.

Mother daydreams a lot. She will be silent for hours and then suddenly say, "Son, you should become a judge! No, no, a doctor to heal the ailing. You will give me medicine for my arms, legs, and back to not hurt after a day at the farm. . . . Farhad, I'd like to see you in an officer's uniform, with stars on your shoulders. I saw a picture of one facing a long line of soldiers saluting him. He looked so distinguished, so dignified. . . . But, no, it's dangerous, they will send you to war. I hate war."

I daydream of going to school, becoming a doctor, and not letting Father die.

~

Cold winters and hot summers come and go, and one spring day when the rumble of the mountain river and the music of long-tailed nightingales resonate in the valley, Mother runs to me and takes me in her arms.

"Son, the government has come! The government has come!" she cries and kisses my forehead. "They want to build a school. Here! In Tali! My Farhad will go to school! How I have dreamed of this day. How I have dreamed of bringing you tea and raisins and watching you study and do homework!"

I stare at her.

"School, books, reading, writing!" she says.

"When?"

"Soon!"

"Tomorrow?"

"No, not tomorrow," she laughs. "First they have to build it."

---

A year later, the school is inaugurated. Every morning, with indescribable passion we students bundle our books and run there in our worn plastic slippers, tattered ill-fitting shoes, or bare feet. And together we learn to read and write.

We study for only three years. After Simin's death, our school dies, too. Obeidullah arrives in Tali and turns the schoolhouse into a Taliban command post and tells the farm owners to plant poppy. Mother, Mobin Khan, and a few others are content with their crops of wheat, beans, fruits, and vegetables. They thank God and continue down their own path.

At night, strange noises come from the schoolhouse. They sound like trembling wails and moans, bitter and drawn out. It frightens the villagers. They bury their heads under their blankets and pray.

The old women who have lived their lives and fear nothing, say it is the sound of black beasts haunted by a curse that denies them sleep.

I grow up with the plight of poppy and opium, the give and take, profit and loss of the farmers, the nightly wails and drones from the old schoolhouse. And the time comes for falling in love. I don't know how long I have been infatuated with Kowsar. I do know that I have always liked everything about her. The way she talks, walks, sulks, cries, and gets angry.

She knows this. Sometimes she can read my mind. Sometimes when I imagine myself holding her, she says, "Hey! Stop dreaming!"

I am seventeen, she is sixteen, when that life-changing day comes.

I'm working the patch Mother and I harvested for onions a few days ago. Tired, I go to the riverbank to rest. It's cool in the shade of the trees and the air is scented with the perfume of pennyroyals and wild jasmines. I like to lie down, watch the river, and listen to the crickets and birds. I like to close my eyes and think of Kowsar until I fall asleep.

I imagine her walking to me.

"Wake up, Farhad," she says.

I open my eyes and look at her.

"Do you like me?"

"Yes, for a long time now."

"Why?"

"Because you are beautiful."

"Which part of me do you like best?"

"All of you."

"Like what?"

"Your eyes."

"They're pretty?"

"They are like crystal clear springs. I want to drown in them."

"How about my lips?"

"They are small and rose pink."

"And my neck? My breasts? My waist?"

"Haven't you heard that song?" I say, laughing. "My beautiful flower, in the dark of my night, come lie beside me . . ."

"Then kiss me," she says.

Her body is soft and delicate, her scent intoxicating. I kiss her lips, her neck, I undress her. She lies naked in my arms.

Her voice wakes me.

"Farhad, I bled!"

I open my eyes. I see us lying there naked. I jolt up.

"What are you doing here?" I gasp, nervously looking around. "What have I done!?"

"You didn't do anything. *We* did something."

She gets up and takes my hand.

"Come, let's go in the water."

She leaps into the river, and I find myself wanting to do nothing but watch her. I cannot believe the body I have seen in my dreams for what seems a lifetime, is so freely naked in front me. I want her in my arms.

"Then, come here," she says flirtatiously.

She is a rebel and makes me want to be one, too. Forgetting my fear of being seen by some villager, Talib, or mullah, I go to her.

"Come under the water," she says, taking my hand. "Let's watch the fish and forget the world."

The icy undercurrent speaks of melting mountain snow. Breathless, we surface. She throws her arms around my neck. I shudder, realizing the gravity of what we have done.

"Please, Kowsar, this is dangerous."

She let's go of me, climbs out of the water, and starts putting on her clothes. I follow her and quickly pull on my pants and shirt and grab my stick.

"I have to go, Kowsar. I'm very late."

"Go," she says softly.

A voice inside me screams, Farhad! Do you understand what you have done? She is no longer a virgin. If she is found out, you will both be put to death. I know, I think to myself, I know what I have done. But it was in a dream, in a fantasy. Perhaps it was God's will. I'll take her hand and go home. I will tell Mother, Kowsar is your daughter-in-law.

"Yes, take me there," she says.

"This was lunacy! Do you understand what will become of us if anyone saw us?"

"Yes, I understand," she says gently. "We gave ourselves to each other. It was beautiful."

Mother is in the kitchen. The moment she sees us, she leaps up and says, "Why are you two wet?"

"We were playing by the river," Kowsar says.

She stares at us. I can tell, a hundred questions are whirling around in her mind.

"Yes," Kowsar says.

"Yes, what?" Mother asks.

"We took off our clothes and jumped in the river."

Mother slowly sits down. She knows all there is to know.

"Auntie Zubaideh, can I give you a hand?"

"Yes," Mother says, sounding lost. "Come sit here."

Kowsar takes a bucket from the corner, turns it upside down and sits next to her.

"Do you like *kachi?*"

"I love the one you make!"

"Have you ever had mine?"

"No. Farhad told me all about it. The way he went on and on, my stomach started to growl."

I want to shout, Mother, don't believe her! She's making it all up!

"Are you going to just stand there?" Kowsar says, looking at me. "Either go and leave me alone with Auntie Zubaideh or sit down and help."

"Serves you right," Mother quietly laughs. "She's on to your laziness."

At a loss, I turn to leave, but she stops me.

"Where are you going? Come, cut the melons, and see which ones are sweet enough for the *kachi*."

"Sit here and learn," Kowsar says. "Your future wife loves *kachi* and you'll have to make it for her."

Mother looks at her, then at me. She smiles, then laughs from the bottom of her heart. I think she has been lonesome for so long that she yearns for a companion, for someone to lend her a hand, to lovingly speak her name, to pour her a bowl of tea when she comes home from laboring at the farm. I scorn myself. As I've grown older, I have spent less and less time at home. I have forgotten about her, neglected her. I go and sit with them.

"Get busy!" Kowsar says with a wicked smile.

I look at Mother, our wet hair and clothes don't seem to be on her mind anymore, but she looks troubled, perhaps afraid.

"How many melons should I cut?" I ask, taking the knife from her.

She doesn't hear me. I know her mind is racing.

"Mother, how many melons should I cut?"

She shifts on her stool and says, "Two, son. . . . Now that Kowsar is here, add one more."

"Mother, you think she's a cow!?"

Mother laughs, but her expression hasn't changed.

"You mean me?" Kowsar says frowning.

"No, I mean the cow!"

"Auntie and I will enjoy the *kachi*, you can feast on the melon rinds."

We laugh. Mother says a prayer and blows it toward us. I watch Kowsar chatting away, and I think, if I were in her place, I would have crawled into a corner terrified of the price I would have to pay for my recklessness.

"What you're worrying about belonged to you," she whispers. "Worry about a wedding instead."

❧

"Did you like it?" Mother asks after we finish eating.

"Yes, very much, Auntie Zubaideh," Kowsar says. "I hope Farhad learned how to make it. . . . But, Auntie, I know there are things you want to say to us."

Mother gathers the dishes, folds the dining cloth, and takes them to the kitchen. She is in no hurry to give voice to her thoughts. When she comes back, she sits and remains silent for a while.

"You know, Kowsar," she finally says. "I have one child and I love him dearly. If a thorn pricks his foot, it pricks my heart. I am happy he loves you. He has picked the best blossom in the field. In truth, if he had asked me to choose a wife for him, I would have gone to Mobin Khan and asked for your hand."

She grows quiet again.

I stare at the kilim, but I see no color or design on it. I know Mother is looking at me. I feel the weight of her gaze.

"What you two did was madness."

"I know," Kowsar says.

I sense her gaze moving away from me. I slowly look up.

"Kowsar, do you understand what you have done?" she says, raising her voice.

"I couldn't help it, Auntie. I had no will of my own."

"How about you?" she snaps at me. "Did you lose your mind, too?"

I have no words to speak.

"Shame on you! Farhad, how could you be so foolish!? How

could you be so irresponsible? The danger you have put yourself and this girl in is immeasurable!"

"Mother, I went to rest by the river. I fell asleep and dreamed of Kowsar. When I came to, she was there, in my arms."

"Are you a child? Can you not tell right from wrong? Do you not understand that this damn country is filled with jackals with ragged lungees. Do you not know what they would do to you two? Are you done with your life and hers? Tired of living? Do you want to have me shamed and in mourning? Mobin Khan devastated and grieving?"

All I can do is look down.

"*Speak!*" she shouts.

"Forgive me, Mother" I say in a voice that rises like a moan from my throat. "God is my witness, I couldn't help it."

"Auntie," Kowsar says cautiously. "We have accepted each other. Today I became his. I'm now Farhad's wife."

Mother leans back, her face dark with anger and fear.

"Auntie Zubaideh, go to my father and ask for my hand."

"With what means? Think, Kowsar! How can a poor widow come up with the bride price a girl's father expects? You tell me, who would ever give their daughter for an empty bag? If I hadn't inherited the farm from Farhad's father, God rest his soul, who knows what our fate would have been. And if I offer the farm, what will we live on?"

Kowsar is fiddling with a button on her dress. I wish she would stop and say something. But she doesn't.

"From the day the school opened, Farhad always told me how you outshined all the other students. I had such hopes for all of you. What dreams I had for Farhad. I imagined him a doctor, a judge, an engineer. None of it came true. A bunch of fanatic cretins and filth peddlers closed the school and poured poppy seed in people's hands. . . . They talk of Islam and religion. What part of all this is Islam?"

Kowsar is still fiddling with her button. We sit in awkward silence, each dwelling on our own apprehensions.

"Don't worry about me," Kowsar suddenly says to me. Then she turns to Mother. "God is kind. Father may not ask for anything. Give him hope, talk of God's benevolence, mercy, and compassion."

"Well, there are no other options. I have to go to him and see what he says. And you, Kowsar, let your mother know. Tell her only that you two want each other, that you won't marry anyone else. And say nothing more. Perhaps she can bring Mobin Khan around and convince him."

Kowsar takes her slippers, tucks them under her arm, and runs out in her bare feet.

"You bad egg!" Mother screams at me. "If you ever do anything this rash, this foolish again, you will no longer live under my roof. I have a son, and then I won't. . . . And pray that no one saw you two. Otherwise, there will be hell to face."

I know she is right. I know whatever I say will be useless. Ashamed, I get up and leave.

~

Late afternoon, Mother goes to her room and closes the door. When she walks out, she is wearing her green dress and white headscarf.

"Where to, Mother?"

"Where do you think? To Mobin Khan, to draw a line around Kowsar. I want him to know we intend to ask for her hand before another kohl-eyed menace descends on us and offers a herd of sheep and a couple of cows for her."

I'm anxious. I realize how critical a moment this is in my life. I fear something going wrong, I fear her father refusing Mother, rejecting me.

"Leave it in the hands of destiny," Mother says. "They say the bond of husband and wife is tied in time eternal. If she is to be yours, she will be. . . . Now come latch the front door behind me, the sheep may wander out."

I see her out and sit on the stoop. She walks briskly down the path, her dress and headscarf fluttering behind her. She, too, is anxious. She takes the footbridge across the river and disappears among the trees. The leaves of the weeping willows, the poplars and barberry trees flutter in the wind like Mother's dress.

My eyes are drawn to the poppy fields. The pods are leaking their milky latex. The valley resembles an opium urn.

# 8

I TUCK MY SLIPPERS under my arm and run out. That strange sense of delirium lingers inside me. My body smells of Farhad. I go to the river, under the trees where it happened. The grass remembers us. Bowed and bent where we lay. The trees, not wanting eyes to see our hideaway, have woven and laced their branches together. The river is still intoxicated. It rolls, dances, and splashes off the rocks. I am suddenly frightened. This place was not safe. Anyone could have seen us. I put on my slippers and race home.

Mother is busy in the kitchen.

"Where have you been, you rascal?" she says without looking away from her work.

"Out."

"You shouldn't go roaming around the valley. The jackals talk with the barrel of their gun."

She waves me in. "Your father is craving mung soup. Come, give me a hand."

She has already browned the flour in oil and added the turmeric and garlic. I take the bowl of beans, drain the water they have been soaking in, and add them to the pot. I stir as they start to sizzle and the garlic and turmeric release their aroma. Mother is searching for something in the pantry when I sense Zubaideh nearby. I fill the kettle and put it next the pot.

"Mother, do we have any candied sugar?"

She swings around and asks, "Who's coming?"

I don't answer. If I tell her it's Zubaideh, she will wonder why her friend has suddenly become so important to me that I'm asking for candied sugar. Having come to believe my intuitions, she closes the pantry door comes over to me.

"Kowsar, is someone coming? Tell me, so I can tidy the room."

"I won't make the soup as spicy as Father likes it, otherwise Farrok will make a fuss."

She hurries out of the kitchen. Seconds later, I hear the rasp of the broom against the rug. I have a good feeling. I'm not worried about Mother saying no, and I want Father to know that Zubaideh intends to ask for my hand.

I'm not sure how my heart fell captive to him. Perhaps love for him took root in me a long time ago. After the school closed and I saw him less often, I thought about him more. It was the same for him. He started coming to the house to see Farrokh, but I knew it was a pretense. I was no better, going to their farm to spend time with Zubaideh, all the while hoping Farhad would be nearby. And so it was, until today. I did not intend to do what I did. I imagine angels drew me there and invisible hands made us one.

I wish God bears witness that we want to be husband and wife. I wish God bears witness that for the first time since her husband's death, Zubaideh is wearing a colorful dress to come ask for me to be her daughter. I wish God bears witness that for as long as there is a world, I want to lay my head on Farhad's chest and listen to his every heartbeat.

I'm adding water to the pot when I hear the front door open.

"Golrokh," Zubaideh calls. "Golrokh, are you home?"

"What a surprise," Mother says, stepping out to the porch. "You look so beautiful! And a new dress! Which side of the sky did the sun rise from today!?"

The green of Zubaideh's dress flashes past the kitchen door. I hear the two kissing each other.

"Sister, how are you? How are Farrokh and Mobin Khan?"

"Thank God, we're all well. And you?"

"All is well. Come, let's go inside."

I peek across the yard. They are already busy chatting. A while later, Mother hurries into the kitchen and starts searching the pantry, then the shelf and the windowsill. Now she runs over to the box of plates and bowls and rummages through it.

I stand there puzzled, following her with my eyes until she stops.

"Kowsar, have you seen our nice china bowl?"

I point to it sitting on the shelf.

"I'm going blind!" she says, grabbing the bowl and hurrying to the bucket of water. She rinses and dries it, then goes to the door and examines it in the light. She fills it from the jug of cool water and hurries out.

I smile. When families come to propose a marriage, they ask for some water as soon as the greetings are over. It is a subtle way of making their intentions clear, and it is considered a good omen. Now, Mother knows.

I pray. God, make Father and Mother's heart keen and kind to Farhad. . . . Father, don't say no. If you do, I will die.

The soup is simmering when Mother shows up at the door.

"Make some tea. Green, not black. Make sure you wipe the tray," she says and hurries back to the house.

I'm still cleaning the tray when she comes back with a small plastic bag.

"Take this. Candied sugar for the tray. Use the china teapot. In the pantry. Then run and wash your face, comb your hair, put on your peach blossom headscarf, and bring the tea. . . . Come in politely and say a proper hello."

I nod.

"And don't linger. Serve the tea and leave."

I again nod.

As soon as she's gone, I wash my face with water from the watering can and run to the house. I comb my hair and find my peach blossom headscarf in the bundle where I keep my clothes. I put it on and neatly tie it under my chin. I look in the mirror. Now I look like the daughter Mother wants.

"Kowsar," I say to my reflection. "I would like you to be Farhad's bride."

I run back to the kitchen, prepare the tea tray, and take it to the room.

"Salaam, Auntie Zubaideh," I say as I walk in and set the tray down on the floor in front of her. And I bend down and kiss her hands.

"May God bring you happiness," she says, stroking my cheek. "May God make your wishes come true."

I serve the tea and put the bowl of candied sugar between the two women.

"Mother, if you need more tea, call me. I'll go check on the soup."

"Go, my dear. May God keep you."

I stop outside the door and listen.

"Sister, who better than you?" I hear Mother say. "And Farhad, may God bless him, is the pride of Tali and the best among our young men. Pray that Mobin Khan gives his consent."

"Golrokh, you can make him putty in your hands," Zubaideh giggles. "No bad deed goes unpunished. If you deny him his due for a week, and there's no pot simmering on the cookstove, he himself will deliver Kowsar to my door!"

I suddenly remember the soup. If I ruin it, Father will sulk just when I need him to be in good humor. I hurry to the kitchen. The flame under the pot is dwindling. I add wood to the cookstove, stir the soup and taste it. Relieved, I sit and think of Farhad and the future. What if we cannot be together? What if Father says no? What if he lays a great obstacle in Zubaideh's way? No. I won't let him. I won't let him decide for me. Today, I went to Farhad and slid into his arms. My silence would be a mistake, it would be my ruin. I will not let Father ask for the impossible. I will say, Father, Ghafoor Khan sold Simin for a herd of sheep, and what became of her? Now he and his wife go around like the walking dead. Their daughter wasted. Their life wasted. Their sheep wasted.

"Kowsar."

I jump. Father is standing in the doorway. The aroma of the soup has him looking excited.

"My girl, pour half a bowl for me while I wash up. I haven't eaten since breakfast."

"Of course, Father. All I will say is, if you eat now, you won't be able to eat dinner."

"I'm no match for mung soup. The smell has me weak in the knees. And don't fret, I will eat it tonight, too. Where's your mother?"

"Aunt Zubaideh is here," I say, avoiding his eyes. "They're in the guestroom."

I point to the watering can. "Shall I pour while you wash?"

"No, girl. Worry about my bowl of soup," he says, walking away.

I fill a small bowl and set it aside to cool a little until he comes for it. But he is already back, his face and hands dripping with water. I want to tell him to dry himself, but I don't. I hand him the bowl and a wooden spoon.

"Girl! This tiny bowl! Two spoons of soup won't even make it to my small intestine!"

I shrug. He hands me back the spoon and gulps down the soup straight from the bowl.

"Mobin Khan," Mother calls from the guestroom door. "Come, Sister Zubaideh wants to talk to you."

My heart drops. I am filled with dread and hope.

"At least bring me a proper bowl of tea," Father says, walking to the house.

The moment that will rule my destiny has come. I take the soup pot off the stove, set the kettle to boil, and put Father's yellow teapot close to it to warm up. My hands are shaking. I know by now the casual chitchat is over and Zubaideh is delicately wording the reason for her visit. He will not give her an answer today. He will think for a while, weigh the positives and negatives of the union.

Only then will he offer a yes or no. How time will drag, how restless and anxious I will be.

"Kowsar," I say, talking to myself. "You have to wait for everything. You have to wait for the water to boil, wait for the tea leaves to steep, wait for the tea to cool. Only then you can drink it. Even a sip of tea needs patience. Be patient!"

But there is an obstinate child inside me. I don't want to wait, she says, stomping her feet. Why should I have to wait when Farhad and I are already wed?

I stop outside the door with Father's tea. He is talking.

"Bibi Zubaideh, who better than you and your son. If there were only one wise and decent young man in the village, it would be Farhad. But I need to also think of my own son. Soon, he will want to take a wife. And, like you, I am of meager means. Give me and Kowsar's mother a few days to think and talk things over."

"Of course, Mobin Khan," Zubaideh says. "Do your thinking. I will come again in a few days, and I will bring a white-bearded elder and a black-bearded learned man. I will not give up. What is in our children's heart is important. If they want one another and we decide otherwise, we have done them and ourselves an injustice. Just before you came, Golrokh and I were remembering Simin, that beautiful, innocent child. Greed is quick to ruin. I have no wealth, but I have Farrokh's love and appreciation. I value Kowsar. Golrokh is worried about her illness, but my son and I accept her as she is. To us, she has no illness."

They are all silent. I walk in and take the small tray to Father.

"Shall I pour?"

"Yes, dear."

I fill his bowl and leave the room, but not the door. I want to hear more, but they are silent, perhaps thinking about Simin. Someone is playing a reed flute out on the road. I cross the yard and look out the door. Farrokh is sitting on a rock, playing a melancholy song. I stay there and listen. Soon, the sun starts painting the clouds a soft hue of rose and flocks of nightingales return to the trees, singing to the tune of Farrokh's flute. I sit, hug my knees, and rest my head on them.

"Farhad," I whisper, closing my eyes. "There's no good news, there's no bad news, there's no news at all. We have to wait. We have to be patient. Good news doesn't come easy in this land of ours."

～

Mother has spread a kilim out on the porch, and we are having tea when the door opens and Zubaideh, wearing her green dress and white chiffon headscarf, walks in. Mother tells me to bring a cushion and bolster for her.

"There's no need," Zubaideh says, sitting down. "I've come to talk to Mobin Khan."

"Well, you can't sit on hard ground and go to battle before tea," Mother says, smiling as she pours tea for her.

"Mobin Khan," Zubaideh says. "All I have in this world is one son. If anything were to happen to him—"

"God forbid!" Mother exclaims. "What has happened?"

"He has lost his spirit and strength, hasn't eaten a morsel of food in a week. He is as pale as a corpse and terribly weak. And all my talking has done no good."

I had imagined Farhad anxious and unhappy, but he is starving himself. I fear for him. My heart breaks for him.

"Kowsar, go inside," Mother says. "Get up and go inside. Now!"

I cannot. I'm shaking. Farrokh pulls me up to my feet. I know all is about to fade into gray.

"Father," I mumble. "I love him."

I feel a heavy weight lifting from my heart. I can breathe.

"Are you all right, Kowsar?" Farrokh asks once we are inside.

I nod.

"Rest for a while. Stay here."

I lie down and wonder, did I really dare tell Father that I'm in love with Farhad? Yes, I did. I boldly spoke those words. Farhad did you hear me? I want to not allow anything to frighten me, to shake me, to reduce me to convulsions and seizures. Farhad, we have each other. We will grow strong together.

Mother comes in and kneels beside me. She feels my forehead. It is not hot with fever, it is not wet with sweat.

"I'm all right, Mother. It didn't happen."

"Get up then. Your Father said, yes!"

I stare at her.

"Believe me! He gave his answer. Congratulations, my girl."

"Tell Farhad to eat."

"Don't worry, Zubaideh will give him the good news. Go kiss your father's hand, and your mother-in-law's, too."

I think to myself, I have a mother-in-law, I am wife to a man who loves me, a man I love. Mother and I walk out to the porch. There is joy in the air and on everyone's face. I go to Father and take his hands. I had never seen them shake before. He has always been my shelter, my haven. Perhaps I knew he would agree, perhaps he knew he would not find a better husband for me. Perhaps as I hold his hands, he imagines me gone. Imagines this house without me. Tears roll down my face as I kiss his hands and he kisses my bowed head.

"May you be happy, my girl," he says with a lump in his throat.

His words remind me of Simin. I think of how fortunate I am. So many fathers in this valley give their young girls to older men and speak Father's words, and most of those girls will take that dream of happiness to their grave. Father, you are a good man.

"Kowsar, what is going through your head?" Mother says. "Come kiss your mother-in-law's hand!"

Embarrassed, I go to Zubaideh and take her hands. "May God have you and Farhad grow old together," she says, as I pay my respect to her. I go to Mother and repeat the ritual. She caresses my face as tears well in her eyes.

"Hey!" Farrokh teases, "I'm your older brother. I count, too! And when, God willing, are you leaving? I want your share of eggs at breakfast."

"Brother, all you get is a kiss on the cheek. As for my breakfast, you have to earn it."

"Mobin Khan," Zubaideh says. "if you have any terms and conditions, tell me now. I want us to settle everything before the elders seal and bless the marriage."

"Like you, I have little. And fate has its own ways," Father says. "I only want you to have a celebration for her marriage. And for people not to talk, put an acre or two of your farm under Kowsar's name."

"Mobin Khan, I will put the entire farm in her name. I was afraid you would ask for it as the bride price. In which case I would be ruined."

"Thank God I have enough sense to know that if I take your farm, my daughter will suffer. I only regret that I can't send her to your home with a dowery."

"Kowsar is worth all the gold in the world. And now, I should hurry home," she says, getting up. "I will give Farhad the blessed news and fry a few eggs. I'm sure he will eat."

—❦—

Two weeks later, Farhad's uncle and a few village elders formalize our engagement. The event also serves as an excuse for Javad Khan and Zubaideh to clear the air between them. Perhaps seeing Farhad building a life for himself has rid his uncle of his greed for Zubaideh's farm.

Geesu stops by every day, and every day she says, "Thank God your wish came true."

She wants me to pray for her fate to be as fortunate. I know she has Farrokh in her heart, and Farrokh plays the flute at dusk, thinking of her. She has never spoken a word to me about this. Perhaps she is afraid of the day she might lose him, the day someone else comes to take her. Her father, Hashem Khan, is a short-sighted stubborn man, and is quick to raise his hand on his wife and child. Geesu could never speak her mind and heart to him.

With only a wall separating our houses, we sometimes hear him beating his wife and shouting obscenities at Geesu.

# 9

AFTER BREAKFAST ONE DAY, when everyone has gone about their day's work and I have finished washing the dishes and sweeping the rooms, Geesu comes to the house.

"Kowsar, did you know Nadim Khan has been ill and bedridden for some time? Bibi Zinat told us when she came to visit yesterday. She said he is not long for this world. It's a matter of days."

My heart drops. I have loved Nadim Khan since I was nine years old, since the year the school opened and he volunteered as a teacher a few days a week. His library was my wonderland. Each book a secret door to other worlds, real and imagined. I remember every moment I spent with him. I remember his kindness and wisdom.

"We should go see him, Geesu. We owe him a lot. I will be grateful to him and to Teacher Sadeq for as long as I live."

She looks down and says nothing.

"Will you go with me?"

"I can't."

"Scared of your father?"

"Of him and the Talibs around the school."

"We can take the mountain trail and avoid that side of the village. It's a beautiful day. I would love to climb up to the ridge and fly away."

"Sister," Geesu says, laughing bitterly. "If you don't fly, I don't know who would! . . . And now you have Farhad."

"And you could have Farrokh. I sometimes imagine what it would be like to have you as my sister-in-law."

Geesu looks away.

I gaze at her profile and think, if I were Farrokh, I would fall in love with her, too. She was small and skinny when we were younger, but in the past two years she has suddenly grown taller, fuller, more beautiful. I adore her round face, the dimple on her chin, and the way her cheeks blush when she laughs. I pray for her and Farrokh. She is loving and kind, and with me leaving home, she could take my place and make it easier for Mother and Father.

"Don't brood!" I tell her. "If you show some courage, the wall between you and Farrokh will come down. Remember that ancient epic about Shirin and Farhad? He carved through a mountain to reach her."

"Not everyone dares accept a suitor before her father has spoken. Mobin Khan is a gem. If it were me, I would have been a corpse within minutes."

"Look," she says, turning around and lifting her blouse.

I gasp. Her back is covered with yellowish-purple bruises.

"He beat me with his stick three days ago. It still hurts."

"Why!?"

"It was laundry day. Mother and I were at the stream for hours. He came home and dinner wasn't ready. He did the same to Mother."

"All I can do is pray for you," I say, my heart breaking for her. "If God wills it and you become my brother's wife, there will be no beating in our home. You will be in peace. Farrokh is a rascal, but he is kind and decent. I think I will talk to Mother. I will ask her to make him her concern after I'm married and ask Hashem Khan for your hand. I just pray he doesn't ask for more than what Father can offer. . . . Now, will you come with me to visit Nadim Khan or not?"

"Only if someone older comes with us. Just to be safe."

"Mother!" I shout. "Nadim Khan is very ill. Geesu and I want to go see him. Come with us so Hashem Khan doesn't lose his temper and some jackal doesn't make off with a pair of chicks."

Minutes later Mother walks in, her hands white with flour.

"In God's name, why are you screaming? I didn't understand a word you said. What about Nadim Khan?"

"He is very sick. It seems on his death bed. We want to go see him."

"You know you are not allowed to go to that part of the village on your own. Those animals don't spare anything that flies the sky or walks the earth."

"That's why we want you to come with us. And we will take the mountain trail."

"Still, we might run into them," she says, hurrying back to the kitchen. "It's time to harvest the poppy farms, which means Obeid is back."

"I wish I had auburn hair, like yours," Geesu says, combing my hair.

"Be happy with what God has given you. Your light chestnut hair is gorgeous, and you cannot find eyes as beautiful as yours in all of Badghis. And I'll bet it's those lovely breasts and that dimple that have driven Farrokh mad."

"Hush! Are you crazy!?"

"I'm not crazy. I'm just tired of being afraid. I think your breasts are beautiful, and I think they have driven Farrokh mad. Why should I be afraid of saying so? Imagine if Simin wasn't afraid, was free to speak. At worst, Ghafoor Khan would have flogged her and locked her in a room for a few weeks. But she would still be alive. And your father who beats whoever is within reach of his stick is nothing but a brute. If you show him your back and ask him to explain why he beat you, perhaps next time he will ask himself that question before he raises his stick."

Geesu turns away from me. I know she loves her father despite his violent nature.

"Don't be cross," I say gently. "I love you, and I hate what he does to you."

She quietly finishes combing my hair and tucks the sides behind my ears.

"Now you are as beautiful as the moon."

I look in the mirror and wink at her.

"Come, let me fix your hair. Mother will come any minute and scold us."

Running the comb through her soft wavy hair that cascades down to her waist, I say, "I wonder what auburn and light chestnut look like together. Shall I braid our hair together?"

"You're being silly, Kowsar."

"If Farhad had long hair," I say, standing next to her and braiding our hair together. "I would do the same with him. Then he would be stuck with me all the time."

"I don't doubt you shackling the poor boy."

We look in the mirror. Our thick braid is strangely striking. Light and dark, coiled together like snakes.

"What madness is this!?" Mother snaps, standing in the doorway. "Undo it immediately! And cover yourselves properly. Headscarves won't do. Put on your black chadors."

Chuckling, we undo the braid and Geesu runs home to bring

her chador. Out in the yard, Mother shoos the hen and her begging chicks s back into their coop, and says, "The poor things want to go for a walk, too."

━

The air is crisp and refreshing. The sun will soon rise higher and shrink and shorten our shadows. On the slopes surrounding the valley, the wheat and poppy fields are in an unending battle. They thrash about in the wind like angry seas. The gusts are calmer further down the hill. The starlings and mynas in the trees chirp and chirrup undisturbed. Mother walks at a brisk pace a few steps in front of us, looking directly ahead. As we approach the footbridge, Geesu nudges me with her elbow.

"Just as I thought," she whispers.

Farhad is there. I smile, as though at a full moon. He walks up to us and says *salaam* to Mother.

"If you are going to our house, my mother isn't there," he says.

"We are actually going to pay a visit to Nadim Khan. He is gravely ill. But give my greetings to Sister Zubaideh."

She sets off again. Geesu smiles at Farhad and follows her, leaving me to have a moment alone with him.

"Come," I say, holding open my chador and wrapping my arms around him. "Kiss me."

He gives me a quick kiss and pulls back.

"Go, Kowsar, this isn't the place for it. Go."

I stand there looking at him.

"Don't be childish. Go!" he says, turning away.

"I saw," Geesu whispers as I catch up with her. "You're asking for trouble."

"Haven't you ever kissed Farrokh?"

"No! We just look at each other and talk with our eyes. When he misses me, he plays his flute out on the road. He knows I can hear him."

"Why don't you kiss him when you're alone?"

She giggles.

At the end of the road, we turn onto a narrow dirt path in a gully that will take us to the highest point of the village. To our right there is a tall cliff wall riddled with holes and furrows where bats and owls sleep during the day. To our left are the farms and fields. Farther up, the path snakes around a ridge. Past the turn, we see a group of boys around a bonfire in the shadow of a boulder. Geesu and I slow down, but Mother continues as before, pretending she hasn't seen them.

"Do you recognize the two facing us?" Geesu says in hushed voice. "Youssef and Nematollah. They are smoking opium!"

Seeing us, they quickly hide their pipes behind them, and Youssef drawls a slow *salaam* to Mother.

"Ghafoor's boy," she says sharply. "What are you doing here?"

"Me?"

"Yes, you!"

"Nothing! I'm not doing anything. Just warming up by the fire."

"You scamp! Who feels cold enough in May to need a fire? Run along and go home!"

Youssef turns too quickly, loses his balance and stumbles. The other boys jeer.

"Pick up your step, girls" Mother says quietly. "They're junkies."

Away from them, she slows down.

"Those ingrates couldn't even walk straight. That wretched Ghafoor. No good has come to his children. . . . Penitence, penitence. God's wrath. This boy used to carry sixty-kilo sacks of grain up the mountain. Now he can barely stand on his feet. Penitence, penitence."

Mother carries on, but I am no longer listening. I'm sad for those boys, for Youssef and Nematollah. I'm sad for Tali. I imagine the village youth, black skeletons in the hands of the wind, the poppy farms soon to be their graveyard.

Sometime later, Mother stops.

"The trail through the valley would have been better," she says, swinging around and walking back. "The outsiders they bring to work the farms are scoring poppy pods in the farms up ahead. Talibs are standing guard."

The moment Geesu catches sight of them, she panics and hur-

212

ries after Mother. I stop, angry that we have to turn back when we are so close to Nadim Khan's house.

"Don't stand there," Mother growls. "Hurry before they see us!"

I quickly go to her.

"God, what sort of an infernal day is this!?"

Mother has hardly spoken when we hear a gunshot and a man shouts, "Halt!"

We freeze.

"Cover yourselves," Mother whispers. "Don't look at them and don't speak. I'll do the talking."

She walks back a few steps and stops, waiting for the Talib to show himself. Geesu and I pull the sides of our chador together, leaving only a small open slit to see through.

"What do you think you're doing?" Mother snaps as the man walks out from behind a rock. "You take us for thieves to shoot and holler like that!?"

With his long scruffy hair and filthy clothes, it is only the Talib's machine gun that sets him apart from a vagrant.

"I'm to take you to Obeidullah Khan," he says, stopping ten steps away.

"Who?"

"Obeidullah Khan, the commander."

"If this Obeidullah Khan has something to say, he can come to us. There are strangers up ahead. It is not proper for them to see us."

"Don't be insolent, wretch!" the Talib snarls.

"Girls," Mother whispers, covering her mouth with her chador. "Walk away. Slowly."

"Well, what are you waiting for?" she retorts. "Go give my message to your commander."

A straight line of bullets pierces the ground inches away from her feet.

"It seems your ears are deaf to reason, wretch—"

"Hold your tongue!" Mother shouts. "If you fed on mother's milk and have the audacity to shoot a mother, go ahead!"

Their wrangling unnerves me. His finger on the trigger terrifies me. I know I must not have an attack. I must resist it at all cost. I grab Geesu's arm. She is trembling like a willow.

"Listen to me," Mother says, now in a calmer, more conciliatory tone. "We are on our way to visit a sick friend. And, seeing strangers up ahead, we were turning back to take a different route. If you are a Muslim, a devout man of faith, you will stand aside and let us go on our way."

"I don't give a damn about your sick or your healthy. I have my orders. If you don't come with your own two feet, I'll drag your corpse to him."

I see four men walking up the trail. It's Chief Abed, with Mullah Sikhdad, Khodadad, and the infamous Obeidullah.

"Mother, Abed Khan is coming," I say loudly.

"Come, Abed Khan," she calls out with veiled relief. "Come and rid us of this stubborn donkey."

The four men laugh, but the gunman is enraged.

"Shut your mouth, wretch, or I'll shut it for you!"

"Run off!" Mother says, waving him away. "And wash that face, it hasn't seen soap and water in three months."

"Step back and shoulder your arm," Obeidullah orders the man as Chief Abed walks over to Mother.

"Abed Khan, I was taking the girls to visit Nadim Khan," she says. "He is in a bad way. And this louse stopped us and dared shoot that machine gun of his."

I imagine Khodadad leering at Geesu and me despite our chadors. I remember the day Teacher Sadeq took me to see him. I remember that dark room. The seed of hatred planted in me years ago runs deeper roots each time I see the man. I want to blind his only eye, go to Simin's grave and say, Sister, Khodadad will never set eyes on another innocent girl.

"You chose this long and steep mountain path over the short trail down in the valley?" Obeidullah asks Mother without approaching us. "And you brought two girls with you?"

"I will not go empty handed to visit a sick friend. I thought the farms on this side of the river would have some melons or other fruits I could buy and take for him."

"Who are these girls?" Khodadad asks, indulging his curiosity.

"One is my daughter, Kowsar. The other is Geesu, our neighbor's daughter."

"By the power of God, they have grown up."

"Girls ripen quickly," Mullah Sikhdad chuckles. "Kowsar's father is making her a bride, but Geesu doesn't have a *sahib* yet. I intend to ask for her hand for my dear son, Nematollah. And Mawlawi, I say this only because I know you to be an avid hunter!"

The two burst into laughter.

"Yes, Mullah, laugh," Mother says scornfully. "What prince of a son you have raised that you want Hashem Khan's daughter for him. Go to the boulder at the bend and take a good look at your dear Nematollah. Open your eyes! Go and see what this money-spinning harvest has brought you. What man would give his daughter to an addict?"

"Sister, what are you saying?" he says, gaping at her.

"Go to the ridge and see for yourself. Your beloved son is flying high in seventh sky."

Without another word Mullah Sikhdad rushes down the dirt path.

"Wait, Sikhdad," Chief Abed calls out, hurrying after him. "I'll go with you. . . . Bibi Golrokh, men from Helmand and Farah are scoring poppy pods. Turn back."

"We will go around, Abed Khan," Mother says, and without a word to Obeidullah, she turns toward the trail that circles the farms. Hardly ten steps along the craggy byway, the Talib shows up again.

"Tell the girls to show their face," he shouts at Mother.

"Why?"

"There is no *why*! Commander's orders. God knows who is under those chadors and where you are taking them."

"You son of a dog!" Mother suddenly screams. "Get out of my way!"

"Don't!" I shriek, as the man releases the safety on his machine gun. "Please, Mother! Calm down. Please!"

"You thug, have you no shame!" she goes on screaming. "Until the day you filthy lot arrived, our girls went without hijab and without fear! Now, blessed by your presence, they suffocate under chadors, and our boys are turning into junkies. And you dare aim that thing at me!"

"Hold your tongue, woman!" Obeidullah shouts, walking up behind us with Khodadad. "And you two, show your face or blame yourselves for what will come."

"Kill me first, then look at their face!" Mother says, defiantly shielding us with her hands braced on her hips.

"I will! As easily as I would kill a sparrow," he says, nodding to the Talib.

"Mother, please!" I say, quickly stepping forward and holding open my chador.

"Here! Take a good look. You, too, Mawlawi. You know me. Surely, you haven't forgotten the kindness you showed me."

"Do you know her?" Obeidullah asks him.

"Yes, she's the one with fainting spells."

"You girl," Obeidullah says, turning to Geesu. "Show your face."

I look pleadingly at her, but she is frozen with fear.

"Geesu, please!" I whisper. "Don't be afraid!"

"Well, well!" Obeidullah says, ogling her as she opens her chador and stands trembling in front of him.

"Hashem's daughter. And all grown up," Khodadad says, laughing. "Obeid, let them go."

"May God strike you with his wrath," Mother hisses at the Talib as we hurry past him.

Shaken and numb, we continue down the trail, our silence broken only by the frogs in the narrow watercourse that ignorant to the world wistfully croak to each other.

Their song drifts me back several years, to the day Geesu and I were playing by the mountain river and saw Nadim Khan sitting on the green, leaning against a tree with his eyes closed. We start to tiptoe away when he softly says, "I'm not asleep."

He puts his finger to his lips and waves for us to go sit beside him, and he closes his eyes again. A while later, he opens them and asks, "Did you hear that?"

Puzzled, Geesu and I look at each other.

"Hear what?" I whisper.

"The frog. Listen. It's singing. Deliriously."

We listen intently and hear it softly croaking at the water's edge.

"Yes," Geesu murmurs. "We hear it!"

"Everyone hears, but there is hearing, and there is hearing," he softly says. "You must learn how to listen and how to hear, how to use your mind and your senses to understand what your ears perceive. All living creatures have a voice, and it is honest, void of deceit and duplicity. When the partridge sings, it sings from the heart. The nightingale sings with love. The goldfinches' silvery twitter is pure and innocent. Cuckoos are lovelorn. And this frog sings from the soul, with flirtation and romance. When you *feel* its song, it will steal you away, intoxicate you. It will make you grasp the meaning of life and living. It will make you understand that you are not alone in this world, that God is not what the ignorant and the devious claim."

All that remains of Nadim Khan is skin and bones. He breathes, his eyes fixed on the opposite wall, perhaps on his books that are now coated with dust. A few of his relatives and friends are there to spend the final days of his life with him. Learning that we are his former students, they offer us their place at his bedside.

"He is not doing well today," one of them says in hushed voice. "He has been grappling with Azrael since early morning."

His face is sallow and moist. His bedding reeks of fever. He is in pain but groans in silence, as though in atonement for his pain-free days.

"Nadim Khan, it's Kowsar. With Mother and Geesu. We've come to see you."

He stirs under his blanket. His eyes move away from his books and turn to me. They are sunken and yellow, their former light dimmed. I take his hand. His fingers are as thin as reed pens. Their tips dark, as though dipped in ink.

His lips move. I bring my ear close. His voice is barely audible.

"You did well to come," he breathes. "I wanted to see you."

"My kind teacher," I whisper, holding back my tears. "Forgive me, I only learned about your illness this morning. The village is no longer safe. I stay home much of the time, and when I go out, I keep to that side of the valley."

"Is my dear Geesu happy? Is Bibi Golrokh well?"

I look at Geesu and Mother. "Yes, they are well."

"Are you still reading, my girl?"

"Sometimes. My old schoolbooks."

"I always wished you would go to university, study the humanities, the sciences, and build a life."

He stops and takes a deep breath.

"But they killed the future," he goes on. "The school, an arms depot, the land poisoned. What could you learn in this infested gorge? You will marry, bear children, and die without having seen anything, achieved anything. . . . I blame the mule at the top who handed your destiny to them.

"Try, Kowsar," he heaves after a while. "Try. They fear your flying. Like *Simurgh*, fly. All you need is the sky they stole. Take it back and try. They will clip your wings and laugh when you fall. Try again."

"I will try, Teacher," I say, tearfully. "I will try."

He closes his eyes and slowly breathes, "I leave you my books. . . . Read *Sophie's World*, learn that freedom is found by choosing to rebel, to dare. . . . Farhad is a good man. Ask him to take you away from here."

# 10

OTHER SNOWY WINTERS pass, but the horror of the night Simin was murdered has not faded in Majid and Halimeh's memory. Halimeh is with child and suffering. She has nightmares and wakes up to her own screams, and every time she climbs the stairs to the second floor, she sees Simin's dismembered body in a pool of blood. Majid has long hoped for a second child, a sibling and playmate for four-year-old Yassin, but he fears Halimeh will lose the child. Doctors and mullahs have failed to help her, and prayers at shrines and houses of worship have resulted in nothing. His wife needs someone to care for her. A capable and kind woman.

My mother, he thinks. I must bring her to live with us, for her sake and for Halimeh's wellbeing.

The next day, Majid travels to Qala-e Naw. In Zulaikha's room he sits at the window and listens to his mother toil—the rasp of the broom against the rugs, the grate of the steel wool against the pots and pans. He watches her carry a large bowl of dough to the mud shed in the corner of the yard that houses the oversized kiln set into a counter. Sometime later, flushed and sweating, she hurries to the house with an armful of steaming fresh bread.

"Son, have some tea," she says, walking in with a tray. "I will see to the dinner and come back to sit with you for a while."

Mother, he thinks, who are you breaking your back for? Is he a husband to you? Is he kind and grateful? After your fifth child, he took a second wife and banished you to the kitchen. That wasn't enough. He married a nine-year-old girl. Then came the fourth wife and he murdered the third. He killed her in my home. In front of my wife and child. I gathered Simin's body with my own hands. From murder to the celestial light that blinded the mawlawi's eye, in this land everything can be concealed under a beard, a title, and a fine white lungee. Memorize a few suras and everyone will stand in reverence and obedience. He and the likes of him ascribe their tyranny to their beneficence and wisdom. But I am that man's son. I see and I know. Any crime and cruelty in pursuit of power, profit, and pleasure. What good is his wealth when you suffer? How will I answer God? I will take you away. I will not leave you to serve his wives and his pious underlings.

Zoleikha returns, wipes her brow, and pours a bowl of the now tepid tea for herself.

"Majid, what is the matter? You don't seem well."

"Mother, I'm taking you away. It's time for you to be with your grandchildren. To watch them play and hear them laugh, to forget the ills of the world. You will wither away here. Even now, your chest wheezes. The day you become bound to your bed, this man will toss you out. I will not wait for that day to come. I will take you away from this house now, even if he turns the world upside down."

Zoleikha quietly cries. She longs for her grandchild and the one that will come. She finishes her tea and sets down her bowl.

"Son, don't think that I don't love my grandchild and her mother. Don't think that I don't want to be in my son's home. I have not had a moment of joy in this inferno. You're right, I have wasted away. My body aches, my hands and feet have no energy left. My fingers have turned into claws. But son, my life is the life my mother and my grandmother lived. The life all mothers and grandmothers live. He will not let me leave.

"Not long ago, I asked him to allow me to come see you for a few days. He went mad. 'If you set foot outside this house,' he said, 'you will pay dearly.' Son, leave me to go on here, and when I am no longer, bury me in Khalishkak. I will thank God that it was your hands that laid me to rest. Say nothing to this brute."

"I will, mother. I will talk to him tonight. I will talk calmly, reasonably. If he understands, fine. If he doesn't, I will wait for him to leave for his office tomorrow, and I will pack your things and we will leave. Let him disown me, take away his house and wealth. I will be happier living in a tent if you are with us.

"Don't stay silent, mother. Tell him it is enough, that you are unwell. Tell him you can no longer stand at the cookstove and bend over the kiln."

"Do you think he doesn't see and doesn't know? He sees and he knows. Mah Jabin doesn't lift a finger, and he lets her get away with it. And his new wife, Salima, is a child and pregnant. Khodadad expects me to go on as long as there is life in my body, and I don't dare defy him. Ever since he lost his eye, he has been even more difficult. His whip is by his side, waiting for one wrong word, one delayed duty."

❧

At night, when Khodadad returns, he sees Majid's shoes in the anteroom.

"Majid Khan, welcome!" he says, standing in the door to Zoleikha's room. "I hope it is good deeds that bring you here."

"Hello, Father. I came to visit Mother."

"Meaning your father doesn't count?"

"To tell you the truth," Majid says uneasily. "I came to fetch Mother. God willing, I will take her home with me tomorrow to spend a little time with us."

225

"What did you say?"

"God willing, I will take Mother to Khalishkak for a short while."

"With whose permission?"

Majid says nothing.

"Look at me! I asked you, with whose permission!"

Majid looks up at his father. Daunted by the forbidding expression on his face, he looks away.

"Halimeh is six months pregnant and having a difficult time. I'm away all day overseeing your properties and Yassin is too young to give her a hand around the house. And Mother is tired and unwell. I'd like to take her to see her grandchild, to rest for a while, and be a companion for Halimeh."

"What audacity! You might as well mock my ancestors! So what if Halimeh is pregnant! What about this house? Who will run it for me? Do you imagine Zulaikha is suffering? She eats from the same pot as us and drinks from the same carafe. She has clothes on her back and a bed to sleep in. What else does she need?"

"Father, she is worn out, tired to the bone. Thank God you are a wealthy man. You can hire a servant or two."

Khodadad strides over to Majid, pulls him up by the collar, and slams him against the wall.

"You cow! Don't give me advice. For seven generations we have not allowed a single stranger near our wives. Have you ever seen anyone cross the yard any further than the guestroom? The world is full of the foul and filthy, and you want me to trust my young wife to them? Go! And never give voice to your juvenile ideas again. Your mother can leave this house in a shroud and coffin. As long as her husband is alive, she has a keeper. Understand?"

Khodadad slams Majid against the wall again and watches him sink to the floor.

"May this be your last foolishness," he shouts, storming out of the room.

"Mother, in the name of the Prophet and the Quran, I will take you away," Majid murmurs. "In the name of God and his guardians, I will save you from this hell."

"I told you there is no reasoning with this man," Zulaikha says, pale and shaken.

"He has insulted me enough. Quietly pack your belongings. I will come with a car on Friday and take you."

"Son, let it be. Let him say whatever he wants. The wind carries away shouts and insults. Don't take them to heart. Come to the kitchen and eat. I cooked lentil rice and lamb for you."

"I've had enough! Enough of not taking it to heart. Enough of what the wind carries away. Every one of his taunts and abuses is a bullet in my chest. If he has no pity for you, then he has none for me. . . . Enough!"

Majid walks out, leaving Zulaikha standing in the middle of the room.

"Son," she calls after him, "where are you going in the dark of night?"

She hurries to the window and draws open the curtain. She can see nothing. He drove away my son, she thinks. He broke his heart. Overwhelmed, Zulaikha breaks into sobs.

"Hush, that's enough tears," Mah Jabin says, stroking her back. "I know you have suffered."

Zulaikha looks at her. Despite her distrust of the woman, she no longer fears her or anyone else.

"I could hardly tell my right from my left when Khodadad put me in the kitchen. My hands would turn blue from the cold and too numb to even peel an onion. I shivered and cooked as he snored under his quilt and *sandali*. He had no pity in his heart. 'You will get used to it,' he said. Yes, I got used to it. I got used to everything, even to his insults and his heavy hand.

"When I was a girl, I imagined husband meant a friend, a companion, a kindred soul. The day I was brought to this house, I didn't know I was going to my prison and to a man who would torment me. Still, I told myself, this is my lot, this is what God has resolved for me. I have endured for thirty years, praying that he will not find fault and punish me with his fists. Now, he has driven away my child, told him that only my corpse will ever leave this house. He cursed at him and broke his heart. . . As God is my witness, I will never again lift a finger in this house, and the next time he berates me, I will take his other eye. If only that poor girl had stabbed the toothbrush deeper into his tainted brain. . ."

Mah Jabin's sympathy suddenly turns into fear. She shudders, realizing that Zulaikha's words are not idle threats. She imagines Khodadad blind and helpless, in need of a hand to feed him, wash him, take him to the toilet. Soon Salima will give birth, and Khodadad will become a deadweight around her neck. She tells herself, I will be the one who pays the price for Zulaikha's revenge.

"I think I just heard him call for me," she says, getting up. "I must go. Try to rest. Majid will come back, and soon all will be forgiven and forgotten. It will be as though nothing happened."

Leaving Zulaikha's room, she quietly goes to Khodadad.

"What's wrong?" he asks impatiently.

"A lot is wrong," she whispers. "Come to my room. I will explain."

In Mah Jabin's room, Khodadad closes the door and says, "What is the matter with you now?"

"Watch out, Mawlawi. You have made Zulaikha a mother scorned and determined to avenge her son. She has sworn to God and the Prophet that she will blind your other eye. And knowing that woman, her words are no idle threats."

"Swear to the Quran that what you have spoken is the truth," Khodadad says, suddenly alarmed.

"I swear. She was crying, shaking with rage. An old woman is like a camel. She will not rest until she has taken her revenge."

229

Khodadad walks out into the hallway. Zulaikha's door is open. He quietly goes to his room and locks the door.

—

It is a night of nightmares for Khodadad. Each time he closes his eyes, he sees Zulaikha clutching a knife and creeping up to him like a phantom. He jolts awake, prays to God and damns Satan. And he thinks, You old bitch! You devious hussy! A whore took one eye, now you want to take the other? Your stomach is full, your bed is warm, your carcass is clothed. Not once have I complained that the food is too salty or in need of salt, is overcooked or undercooked. What are you lacking that you so desperately want to go to Khalish-kak? Your son has a wife, and she has him on a leash. What woman has ever loved her mother-in-law for Halimeh to now love you? Do you think she will tend to you? Pamper you? No. She will put you to work. . . . And a pious woman goes from her husband's house to her grave. Wretch, your first and last home will be this and no other.

He tosses and turns and imagines himself blind. A man whose world will be nothing but darkness, a man who will no longer see his beautiful young wife and will never lay eyes on the child she is bearing for him. A man stripped of power and position and a target for deception and deceit.

"No," he hisses. "I will not allow it."

Near dawn, Zulaikha wakes up with a heavy heart and her fury all but forgotten.

Perhaps it was for the best that he insulted my son and drove him away, she tells herself. One day soon, I will talk to Khodadad and beg for his permission to go to Khalishkak for a few days. He might take pity on me. God is kind and merciful.

She dresses and goes out to the shed and starts a fire in the kiln. It's time to bake fresh bread for Khodadad's breakfast. The first light of day is only now breaking and roosters near and far are crowing *azan*. Now and then, she hears a motorcycle speed by.

Khodadad quietly tiptoes out of the house and keeping to the shadows walks over to the shed. The fire is already burning bright. Red flames lick from the gaping mouth of the kiln. Zulaikha is standing there warming her hands, waiting for the roaring flames to ebb before she adds a handful of tinder for a gentle and steady heat. Crouching down, Khodadad sneaks up behind her, snaps his hands around her ankles and yanks her legs out from under her. Before she can let out a scream, Zulaikha plunges into the kiln, her fingers desperately clinging to the rim. She feels the flames scorching her face and scalp and setting her dress on fire. She feels her legs as Khodadad swings them up and pushes the rest of her body into the pit. And she feels nothing more.

Khodadad quickly puts the large clay lid over the kiln, takes a step back and a deep breath of relief.

"Now try to blind me," he sneers. "Your forefathers be damned!"

Soon the roar inside the kiln quiets down and the smell of burned flesh fills the air. Khodadad hurries to the storage room and returns with an armful of oak logs. He throws them in the kiln and waits. As the slow-burning wood begins to crackle, it releases its sweet scent.

Back in his room, the mawlawi goes to bed and soundly sleeps. It is later that he wakes up to Mah Jabin's jarring voice.

"Zulaikha! I smell kebab. Are you grilling liver for breakfast? Hurry up, I'm faint with hunger."

"Stop shrieking!" Khodadad shouts. "Zulaikha has gone away. Go brew the tea."

# 11

NADIM KHAN IS BURIED with no more than a dozen mourners present. The graveyard is south of our home. From the hill there is a clear view of it. Geesu and I, choking back our tears, are again standing on the rooftop, watching.

"If he were rich and gave alms and handouts, there wouldn't be an inch of room left in the graveyard," Mother later says. "May God absolve his soul."

———

A few days later, his relatives come to bring me his books.

"Other than his house, these were the entirety of his assets," one cousin says.

I carry the cartons inside and put them next to the alcove where I keep my things. I draw open the curtain and see my old school-bag. Cinderella is clouded by a layer of dust. I wipe it away with my hand. She smiles at me. She is still small and slim. There was a time when I was small and slim, too. I am now taller, fuller, and going through puberty. I feel I have left behind so much in my life. Hopes and dreams that had flowered in my heart.

Seeing Nadim Khan's coffin the day of his funeral, took me back in time and brought the past to life again. I look at my schoolbag and wonder if I can just as easily wipe away the dust that has settled on my hopes and bring back my dreams. May God rest his soul, Nadim Khan was right. Farhad must find a way to take me away from this gorge.

Let's assume I stay, I marry Farhad. Then what? It is as clear as the day is bright. What awaits me is the same destiny as my mother, as that of all the women in the village, as that of all the women in Badghis. And Farhad's fate will be similar to that of the men. Shepherding, farming, breaking his back to provide a meager life of near poverty for his family. He will leave his youth among the boulders and grow old and gray before his time.

I stack some of the books in the alcove and leave the rest in the cartons. I find *Sophie's World* among them. I brew some tea in Father's yellow-china teapot and take it to the room on the roof. Sitting by the window, I open the book and start to read. It doesn't take long for me to find myself relating to the story. Sophie, too, is searching for answers, searching for something that so far does not exist, has no shape, and no name. The unknown nudges and urges her to discover, to unveil mysteries. An invisible hand guides her to learn about the universe and the world around her, to learn of ciphers and secrets. A few chapters into the book, I stop and look out at Tali. It is near dusk. The birds are returning to perch on their trees and rest away the day's fatigue so that at dawn they can again fly and feed and sing all day. The trees are pleased that they have come. They arch their boughs for them to settle down, create a ruckus for an hour or so, and then sleep to the lullaby of the breeze and fluttering leaves.

The men, too, are returning from the farms and mountains. Many are strangers. Their dialects, clothes, and lungees are different from ours. As though the poppy tears have seeped into their veins, their gait is sluggish, with no eagerness to reach their lodging at the school. With the classrooms having reached their capacity, the Taliban have set up tents for them in the playground and around the building.

I see dust rising in the air outside the front door as Farrokh hurries home with his sheep and rushes them to their hold. My eyes are drawn to the neighboring yard. At the sound of Farrokh *heyheying* the sheep, the house door opens and Geesu walks out. She's wearing her red headscarf and yellow flowered dress. In the fading light, she looks like she's floating across the yard to their guestroom. Theirs is built next to the front door, with a wall in front of it blocking the yard and the house from visitors' eyes.

I watch Farrokh go to the kitchen and return with a watering can. He squats down next to the narrow gutter and washes his hands and face and slaps the dust off his clothes.

"Mother!" he says loudly. "Toss me a towel. And make some tea, I'm awfully thirsty."

Mother hurries out with a towel and goes back to her kitchen and her stove. Farrokh quickly dries his face and hands, throws the towel on the clothesline, and quietly goes to the ladder leaning against the wall between our house and Hashem Khan's. I chuckle. Now I know the secret behind the ladder that one day appeared there and was never removed. He climbs up and nimbly jumps down the other side, behind the wall blocking the guestroom. I watch them fall into each other's arms and passionately kiss. I smile at Geesu's newfound daring and abandon.

Her father's voice goading his sheep to the house ends the secret rendezvous. Farrokh quickly climbs up the wall and down the ladder.

"Mother is tea ready?" he shouts as he steps off the last rung.

"Yes. Come and take it. And where is that rascal, Kowsar? She always disappears around dinner time."

"Mother, she's done. Off to her husband's house," he chortles. "Start worrying about the wedding instead."

I open the window and call Geesu before she goes back inside.

"Come over for a chat," I say. "And tea is ready. Come have some with me."

Leaving the kitchen with his tea bowl, Farrokh looks up at me and asks, "What did you say?"

"I was talking to Geesu. She's coming over to have tea with me. And it's girls only."

"You, dog!"

I laugh and close the window. A few minutes later, Geesu joins me upstairs. The moment her eyes fall on the window, she blushes and stares at me.

"You saw!"

"Yes. I saw you carefree and happy. You two are a perfect for each other."

She sits on the windowsill and sighs.

"What is it?"

"I'm afraid."

"Of what?"

"Of the day I learn Farrokh and I cannot have each other."

"Why not?"

"I don't know, I'm just afraid. And I can't shake it off no matter how hard I try. . . . Aren't you ever scared of something unknown, scared without knowing why?"

"Yes, I am scared, but I know why. The more I learn about the rest of the world, the more I fear my own."

"I grew up afraid of Khodadad, Mullah Sikhdad, and the Taliban. Now I'm afraid of my own parents," she says.

"Why?"

Geesu says nothing for a while, she just watches the starlings darting from tree to tree.

"Father is stubborn and has strange beliefs," she finally says. "And Mother is simple and superstitious. No matter what Father says, she nods and agrees. And they don't listen to anything I have to say. They ignore me, thinking I'm young and ignorant. . . . Last night Father was saying the starlings have evil eyes, that they bring bad luck. He claims every time they migrate to the valley, we suffer some misery. A few years ago, grasshoppers destroyed the crops, before that, worms infested the melons, and now the Taliban and their opium have made our farms *haram*. I said, 'How do you know the starlings brought the grasshoppers and worms? It wasn't the starlings that planted the opium. It was our own people. And it was Obeidullah and Mawlawi Khodadad who gave them the seed.' He was furious! He shouted, 'You're barely a hand tall and you think a couple of days in a classroom have made you wise and give you the right to lecture and question me? Thank God they closed that damn school.' And he called me a bitch!"

She laughs bitterly, shakes her head, and says, "As for my mother, a few days ago she got a talisman from some old woman and told me to tie it to my pants' drawstring and make sure I don't lose it. Otherwise, the old woman had told her, I will be 'a stone in a sling, flung far, and lost.' Well, I threw the talisman in the cookstove furnace. This morning, I woke up and saw her checking my pants. I told her I lost it. She burst into tears!"

We sit quiet and watch the birds disappear in the trees.

"My parents are kind," I say after a while. "And they listen when I talk. But as far back as I can remember, they referred to me as a wretch, helpless and hopeless. It made me terrified of life. Even a cat's meow would make me panic and faint. Sometimes I wonder if that's why I started having the attacks. I didn't know wretch is what all women are called. . . . But Geesu, God grants us only one life. We have to struggle and fight for what we want. Don't expect miracles. Our parents will not change. Remember the proverb about the fox that was born in a well and believed it was the entire world? Well, to them Tali is the entire world."

I'm expecting Geesu to agree, to say, Yes, we have to fight for what we want.

"Kowsar!" she says instead. "What if others saw us, too!"

＊

Zubaideh comes to the house one day and tells my parents that Farhad is now of age and it's time for her daughter-in-law to go to her husband's home. Mother and Father, worried about the Taliban's growing presence in the village and my recklessness, agree. Father says she should arrange a ceremony and take me.

Zubaideh quickly sells two of her best sheep and tells me she will take me to Qala-e Naw to buy new clothes. She borrows a burqa from a friend and gives it to me to wear on the trip.

"I don't want evil-eyes to see my son's beautiful bride," she says. But I think it is other eyes she is worried about.

Two days later, Zubaideh, Farhad, and I walk to Jawand and board a minibus to Qala-e Naw. I lift my veil to see better and pull the sides of the burqa closer over my cheeks. I breathe in the cool breeze blowing through the half-open windows and remember traveling this road with Father and Teacher Sadeq. That time, the fields and meadows were barren and bare, but spring has come and they are now lavish with tender greens and wild tulips.

"Farhad, look at the tulips," I whisper, taking his hand. "Aren't they beautiful!"

"Yes. Very."

"Would you have liked to run through them with me?"

"Sh! People will hear you."

"Would you have liked to roll on the grass with me?"

Annoyed, he turns away and doesn't answer. But I am drunk with the beauty I see. I want the minibus to stop. I want to tear off this confining burqa and run like a wild gazelle. The warmth of Farhad's hand currents under my skin. I want him to kiss me.

"Farhad," I murmur, "kiss me."

He doesn't move. I wonder if I actually spoke those words.

I want to say them again, a little louder. No, the voice inside me warns. Not here. But my heart doesn't care. I look at Farhad. I desire him. He knows it and refuses to look at me. I feel the ache, the want inside me.

"Farhad."

He slowly turns and looks at me. "Have you lost your mind!?" he sternly whispers.

"Yes," I breathe.

"You are insane!"

Offended, I sulk. That impossible feeling fades. I pull my face veil down and look at the passengers. Their expressions are grim, sullen. They don't seem to take pleasure in the nature around us. I think they don't see its splendor.

"I'm sorry," I quietly say. "I couldn't help it."

He gently squeezes my hand.

I turn and look out the window.

❧

As we arrive in the crowded and chaotic town, sadness settles over me. Harsh memories return as we drive past the turquoise blue arch at the entrance of the Department of Education. Sometime later, the minibus stops. I automatically follow Zubaideh and Farhad out, and we head down the street to where there is a row of shops. Farhad stops and talks to a shopkeeper. I pay no attention. My mind is revisiting the past. He turns and says something to me. I nod. Further down the street, we stop at a grill house. Smoke and the smell of kebab waft from its open door and windows. Farhad talks to a young, dark-skinned boy with a greasy napkin flung over his shoulder and then climbs up the narrow stairs on the outside wall of the restaurant that lead to the rooftop. Zubaideh, thinking that it's car-sickness that has me listless and quiet, holds my hand as we follow Farhad. A minute later, the young boy shows up with a keychain.

"The room facing the street is more expensive," he says.

"How much is it?" Farhad asks.

"Two hundred fifty."

"And the other one?"

"Two hundred."

"I'll take the one overlooking the street."

The boy unlocks the bolt and hangs it and the key on a hook inside the door.

"Lock it when you go out," he says, and holds out his hand. "Two nights upfront."

Farhad pays him, looks around the room, and asks for a third mattress.

"Yes, Sahib. Do you want the kebab and tea now?"

Farhad nods and ushers us in. The room reeks of dipping

tobacco and unwashed socks, but it's clean. Zubaideh takes off her black chador and hangs it on a hook next to an old, oxidized mirror.

"Kowsar are you all right?" she asks as she helps me off with my burqa and hangs it on the same hook.

"I'm fine, Auntie."

"No, you're not. You're very pale."

We sit on the frayed and faded green floor cushions at the front of the room. The rug is in no better condition.

"Mother is right," Farhad says, feeling my forehead. "You have a fever."

"I'll be fine. It's the bus ride. It made me a little nauseous."

I get up and open the window. The loudspeakers of restaurants and teahouses are each playing a different music. Afghan, Indian, and Iranian songs, some contemporary, others traditional. A discordant and jarring mix. The cars, bicycles, and motorcycles add to the clamor, constantly blowing their horn at pedestrians who haphazardly cross the street. No one seems to mind. People are busy shopping, haggling, going about their business.

I sit at the window and look at the shop across the street. It sells burqas. I had never worn one until today. I never knew how difficult it is to walk in them and to see through the face veil. The shop has steel blue, olive green, taupe, and black burqas on display. I wonder what difference the color makes when the woman vanishes under it. Perhaps people from different regions prefer one color over the others. Perhaps there is some fashion at work.

From where I'm sitting, I can see the tip of the turquoise arch. I think of Teacher Sadeq and wonder what became of him. I think of how different the fate of the school and all its students could have been. I think of dear Simin. Oh, how I despise this town.

I feel my fever worsening. The noise outside is now unbearable. It's like molten lead pouring into my ears and burning its way through my nerves. I know I will soon be overcome. I quickly close the window and get up to go to Farhad, but I fall and feel my body convulse. I see Zubaideh and Farhad's silhouettes through the gray haze.

"Kowsar, can you hear me?" Farhad asks.

His voice is somewhere in the racket rising from the street. It is low, then high, his words drawn out. I am aware of my surroundings. I feel Zubaideh's hands lifting my head and resting it on her lap. Her face fades in and out. I resist the force that is pulling me away. I hear the door open and close and feel cool water sprinkling on my face.

"Try to drink," Zubaideh says.

I feel the plastic bottle against my lips. I take a sip. She caresses my face and strokes my hair until I feel the gray slowly lift. I lie there for a while. Then Zubaideh gently helps me sit up and brings a bolster for me to lean on.

"I'm all right," I say.

Farhad looks at me. He doesn't believe me.

"I'll take you to a doctor. I saw a sign for one nearby."

"No. It's going away."

He wants to argue with me, but Zubaideh stops him.

"Don't fret, it was the car ride," she says. "And Kowsar hasn't had anything to eat since breakfast."

I close my eyes and rest until I hear a knock at the door and the boy comes in with the tray of food and tea.

"Enjoy," he says on his way out. "And call me if you need anything else."

The smell of the kebab makes my mouth water, and Farhad stares hungrily at the steaming strips of meat arranged on the flat bread. But custom calls for us to wait for Zubaideh to say a prayer and start to eat before we do.

"In the name of God," she says, biting into a chunk of kebab she has rolled in a piece of bread.

Farhad and I greedily reach for the meat.

"During the trip with Father and Teacher Sadeq," I tell them in between mouthfuls, "I only smelled the meat grilling on charcoal in restaurants, but I couldn't ask Father to buy some. Today, I finally taste it with you. Good thing you asked for my hand, Auntie."

They both laugh and Zubaideh says, "Later, if you feel up to it, we can go for a walk and take a look around the bazaar."

I nod as I chew, but after our meal and the tea, I still feel the strain of the attack.

"Better?" Zubaideh asks. "Can you go for a walk?"

"Yes," I reply.

At the bottom of the stairs, we run into the young boy.

"Whey, hide, wool, pistachios. If you have goods to sell, my boss will pay a fair price. Don't sell to strangers."

"We have nothing to sell," Farhad laughs, patting him on the shoulder. "God willing, next time."

I walk along the sidewalk, and yet I don't. Simin lingers in the folds of my mind. You took the peril that was to be mine, I say to her in my heart. If it were not for you, if I had not fainted that day, it could have been me buried in that grave. I feel angry. I feel the rebel inside me, the daring, rash Kowsar. The Kowsar who doesn't believe in subservience and subjugation, who doesn't believe a woman is a pitiful wretch, to be done with as a man wishes.

We walk for a while until we reach a stretch of clothing shops. Zubaideh walks into one and looks at their dresses. She picks out a few and looks them over.

"Do you like any of them?" she asks. "And don't worry about the price, there's plenty of room for haggling."

I tell her I don't feel up to trying them on, that perhaps we can come back tomorrow. She seems to have already guessed.

"Then let's go find a jewelry shop," she says. "I want to sell my silver and Qajar gold coins."

I have asked her several times to not sell them. But each time she argues, "I'm bringing a bride to my house. Her clothes and household goods must be new."

Zubaideh and Farhad set out ahead as I weave my way through the crowd and follow them. Soon the sound of blacksmiths' hammers and coppersmiths' mallets add to the commotion, then steadily fade as we continue down the street. Minutes later, I freeze. I'm in front of the Department of Education. I stare at the arch and feel myself being pulled inside.

The quad, the long corridor, the office doors are all familiar. I walk to the far end of the building and go out the back door that leads to the planted courtyard. I look at the small building on the other side. The Department of Religious Studies. I cross the yard and walk in. It is quiet inside, the end of the workday is near. A middle-aged attendant is sitting outside the department director's office rolling his prayer beads. Seeing me approach, he quickly stands up as though he recognizes me despite my burqa. He says hello and opens the door. Without a speaking a word, I walk in. Mawlawi Khodadad is praying on a prayer rug spread next to his desk. He looks up at me and is visibly agitated. He cannot break his prayer, but his voice rises and falls as he rapidly recites the verses.

Now and then he muddles his words, some get stuck in his throat and emerge garbled. Hard as he tries, he cannot continue. He gets up, quickly folds the prayer rug, and goes to the door.

"Ramazan, you can go. Only twenty minutes before the day is done."

He closes the door and locks it.

"Didn't I tell you never to come here again!" he says.

I stare at him. No, I'm not imagining it. Mawlawi Khodadad with a blind eye is standing in front of me. I don't understand why I'm here or what I came here for. With my own two feet I have walked into a snake's pit. Kowsar, I warn myself, he is going to take off your burqa, and there is no escaping him in this locked room.

"I told you, never come here again," he says, moving closer. "I told you, if there is ever anything, just call me!"

He has me mistaken for someone else. I must remain silent.

"The door is locked, take that thing off, and tell me why you did such a foolish thing."

I am certain of his fury if he realizes I am not who he thinks.

"Nazy, stop teasing me," he says as he wraps his arms around my waist. My heart is pounding wildly. "You know what your flirting does to me. Damn you, I want you, I want to undress you, slowly..."

I know I have only a few seconds before I am found out. My eyes desperately look around. On the side table next to me there is a cup with pens in it, and a pair of scissors. I slowly reach for it.

Running his hands over my body, he quickly realizes I am not his Nazy. He pulls back and squints his eyes. He cannot see through the tiny holes in the face veil. He reaches for it. I raise my hand and stab the scissors into his eye. He screams, cups his face in his hands, and drops to his knees. His lungee falls and rolls under the chair.

It all happens in a flash. I look at him. Mawlawi Khodadad yelping at my feet, blood streaming through his fingers. I have to silence him. There is a glass pitcher on a table across the office. I run and grab it, and I pound it on his head. He sprawls out on the floor.

I quickly unlock the door and peek up and down the hallway. It's empty. I tiptoe out of the building and hurry across the courtyard. The corridor is crowded with office workers leaving for the day. I slow my steps. Out on the street, the same commotion greets me. A voice inside me says, Kowsar, you avenged Simin, avenged all the girls he devastated, avenged the children whose future he destroyed. Hurry, Zubaideh and Farhad must be searching for you.

I'm shaking with fear and shock, yet I feel strangely exhilarated. I want to tear off my burqa, run, and scream, Simin, the tyrant is blind! Completely blind. Blind and helpless. The jackal who set eyes on you will never see anything but a black bottomless pit. He will forever howl, forever desperate to know the woman who lay his life to waste. It was Mawlawi Khodadad who said, "A woman is safe under a burqa." In this case, he was right.

I search for Farhad and Zubaideh on the sidewalks. I cannot

find them. I hurry in the direction they were going, poking my head into shops they might be in. It is useless. I turn around and rush back toward the grill house. Then I see them up ahead. I pull up the hem of my burqa and run. The moment Zubaideh sees me, she slaps her hand on her chest and sinks down in the middle of the sidewalk.

"Auntie Zubaideh, I'm sorry!" I say, kneeling in front of her. "All of a sudden, I lost sight of you. I can hardly see through this damn veil."

She wipes the sweat off her face with her chador.

"I knew you would give us a fright in this damned town," she says scathingly.

"I'm so sorry! I was scared, too."

I hold her under the arm to help her up and look to Farhad for help. He is standing there, staring at me.

"Farhad, forgive me. I know I frightened you."

He is still staring at me.

"You shouldn't have worried. You know if someone so much as looks at me sideways, I will pluck their eyes out."

Back at the grill house, I ask the young boy to bring tea up to our room.

"Black or green?"

"Green."

"With cardamom?"

"Yes."

"With sweetened milk?"

"No. Candied sugar."

Farhad pushes me toward the stairs. "Hurry up before he asks white or yellow."

In the room, I take Zubaideh's chador and hang it up. She sits down, leans against the wall, and closes her eyes.

"I shouted at Farhad for letting you out of his sight," she says.

"Forgive me," I say, kissing her hand. "I don't know how I managed to lose you. I looked for you up and down the sidewalks, I looked in the shops. I finally gave up and hurried back here."

The knot on her brow slowly softens.

"Don't think I'm going to kiss your hand, too," I say, walking over to Farhad. I hold his face and kiss his lips. "Delicious!"

Zubaideh chuckles, "The poor boy turned the color of death when you disappeared."

"I love him more than I love myself, Auntie. I will never leave him. And I want you to please listen to me. Don't sell your silver and heirloom coins. One dress and one pair of shoes is enough for me. And I don't want an elaborate celebration."

"My girl, there are certain things we must do. People talk."

"Let them talk. I don't care. I want my own life, and it will be hell if I have to worry about who says what."

"All right, I won't sell them," she says, sounding almost relieved. "But you must accept them as my gift to the bride."

"Thank you, Auntie, I will treasure them."

There's a knock on the door.

"Green tea with cardamom, and a bowl of candied sugar. Yellow and white."

"Farhad," I say as we sip our tea. "Let's visit Teacher Sadeq tomorrow. He lives nearby."

—

Teacher Sadeq's mother opens the door. He is not home. Her son is now teaching at a school in a distant village and only visits once every two months. I imagine that gentle man standing in front of a blackboard, facing his students, devotedly educating children who never dreamt they would one day learn to read and write. His mother invites us in, but we thank her and say we will trouble her another time when her son is home.

We walk away disappointed, and I tell Farhad to instead take me to Haji Zaman's Bookstore. To go there, we must pass by the blue arch. Armed soldiers are standing guard in the quad at the entrance to the building. By now news of Mawlawi Khodadad has spread throughout enemies fighting against the Taliban, others think it was certainly one of the men he cuckolded. There are even those who believe a celestial light has again shined on him.

Let them think what they will, the voice inside me says. It was a feat rubbing that murderer's nose in the dirt. Simin's spirit rests easy now. And the truth, I will take to my grave.

~

Haji Zaman now sells the works of Afghan writers, too. I would love to read their books, to see what and where they write about. With no money of my own, I settle for *In the Time of Bukhara* by Wasima Badghisi. She is from our province.

We leave for Jawand. This time I have something to read on the long ride. I raise my face veil and open the book on my lap. It is a collection of short stories. Stories about our towns and villages, about familiar people, about melancholy, the poor and suffering. The heroes of her stories are not trying to discover the philosophy of life and the meaning of reality like Sophie. They are struggling to survive. Filled with heartache and longing, spending the entirety of their life striving for a small measure of comfort and happiness, and in the end finding neither. Her heroes are cut from the same cloth as Geesu, Simin, and me. Wasima's stories reflect Zubaideh's life, the lives of Homeira and my mother.

In her stories the wind is wild, the rivers turbulent, the moon icy, and the sun troubled. And the women love more than the men.

I lose myself. I don't know how long we have travelled, what Farhad has said or Zubaideh whispered.

Two days after our return, news of Khodadad's blindness arrives in Tali. In the evening, Geesu peeks over the wall and calls me.

"Why are you huddled indoors with a book? Come, there's news!"

"What have you heard this time?" I laugh, leaning out the window.

She cups her hands around her mouth and in a hushed voice says, "Someone took Khodadad's other eye!"

"What?"

"Yes! Simin's cousin told me. He's completely blind! She said she wishes he had been lamed and crippled, too. Come over so we can talk."

"I can't, Sister. Mother isn't feeling well and I'm stuck cooking dinner. I have a pot on the stove."

"What are you making?"

"The two things I can cook well. Rice with mung beans and a fresh herb omelet. Come eat with us."

"Call me when it's ready."

I sit there for a while longer and watch the mountain river in twilight.

～

The closer my wedding day comes, the more passion I feel for Farhad. I know love means affection, devotion, and friendship, but what smolders inside me is more than these. It's irrational and irresistible. I feel without him I will be nothing, every moment of my life empty.

"Among a hundred girls, why did you choose someone this stubborn?" I ask him one day.

"Kowsar without stubbornness wouldn't be the Kowsar I love," he says.

Our wedding is simple and without fanfare. Zubaideh had a lamb slaughtered and has cooked a huge pot of stew. Her neighbors have been busy with the festivities, baking bread at their kilns. Others have helped clean the house and brought their rugs and kilims, cushions and bolsters.

Geesu powders my face and puts rouge on my cheeks, all the while singing:

> *A friend and kindly mate is gold*
> *Splendid as spring water cold*

*Your pain and sorrow he knows*
*Your melancholy away he throws.*

"You are cheerful today!" I say, laughing.

"My dearest friend is going to her house of fate and fortune. If I were not jumping with joy, who would!?"

"Then sing something for Farrokh."

"No, you will sing for both of us the day we get married."

Combing my hair, she sings a love ballad anyway.

"I never knew you know so many songs."

"Farrokh finds comfort playing his flute, I find comfort singing these little songs. You know better than I do, a mountain girl doesn't give her heart easily, but when she does, it's with her soul."

I once talked to Mother about Geesu, suggesting she would be a perfect match for Farrokh. Mother said Father's purse is small and Hashem Khan is the kind of man who would ask for a hefty bride price. "Better to find Farrokh a girl whose father won't take Mobin Khan's arm from the shoulder," she said.

Geesu helps me on with the dress and matching pants Zubaideh bought for me in Qala-e Naw. The dress is emerald green and adorned with beads and glittering sequins. I have never owned anything this beautiful. Geesu takes the mirror off the wall and holds it in front of me.

"Look!" she says.

"Is this really me!?"

"You look more beautiful than ever. As beautiful as a pomegranate on a tree."

I can hardly recognize myself. I never imagined that one day I would wear a dress I could only dream of, that my face would be powdered and my cheeks rouged.

"Will Farhad like it?"

Geesu hangs the mirror back on the wall and goes to the door.

"Prince Groom," she calls out. "Are you there?"

"You mean me?" Farhad asks.

"No," Farrokh teases. "She means me!"

"Wait your turn!" Gessu quips.

The guests laugh, but I'm anxious and insecure. What if Farad doesn't like the way I look? I childishly run and hide behind the curtain. But Geesu cheers and yanks it open when Farhad walks in. He stares at me.

"What?" Geesu giggles. "Never seen a bride before?"

"Yes, but where is Kowsar!"

"You don't like my makeup?"

"I do, I do. You look beautiful, but for a minute I didn't recognize you. With the green dress and red cheeks, you look like a pomegranate on a tree."

"That's what Geesu said! Should I wipe it off?"

"No! I like it. It's nice."

I walk up to him. I want to throw my arms around him and kiss him. He reads it on my face and steps back.

"You two have been locked up in here for hours. There's a limit to makeup and fussing over your hair," he says. "The white-beards are waiting. They want to perform the ceremony, eat, and leave."

He grabs my hand and pulls me out of the room.

Mothers always tell their daughters that they will one day fly from their nest, that they will marry and leave their father's home, but I never knew how painful this would be. The moment I step into the guestroom and see Mother and Father, my knees weaken, and something pricks my heart. I am leaving these angels, I think to myself, I am leaving them forever. I won't be there to help Mother and take Father his tea. I have been so happy, counting the seconds for the moment I become Farhad's wife, but now my legs don't want to take another step. Tears roll down my face as I throw myself in Father's arms. He kisses my forehead.

"Go, my girl," he says, his voice cracking. "May you be happy. May God have you two grow old together."

Father and I have been good friends, Mother and I have been close. I know my absence will not be easy for them. I had a trying childhood. As an infant, I was sick and temperamental, as a child with an unpredictable illness, I was demanding and in need of care. How many nights did I rob them of sleep? How many days did they spend in anguish? How often did I drive them mad, first with my peevishness, then with my petulance?

Every night when Father came home after a long day of labor, I imagined Rostam, the hero Persian epics, has returned and no ill or evil can touch us. And now, I don't want to leave his arms. But he takes me by the shoulders and turns me to Mother. Her eyes are brimming with tears. She knows that with me gone, the burden of life will be heavier for her. I put my head on her shoulder. Her scent makes me cry. I kiss her hands.

"My girl, let Mother not see your tears. Give your pain to me and go. May God give you happiness and good fortune. May God protect you."

"Come kiss my hands, too!" Farrokh says impishly.

"You scamp!" I say, wiping away my tears. "You better come get news of me every day."

"I will, when you cook lamb stew."

I laugh and kiss him on the cheeks.

"Pray for your sister. And think of a wife who can be Mother's friend and helper," I say winking at him. "Until then, dear brother, fill my shoes as best as you can."

After the elders have performed the religious ceremony and our parents have declared their agreement to the marriage contract,

Farhad and I walk out into the yard. Some of the guests have gathered there, with the rest waiting outside the house.

"Uncle Pordel," Zubaideh shouts. "Play!"

Out on the road, the father and son village musicians beat the tambour and blow the hornpipe, playing a festive song. A few of Farhad's friends run into the yard, dancing and stomping their feet so feverishly that I forget my parents' tearful eyes and my heavy heart. The women drape a long green chiffon scarf over my hair, Farhad takes my hand, and we join the people outside. Seeing us, Pordel and Khoshdel play even more passionately. I imagine the entire valley must be shaking with the beat of the music.

I'm cherishing the joy and revelry around me when suddenly my heart drops. I sense trouble. I say nothing to Farhad and pray that for once my premonition is wrong. As everyone leaves the house, the musicians lead the cheering crowd down the hill. Not far from the river, Pordel abruptly stops playing. His son beats his tambour a few more times, then he, too, stops. They are staring at the dust rising in the air some distance away. We all stop and in silence turn our gaze in that direction.

Minutes later, Obeidullah and a squad of armed Talibs on horseback emerge from the haze. The fear they strike in us is palpable. We hardly breathe or blink as Obeidullah dismounts.

"What is going on here?" he asks, standing insolently close to Father.

"Obeidullah Khan," Father stammers. "It's my daughter's wedding."

"Move away from the wretches!" he says, grabbing Father by the collar and pulling him a few steps away.

"Obeidullah Khan," Zubaideh says, stepping forward. "He has done no wrong! I am the groom's mother. I arranged the celebration, and I asked the musicians to play. Say what you have to say to me."

He tilts his head and scowls at her. I grip Farhad's hand.

"So! You are the cursed sinner."

"If music that is our ages-old tradition and the heritage of our forefathers makes me a sinner, then, yes, I am!"

Obeidullah shoves Father aside and glares at us.

"Latif," he shouts. "The instruments."

Taking his machine gun off his shoulder, the man walks over to Pordel and his son, and snarls, "Put those things down and get out of the way."

The two quickly drop their instruments and have hardly taken two steps back when a burst of bullets shatters the tambour and hornpipe. The man grins and slings the machine gun back on his shoulder.

"All done, Commander," he says to Obeidullah who is leering at Geesu.

"Bring me that girl. The one with the light-colored hair."

I turn to Geesu. All color has drained from her face and she is visibly trembling. People gingerly move away from her.

"Come!" the man shouts.

"Geesu, don't panic," I say quietly.

"You're the one on the mountain that day," Obeidullah says as the Talib pushes her forward. "Whose daughter are you?"

"Hashem," Geesu stutters. "Hashem Khan."

Obeidullah mounts his horse and taking the reins, he warns, "This is your only warning. From this moment on, no more music. And let me never see another wretch without proper hijab."

He leads his men away in another fog of dust, and we remain there with the broken tambour and hornpipe, mourning music and hungering for a moment of joy.

"Let's go!" Zubaideh goads everyone. "Don't stand here looking miserable! He won't let us have music? So what? It's not the end of the world!"

# 12

THE ROAD OUTSIDE Mawlawi Khodadad's house is buried in darkness. There is not a soul in sight. With no electricity, night surrenders Qala-e Naw to its ghosts. People lock their doors and unchain their dogs. In every house Majid passes one starts to bark, warning its owner of a phantom roaming the streets.

"Yes, I am an idiot," Majid says under his breath. "Yes, Father, I am everything you say I am. Go on! Call me whatever you want, do what you will. But I will take my mother away. I will take her in a way that will leave your jaw hanging. Curse me, disown and disinherit me. You have already driven me out of your life, thrown me away, exiled me to Khalishkak to count your sheep, to go from one shepherd to another and warn them of wolves, thieves, and bandits, to caution them never to turn their eyes away from Mawlawi's herds. . . . Enough! You who won't spare a mother for her son can go protect your own ill-gotten wealth. . . . Mother, sleep sound and gentle. I will come for you tomorrow."

He turns onto the main street flanked by trees hunched as though under the burden of the night and gazes at the pale flame of oil lamps hanging above shop doors. When he arrives at his friend's inn, he sits on the ground outside the door. "What do you think, Father?" he murmurs. "Do you think I'm still an eight-year-old boy? Do you think I don't know you? Do you think I will let you work my mother to her grave? Do you think she has no one to protect her like young Simin?"

His eyes focus on a small rock. He picks it up and knocks it against the steel door. A window opens on the second floor.

"Who is it?"

"Golab Khan, it's me. Majid. Come open the door."

"What happened? Your mawlawi kicked you out?"

A minute later, his old friend comes to the door.

"I had a fight with *your* mawlawi. He refused to let me take Mother to the village."

"The rooms are all taken," Golab Khan says as they walk in. "People bringing their sick to town. I can set you up on the roof. It's a pleasant night."

Majid nods as Golab hands him a small rug and brings a mattress, pillow, and blanket.

"The stairs are at the end of the hallway. To your left."

As they spread his bedding, Majid tells Golab everything that led him to leave Khodadad's house.

"I will take her in the morning. By nightfall, I will either be in my bed or in a coffin."

"Be careful, he is as ruthless as can be. And take your mother only if she really wants to leave. Anything forced comes to no good."

"I've known you since we were boys. If a bicycle tire bursts at the end of road, you'd lose your bowels sitting up here. I'll face the risk, come what may."

"Imagine yourself a lion, a dragon, a creature of unparalleled courage. Fine. But are you match for the mawlawi? Don't forget, the governor, the head of security, directors and officers, all stand with him."

"They stand with him because they believe him to be a man of God, because they believe he has revelations from the Prophet, and because they know he can easily issue a fatwa for their death as nonbelievers."

"Well, whatever he is and whatever you do, don't ever say I didn't warn you," Golab says before leaving him. "My advice: Don't get your ass into battle with a bull."

❦

The morning *azan* wakes Majid. He gathers his bedding, says his prayer, and joins Golab Khan as he goes about the business of running his inn. At eleven, he gets up, shakes his shawl, and prepares to leave.

"May only good fortune await you, my friend," Golab says,

forcing a smile. "I will come see you in Khalishkak after Ramadan. Have the upstairs room ready."

The streets are crowded and the shops and teahouses bustling. People absorbed in their own worries hurry after one thing or another. Cars blow their horns and the loudspeaker outside Golab's inn blares a chant by Amir Jan Saburi.

Majid is deaf and blind to it all. Haunted by the words his father spat and shouted the day before, unrest churns inside him. When he arrives at the house, he lets himself into the front yard. The smell of smoke lingers in the air. His mother is neither at the kiln, nor in the kitchen. Majid goes to the front porch and calls her. There is no response.

"Mother," he calls out loudly. "Where are you?"

"*Mother* is not here," Khodadad barks from his room. "She left early this morning."

"Left? Where to?" Majid asks, trying to veil his shock at his mother's absence and his father's presence in the house.

"How would I know? You're the one who tempted her to leave. She probably went to Khalishkak."

"She wouldn't go without me. She wouldn't know how!"

Khodadad leans out the window and grins at Majid's anxious face.

"All she had to do was walk to the car, stand at the corner, and tell the drivers where she wanted to go."

Majid hurries out and minutes later is in the last car heading in the direction of Khalishkak. Excited, he thinks of his mother who by now must have arrived in the village. He imagines her happily chatting with Halimeh and laughing with her grandson. He sees his wife celebrating the end of her loneliness by bringing plates of pistachios, pumpkin seeds, and sweets for her mother-in-law, insisting that she have some of each. The car speeds along the narrow dirt road that snakes its way through the thick of wild rue and thorn bushes. Majid rolls down the window a crack and inhales the fragrance of the wild shrubs the brisk wind blows into the car.

Mother, he thinks, I will not allow you to lift a finger around the house. Rest, shed your decades-old fatigue. Soon, Halimeh will give birth, and you can sit with your grandchildren and lull them to sleep.

&#x2767;

"Where is Mother?" he asks, walking into the house.

"Mother?" Halimeh says, surprised. "Was she supposed to be here?"

"I went to the house to pick her up, but Father said she left for Khalishkak early in the morning."

"But why would she leave knowing you were there to bring her?"

"Father and I had a terrible fight last night and I walked out. She probably assumed I came back home. He said she must have taken a hired car."

"What if she's lost! What if they took her somewhere else?"

"God," Majid groans, dropping down on a cushion. "What do I do? Where do I search?"

"Which car did you take?"

"The last one going to the pistachio farms. The one that comes directly to the village had already left."

"Go find Gamaroldin. She might have come in his car."

"What are you talking about?" Majid shouts. "If she had, she would be here now!"

Still, desperate to do something, Majid runs to Gamaroldin's house. But he had no passengers that match Zulaikha's description. Walking back, Majid thinks his father must have lied to him and his mother never left Qala-e Naw.

"I swear, Father," he growls under his breath, "if you invented that story, you will see no man as vengeful and vicious as me. You have taught me well. To God I vow, I will make you pay."

Back home, Halimeh brings him a bowl of tea and sits with him.

"She probably went to the bazaar or someplace in town and that hateful man intentionally misled me," he says. "I don't know. I have to go back."

"He must have lied," Halimeh says, relieved. "But wait a few days for Khodadad's anger to ebb. By then whatever has happened will come to light."

◆

Three days go by with Majid plagued with one thought. What if Father told the truth, what if Mother left that morning? She could be somewhere lost, perhaps hurt? But, no, he argues with himself, Mother would never do anything so rash, she would never just wander off.

I should not have spoken so angrily to Father, he scolds himself.

◆

Majid is preparing to travel back to Qala-e Naw when news arrives of an attacker blinding his father's other eye.

"When I arrived there this morning, the whole town was talking about it," Gamaroldin tells him. "But no one knows who did it. One man says it was one of his wives, another says it was a government agent, a third claims it was his enemies' doing." He pauses and quietly chuckles, "Of course, some believe it was that blinding celestial light again! ... None in heaven or on earth know the unseen except for God the All Mighty."

"What if it was Zulaikha!" Halimeh cries, hearing the news. "Khodadad will cut her to pieces!"

"That is what terrifies me."

---

When Majid arrives at the house, there is commotion in the front yard, and the guestroom is heaving with Talibs, mullahs, and government officials. A few of Khodadad's close friends are cooking cauldrons of soup over pit fires. Alms for the poor. A few others are in the kitchen preparing meat and rice dishes for the dignitaries and senior officials of the province who are coming to extend their respect and offer words of consolation to the mawlawi.

Majid sees Khairullah across the yard and makes his way over to him.

"Khairullah, where is my father?"

"In Salima's room, at the end of the hallway. Mah Jabin is there, too."

"Who was it this time?"

"Only God knows and the mawlawi."

Walking down the hallway, Majid sees a padlock on the door to his mother's room. Fear washes over him. She really is missing. In Salima's room, he finds his father resting on a long floor cushion and slouching against a bolster. His face is ashen and gaunt, and there is a dark bloodstain on the white bandage over his eye. A cane is on the cushion next to him.

"Khodadad Khan," Mah Jabin says, standing up. "Majid is here."

Khodadad braces his hands on the cushion and sits up.

"Come, son," he says, patting the cushion. "Sit with me."

Majid sits down and looks at his father's faintly trembling hand groping for his. He takes it and asks, "Father, what happened? Who did this to you?"

Khodadad's lips quiver, but he says nothing. Majid looks at Mah Jabin and Salima and motions for them to leave.

"They're gone, Father. Tell me."

"I don't know who it was, son," Khodadad groans, wiping his nose with a handkerchief. "She was wearing a burqa."

"*She!?*"

"A woman came to my office late in the day with a petition for something or other. As I reached over the desk to take the papers from her, I suddenly felt fire in my eye, and everything went dark. She stabbed me with a pair of scissors. I screamed and shouted, but everyone had left for the day. I crawled my way out into the courtyard, calling for help. Finally, a janitor heard me and came running."

"What a horror! . . . The police will surely find her."

"How? I can tell them nothing about her. No clue for them to follow."

"I am terribly sorry, Father. But I'm sure my mother is tending to you day and night."

"Your mother!" Khodadad says, feigning surprise. "Isn't she in Khalishkak?"

"No! I hurried back to the village, but she wasn't there. I thought you were angry with me and fabricated that story."

"Son, how could you think that? You are my son, my flesh and blood. My entire wealth is in your care!"

"Then where is she? Where could she have gone?"

"I don't know. She was furious with me for speaking harshly to you. In the morning, she took a few things and left without a word. If she's not in Khalishkak then the only other place she could have gone is to her relatives in Qadis."

Suspicions and speculations invade Majid's mind. Could it have been his mother who put on a burqa and went to Khodadad's office? Yes, he thinks, it must have been her. She was devastated being denied some time with me and Halimeh. And watching Father insult and humiliate me enraged her even more.

"It wasn't your mother," Khodadad says, having read his mind. "The woman was young and tall. I lived with Zulaikha for decades. I would recognize her among a thousand women in burqas. And she has a kind heart. She could never commit such violence. Wherever she is, sooner or later she will come back."

"No, Father. I can't just sit and do nothing, hoping one day she will show up. I will go to Qadis. If she's not there, I will turn Badghis inside out until I find her. And if I don't—"

Majid frees his hand and gets up.

"Where are you going?"

"I told you! To Qadis."

"But wait, son. Don't go alone. Tell Khairu to come here. I will have him go with you."

Majid finds Khairullah among the crowd in the front yard and sends him to Khodadad. A few minutes later, he comes back smiling.

"Majid Khan, wait for me in the car," he says. "I'll be right there."

---

As Khairullah drives, Majid prays he will find his mother in Qadis. Gazing out the backseat window, his thoughts drift to all the inexplicable incidents of the past few years. Hardly listening to anything Khairullah asks or says, he replies only with a *mhm* or an *aha*. Some time passes, and then some more. Majid comes to when the car stops. He looks around. They are above a cliff and the terrain is unfamiliar.

"Khairu, where are we? Did you make a wrong turn?"

Khairullah climbs out of the car, reaches under his jacket, and pulls out a gun.

"Get out of the car," he says quietly as he opens the rear door.

"Khairu, have you lost your mind!?"

"I said get out of the car."

Confused and dumbfounded, Majid gapes at him. He sees Khairullah raise the gun and pull the trigger. There is a deafening blast, and pain stabs through his right shoulder. He looks down at the warm blood coloring his shirt, and stares at Khairullah in disbelief.

"Why Khairu? You and I are—"

Another bullet pierces his left shoulder.

"Get out of the car!" Khairullah shouts.

Majid stumbles out.

"Now, walk!" he barks, holding the gun to the back of Majid's head and shoving him toward the cliff.

Majid staggers forward, knowing that his father has ordered his death, that Khairullah was sent to stop him from searching for his mother. And that could only mean one thing.

"Khairu, I have a wife and child, and another on the way. If you do this, they will have no one, they will have nothing."

"Some other man will enjoy your beautiful young wife," Khairullah says, pushing him closer to the edge of the cliff.

"Did he have you kill my mother, too?"

"No. Say your last prayer."

"God is in my heart, not on my tongue," Majid says, his voice trembling. "You're the one who should pray for absolution."

The gun goes off again. The bullet rips through his left ear and he falls face down. Khairullah holsters his gun, grabs Majid's ankles, drags him to the edge of the cliff.

Majid plunges down. His body bounces off rocks and soon disappears among the wild fig trees in the valley below.

# 13

I AM HAPPY in Farhad's loving embrace, in Zubaideh's home, my home. I am no longer sitting in anticipation of an uncertain tomorrow for my dreams to come true. I know they will. I have become patient. I savor the moments of my life. With Farhad, I am no longer waiting for days and nights to end.

After the wedding, I share my hope with him and Zubaideh. I tell them that I want Farhad to someday take me to Herat, that I want us to continue our education, finish school, go to university, and make something of our lives. Zubaideh smiles proudly.

"God willing," she says. "We will sell three of the sheep to pay for it. Let's pray the government people there have more brains and allow you to go to school."

Excited, Farhad and I talk about it. When? How? What about Zubaideh? We can't leave her all alone. We will find a way, we both say. I dream, I fantasize.

My happiness is short lived.

As the sun ducks behind Tiq-e Barik peak and the sky is dressed in red, gun shots frighten the nightingales and starlings out of their trees. I'm with Zubaideh in the kitchen, cooking *gurooti*. We run out to the yard, but we hear nothing more. No shouts or screams, no commotion. Just the birds' cries and the agitation of their wings as they circle above the valley.

"It's nothing," Zubaideh says. "Probably some kohl-eyed thug high on opium. Come, the pot is going to boil over."

I gently stir the *qurut* as she tears the bread into small bites and tosses them into three bowls. We are both quiet, shaken by the gun shots that we seem to not grow accustomed to.

"Auntie, didn't the noise sound like it was coming from the hill-top across the river?"

"No, I don't think so," she says. "It was farther away."

We pour the *qurut* over the bread and take the bowls to the house.

Farhad meows as soon as he picks up the scent.

"All we need is for you to turn into a cat!" I say.

"Cook lamb and I'll turn into a leopard and roar."

"Did you hear the gunshots?" Zubaideh asks.

"Yes. It was probably one of Obeid's dogs, shooting cross-eyed at the poor birds."

"That's what I thought," she says, spreading the dining cloth on the floor.

"Do you want some onion with it?" I ask Farhad.

"*Gurooti* isn't *gurooti* without onions!"

"I've garnished it with fried onions."

"It's much better with raw onion."

I take the lamp and go to the kitchen. I peel and cut an onion into four and take it back.

"You cut it with a knife!?" Farhad complains. "You've killed the taste! You're supposed to break the onion by pounding on it with your fist! Bring another one and I'll show you."

I bring a whole onion and Farhad thumps his fist on its head, splitting it in two.

"This way, its juices are released, and the flavor is not ruined by a metal blade."

I nod and smile, and I don't tell him that my hands are small and not strong enough to smash an onion.

We have finished eating and Zubaideh and I are clearing the dishes when I see Farrokh through the window racing across the front yard. He bursts into the room and sinks to the floor. My heart drops.

"What has happened?" I cry.

"Nothing good," he says, his voice cracking. "Did you hear the gunshots?"

"Yes!" Farhad says. "Speak!"

"It was Obeid. Behind Hashem Khan's house. He shot his gun and yelled 'Geesu is mine!'"

I stare at him.

"Meaning what?" Zubaideh asks. "How can a girl belong to some man because he shot a few bullets outside her father's house?"

"I don't know," Farrokh moans. "He had brought Mullah Sikhdad with him. They told Hashem Khan that by shooting his gun, Obeid has put a claim on Geesu, and Hashem cannot marry her to anyone else. Mullah Sikhdad said that it's the Talibs' custom and he should accept the proposal. . . . But I love Geesu, and she loves me. We want to be husband and wife. And now—"

I feel faint. His voice is dragged and drawn. I hear myself scream. The room spins, the bowls fall out of my hands. I can make out Farhad's face. He pulls me up and leans me against his chest.

"You know how sensitive she is, you know she can't tolerate shock," I hear Farhad say angrily. "You shouldn't have told her. Not like this!"

I know Farrokh's broken heart is even more wounded. I see his silhouette move away and vanish in a dark thicker than tar.

"Don't panic, son. I'll bring some water."

I see a halo of yellow light move away. I feel Farhad's lips on my cheek. The voice inside me says, be strong, Kowsar. Be strong. Tell Farhad, You coward! If you have any honor, take your mother's rifle and we will go kill that opium peddler. And if you don't have the guts, I will do it. . . . I see Zubaideh holding a bowl against my lips. I drink. I have spoken those words out loud. Farhad is shaking.

"Son, take the bowl and give her some more."

"Drink," I hear him say.

Their voices are clearer. My vision is less blurred.

"I cannot sit by and watch Geesu and Farrokh devastated, their lives destroyed," I mumble. "Do you understand?"

"Yes, I understand. Just stay calm. We will think of something."

"Please, go and bring Farrokh back," I say, holding back my tears. "He shouldn't be alone."

"I won't leave this room until I know you are well again. Mother, brew a pot of tea and let's figure out what to do."

Zubaideh takes the lamp and leaves us in the dark.

"Kowsar," Farhad says, holding me tight. "It kills me every time you have an attack. It terrifies me knowing something might happen to you."

"I know. But Geesu and Farrokh are in love, too. Imagine how terrified Geesu is, how helpless Farrokh feels."

"I understand, Kowsar, but this is a mess. A ruthless warlord is involved."

"If they give Geesu to him, she will break. We must find a way. . . . They are a plague, ravaging our lives."

I know what Farhad is thinking. He is relieved that I wasn't Simin, that I'm not Geesu. That we are married.

"As long as they are here, this will not end," I say. "Tomorrow it will be another girl, and what happiness we have will again turn to poison. Like today. In the kitchen, I was happy cooking with my gentle mother-in-law and thanking God for the blessings we have. Hardly an hour later, Farhad came with horrible news."

"God is merciful," Zubaideh says, walking in with the tea. "He will show us the way, grant us a solution."

I burst into tears. I get up, I want to be alone and cry for as long as I want.

"Don't," Farhad says, taking my hand. "Sit with me and cry."

"But I don't want you here. I want you to go and find Farrokh. Don't leave my brother alone."

"Then stop crying and drink some tea."

I pull the tray toward me and fill two bowls. I put one on the windowsill next to Zubaideh, and I take a sip from the other one. Farhad looks at me.

"I won't pour any for you. Please go. Find Farrokh and bring him here. And take a walking stick, it's dark."

Worried, Zubaideh looks out the window as Farhad leaves. But the night is moonless and dark. Deep in thought, she sits there under the window.

"Drink your tea," she says sometime later. "It's getting cold."

I pick up the bowl I had abandoned and reluctantly drink.

We pass two dreadful hours waiting for Farhad to return.

"I looked everywhere," he says, standing breathless in the doorway. "I couldn't find him."

I look at him, desperate and afraid.

"Kowsar, don't do this to yourself," Zubaideh gently says. "He is probably curled up in some corner, wanting to be alone with his heartbreak. We will get news of him tomorrow. Prepare your bedding and get some sleep."

She leaves with the tray, and I stare blankly at Farhad as he unrolls the mattress and makes our bed. I lie down and think of Geesu, of her heart that has been so full of hope, of the love ballads she sings. I think of the nights she sneaks behind that short wall to kiss Farrokh and hurries back to the house.

"You know I will die if I am not with him," she said one day. And I consoled her, told her to not be afraid, to have courage.

"Kowsar," she said. "Pray for me. These mountains are now full of jackals."

The faint sound of a reed flute breaks the silence. I know it's

Farrokh mourning with his music. He plays for a long time, and I silently cry.

"Farhad are you awake?" I whisper when the music stops.

"Yes."

"Did you cry, too?"

"Yes."

"I love you."

"I love you, too."

"What is going to happen?"

"I don't know."

~

Zubaideh comes in early the next morning with the breakfast tray and dining cloth that smells of the freshly baked bread kept warm in its folds.

"Wake up!" she says. "It's almost noon!"

Remembering the night before, I jolt up and shake Farhad awake. I look out the window. The first rays of sun are only now shining in. Farhad and I go outside and quickly wash. By the time we join Zubaideh, she has prepared the spread and filled our bowls with milk. As hungry as I feel, I have no appetite.

"Eat this," Farhad says, giving me a piece of buttered bread.

"Someone was playing the flute last night," Zubaideh says.

"It was Farrokh, Auntie. It made us cry."

"I can tell by your red, puffy eyes. I could hardly sleep myself, worrying about what will become of that innocent girl. I got up long before dawn and busied myself baking."

We eat the rest of our breakfast in silence. Zubaideh and I are clearing the dishes when there is a knock on the front door. She hurries out and returns with Mother. She is pale and crying.

"What is it?" I ask, dreading the news she brings.

Mother throws off her chador and drops down on a cushion.

"They ran away," she says, burying her face in her hands. "Farrokh and Geesu ran away last night."

I freeze. Farhad and Zubaideh stare at her.

"What are you saying, Golrokh?" Zubaideh says. "Ran away where?"

Not bothering with a handkerchief, Mother wipes her nose with the edge of her robe.

"God only knows. I woke up this morning and found his bedding untouched. He took his backpack and a few clothes. Zubaideh, what am I going to tell his father? He still doesn't know. Even worse, what am I going to tell that foul tempered Hashem? If only Farrokh had enough sense not to take someone's daughter with him."

She turns to Farhad and says, "Son, if news of this spreads in the village and reaches the ears of that son-of-a-mule Obeid, we will be doomed and done for. Go find them. Take Mobin Khan's horse and go after them. Tell them to not do anything stupid, tell them to come back and let their parents find a solution."

Farhad looks at me and his mother.

"How do you know they have run away?" Zubaideh asks.

"Last night he told me everything. He told me they have been in love for a long time. That now the only thing they could do was run away. My heart almost stopped. He asked if I had any money to give him, he asked me to pray for them. . . . I begged him to be patient. I begged him to wait. I told him we will find a way. I said, maybe Hashem will refuse to give his daughter to that man. He argued with me. He said, 'You know these savages. No one can say no to them, much less Hashem Khan.'

"They must have gone to Jawand to take a minibus. We have relatives in Morqab, Ab Kamari, and Qadis. Please, Farhad, take the horse and go after them. Tell them not to ruin their lives and destroy ours. Beg them to come back, for the love of their mothers, for the love of God!"

I imagine Farrokh, feeling lost and desperate. I think, perhaps he made the right decision, perhaps escaping is the only hope they have, their only chance at being together, the only way to save Geesu. I don't want Farhad to search for them. Returning would mean walking to the scaffold.

285

"Mother, I knew Farrokh and Geesu were in love," I say. "He came here last night. He told us it was Obeidullah who fired his gun and explained that barbarian's intentions. You are right, Farhad should go find them, and quickly."

"God, where did this curse come from to torment us?" Mother grieves as she quickly throws on her chador. "Hurry, Farhad. I will saddle the horse and wait for you outside the house."

The moment she steps out into the yard, I turn to Farhad and say, "Go. But if you find them, do not tell them to come back. Tell Farrokh to go to our relatives in Ab Kamari and hide out there. They are good people. If they know his life is in danger, they will shelter them, at least for a while."

Farhad nods and is about to leave when I remember Farrokh has no money. I stop him and run to my trunk. I take my silver ring and earrings, Zubaideh's gold coins, and the money relatives and friends gave me as wedding gifts.

"Give these to Farrokh. May God watch over them."

Farhad looks to his mother.

"Take them and run!" Zubaideh says.

"Walk up and down the bazaar pretending you are looking to trade," I shout after him as he hurries across the yard. "The minibuses come sometime between ten and eleven. If they are waiting there, they will see you."

# 14

WHEN I REACH Mobin Khan's house, my mother-in-law is waiting outside with the horse. I can tell she ran all the way. Beads of sweat shine on her face.

"Go with God," she says, throwing the reins to me. "Beg them to come back quietly. Tell them if they don't, Obeidullah will take his vengeance on their fathers."

I nod, quickly mount, and quietly ride down the path. At the foot of the hill, I drive the horse to a gallop and slow down to an easy trot when I reach the river trail, careful not to attract attention and raise curiosity.

Daily life in the village is only now starting. Girls are coming to the river with their buckets and watering cans. Boys are leading their sheep to pasture lands. My greatest worry is riding past the school and its surrounding area. God is with me. It is quiet around the Taliban outpost. It seems early morning is the best time of day to collect the opium sap.

Clear of the village, I press the horse into a canter. "Go like the wind!" I tell it. "I need your strength today."

I think of Farrokh. I don't remember when my friendship with him began. We grew up together and share many memories, good and bad. We were playmates as little boys. A few years later, we shepherded our sheep together. We would talk and joke around. I am not sure why Farrokh never told me about Geesu. Lately, I had noticed he was less lively, often pensive. I could tell his heart was heavy. One day I asked him if something was troubling him. He only sighed and said life doesn't always go the way we want it to. Then he laughed and said no more.

Pushing the horse to go as fast as it can, I look to my left and right for any sign of him and Geesu, even though I know that if Jawand was their destination, they would have arrived there hours ago.

At the bazaar, shops have opened and the music blaring out of teahouses is prevailing over the loud drone of the generators. I leave the horse at the stables and hurry to the minibus stop. Two are already there. I ask one of the drivers if any have left. He tells me one headed for Qala-e Naw half hour ago. I'm certain Farrokh and Geesu have flown the coop and I will have nothing but bad news for Kowsar. Still, I harbor some hope that they might be going in a different direction. I go to the teahouse across the way from the stop. I order a pot of tea, sit on the wood platform outside, and keep my eyes on the bazaar, carefully looking up and down the road. The tea arrives. Thirsty from the ride, I gulp down my first bowl. I'm pouring a second one when a shadow blocks the warm morning sun.

"Pour one for me, too," Farrokh says.

I leap up and clasp him in my arms.

"I had little hope of finding you! I imagined you already gone and us worried sick forever."

"Gone where?" he sighs, sitting across from me. "Leaving isn't easy."

"Where is Geesu?"

"Inside, sitting with a family traveling to Qala-e Naw. How are things in the village?"

"No one is aware. For now, there's no talk. Your mother came at the break of day and told us you two have run off."

"And she told you to come find us and convince us to go back. She said God is kind and a solution will be found."

I don't answer him. Instead, I call the server and ask for another pot of tea.

"Two pots, with sugar," Farrokh tells him. "And two breads."

I look at him and only now notice his parched lips.

"You haven't had anything to eat or drink?"

"No."

"You don't even have money for tea?"

"No," he laughs grimly.

"Where were you going to go with empty pockets!?"

"I went to Hassan Khan's shop at the other end of the bazaar. He's an old family friend. I told him Father needs a short-term loan, a thousand afghanis. I said he'll pay back half of it in a month. Hassan Khan agreed, but said I have to wait until noon. This early in the day, he still hasn't sold anything to have the cash."

The server returns with our order. "Take one tea and bread to the woman in a gray burqa inside," Farrokh tells him.

"Kowsar is terrified. She loves you, and Geesu has been a sister to her all her life."

"Farhad, I did this for Geesu. Her life has become a nightmare. She was going to kill herself last night, set herself on fire. I snuck over the wall to see her. She said she will never let that Talib touch her. She had hidden a can of kerosene on the roof. I knew she would do it. Especially after Simin... Do you understand? I had no choice but to take her away."

I look at him. My heart aches for them.

"Running away is worse than staying, staying is worse than running away. What was I to do?"

I have no answer to offer.

He pours some tea, tears off a piece of bread and devours it. I want to tell him to sweeten his tea, it will give him energy, but I can't bring myself to speak.

"Last night, I realized I hate Tali. I realized when disaster strikes, no one will lend you a helping hand. I was desperate, I came to you and Kowsar, believing that of all people you two would help us. Instead, you got angry and berated me."

"Forgive me, Farrokh. I panic when Kowsar has an attack."

I reach for the sugar bowl and add some to his tea.

"You will need the energy."

I let him drink his tea in quiet. Then I say, "Bibi Golrokh wants me to take you back, but Kowsar asked me to tell you to leave. You decide."

"Mother is afraid of Obeid. She's afraid he and his thugs will come after Father. Geesu be damned, she thinks, Farrokh is young and there are plenty of other girls. But Kowsar understands, she knows what Geesu is going through, she knows leaving is our only option and staying means certain death for me and God knows what for Geesu."

I reach into my pocket and take out the money, the jewelry, and the gold coins.

"Your sister sent these for you. They're worth enough for you to make it for some time. She said you should go to your relatives in Ab Kamari and stay there until we figure out what to do."

"Yes, I think I'll do that," he says, tears welling in his eyes. "The first thing I must do is find a way to marry Geesu. I want her to be my lawful wife. I want her to stop being afraid, to know there is someone who will protect her."

A young man comes over and asks him, "What happened to the family heading to Qala-e Naw? The minibus is leaving."

Farrokh quickly downs the rest of his tea and takes what's left of the bread.

"Now that I have money, we can take the same minibus as the family Geesu is with. It's safer for her to travel with a woman."

He hurries inside and I watch the family walk out and go toward the minibus. Farrokh and Geesu follow them. Seeing her, I feel my bones burn. Hidden beneath a burqa, she is leaving herself in the hands of fate. Seeing me, she breaks into tears.

"Farhad, tell Kowsar I will never forget her, I will always love her. Tell her I will see her in another world. Tell my parents I beg their forgiveness. And pray for us, Farhad. Pray for us."

The driver is honking the horn. They run to the minibus. I watch it drive away and disappear in a haze of dust.

I am in no hurry to return to Tali. I want to arrive around sunset, so that I can tell Kowsar's mother, I searched all day, but didn't find them.

After prayers, I ride back, allowing the horse its leisurely gait.

〜〜

Riding up the hill to Mobin Khan's house, I see Bibi Golrokh sitting at the window of the rooftop room, waiting for me. She disappears the moment she sees me.

"Did you find them?" she asks, swinging open the front door.

"No, I'm sorry. I looked everywhere, but there was no sign of them."

"We are ruined!" she groans, covering her mouth with the length of her headscarf. "What are we going to say to Hashem Khan? What are we going to say to that son-of-a-mule Obeid? How can we ever hold our head up again in the village? God, you should have taken my life and not let me see this day."

Looking like a lost soul, she takes the reins from me and is leading the horse inside when I ask, "Aunt Golrokh, any news in the village?"

She drops the reins and turns back.

"I don't know about the village, but there was bedlam here. Before sun-up, Geesu's mother came over, terrified and shaking so badly she could hardly talk. I snuck her to the kitchen. Mobin Khan never comes there. She told me Geesu has run off with Farrokh. I said nothing. The poor woman knew her daughter was in love with our son. She said, 'Golrokh, you have to save me. Hashem still doesn't know, but when he finds out he will blame me and beat me to death. If you know where they've gone, tell Farrokh to bring her back. No good will come of this. When that Godless Talib finds out, he will send his men after them. Your son will be stoned, and God only knows what Obeid will do to Geesu before killing her, too.'

"I told her Mobin Khan still doesn't know, and that you've gone looking for them. I told her to keep Hashem in the dark until you come back. But a few hours later, I heard that animal shouting and the poor woman howling and begging him to stop. Then he stormed in here like a wounded viper, waving his slaughter knife and screaming, 'Bring me my daughter!' Mobin Khan was sitting at breakfast. He ran out in shock and shouted, 'Golrokh, what is his daughter doing here?' I died a thousand deaths telling him everything. I tried to calm Hashem. I told him our children love each other, that I was going to ask for Geesu's hand, but then evil rained from the sky and a Talib descended on us.

"Mobin Khan burst out laughing and said, 'So it's true that a lion breeds a lion! Where is my son for me to kiss him and say you've made your father proud!'

"'Don't mock me, you old cow,' Hashem screamed. 'If it were your daughter, you'd be yelping like a dog! I've never taken another man's life, but I will spill your blood in front of this wretch!'

"'Spill my blood if you will, but it won't untangle the knot we're in. Don't forget Obeid and his militia. Now, let's sit quietly and think of what to do.'

"Hashem quieted down a little. Mobin Khan paced up and

down the yard for a few minutes. Then he said, Farrokh has never gone farther than Jawand, and he has no money. They couldn't haven't gone far. Maybe they have gone to the mountains and are hiding in one of the caves, or walked to Buzghalak, to his cousin's children. He told Hashem they should go find them and bring them back, then worry about everything that's to come.

"Hashem started to cry. He said if God hadn't cursed him with a daughter and had blessed him with a son instead, none of this would have happened. The two of them went to search the caves and wherever else they can think of."

Aunt Golrokh takes the horse to the stable, and I, with a world of worry, head for home. The poppy farm laborers are returning to the village reeking of opium sap and looking like ragged scarecrows no bird would fear. Crossing the footbridge, I see Kowsar sitting at the window, just like her mother. I pick up my step and thank God we have each other. I'm hardly at the house when the front door flies open, and she tears out with no chador or headscarf. I nervously look around and run and drag her back to the house.

"What's the matter with you?" she cries.

"Get inside!"

In the yard, I kiss her frowning brow.

"I found them. They took a minibus and left for Ab Kamari."

295

# 15

LATE AT NIGHT, Mobin Khan and Hashem Khan return empty handed and ill-fated. Hoping that hearing the news from Geesu and Farrokh's shamed and aggrieved fathers would lessen Obeidullah's wrath and ease his vengeance, they decide it is best for them to go to him in the morning and deliver the news themselves.

Obeidullah is enraged. The two terrified men are held and publicly flogged with leather straps. The Talibs heckle, the villagers look away in fear and disgust.

"This, I vow," Obeidullah shouts. "I will not rest until those two are found. Praise to God, we are now in every town and village across this country. We will find them even if they have crawled under the earth."

And he laughs as the two men stumble away.

❦

A week later, Mawlawi Khodadad, wearing dark glasses, arrives in Tali with a legion of heavily armed Talibs. With the poppy tears dried to a sticky brown paste, pressed into bricks, and dried under the sun, time has come to pay the farm owners and laborers and haul away the raw opium.

His men, taking turns to guide the mawlawi by the arm, carefully lead him down the trail to their shouts of "*Allah o Akbar.*" Obeidullah and Mullah Sikhdad greet him and lead the way to Chief Abed's house as a crowd of Talibs gather and chant, "Glory be to God. I seek forgiveness from God."

Comfortably settled in Abed Khan's guestroom, Khodadad holds up his hands in prayer and recites lengthy verses of the Quran in a mangled mix of Persian and Arabic, then he runs his hand over his beard and the gathered guests intone, "Amen."

"Welcome, Mawlawi Sahib," Mullah Sikhdad says, sitting next to him. "Ever since your first visit to Tali, we have been blessed with gains and good fortune. It is true that in the shelter of a man of God and position, one will never go without. May God not deprive the pious of your haven, may God bring bounty wherever you tread."

"Amen," the men repeat.

"May God not deprive me of your support," Khodadad says gravely. "I *am*, because you are. An elder of position without disciples and devotees is not an elder of position. May God bring you blessings. There will be recitations of the Quran after evening prayers. Tell the needy and the suffering that Mawlawi is here today and tomorrow. God willing, there will be enough time for me to see them all. For now, there are matters I must discuss with Mullah Sikhdad and, in good time, with Obeidullah Khan."

As the room clears, Mullah Sikhdad pours a bowl of tea and puts it in Khodadad's hand.

"Tell me, Mawlawi Sahib. They have all left."

"Fortunately, everything is progressing as it should. When well-wishing devout men received news that divine light has affected my sight again, they asked for my patronage and requested that I attend to the jihad and oversee the revered scholars of Islam. Hence, I have ordered that religion schools be built in every town and village near and far. I want our sons to be correctly educated. They will also be instructed in jihad and receive arms training. I want you, Sikhdad, to sit with Abed Khan and plan for one in this valley. Of course, the schoolhouse you already have is the perfect location for it."

"That is excellent news, Mawlawi Sahib. May God reward you for your wisdom and benevolence."

"As the old saying goes, you can't hold two watermelons in one hand. So, I have left the Department of Education for this higher calling, but you need not worry. The director who has replaced me will continue with the same accounting system as before. Continue sending your monthly reports. Salaries for teachers, all other expenses, as well as your compensation will be sent to you."

Every word Khodadad utters is a seed of new hope sprouting

in the mullah's heart. He clutches Mawlawi's hands and fervently kisses them.

"May God give you a palace in heaven and as many *houris* as your heart desires."

—◦—

After the food prepared as alms has been served to the poor and Khodadad has rested, Obeidullah comes to see him. With the door closed and their voices hushed, they discuss the opium crops and harvest Obeidullah has overseen in the region, and he leaves to settle the accounts and prepare the transport of the opium.

The next day, the villagers gather to watch the army of Talibs on horseback and the caravan of donkeys with their burden of opium. Before leading them out of the valley, Obeidullah turns to the crowd and says, "For sixteen years, the foreigners and their lackeys have fought to annihilate us, but we are stronger and greater in number than ever before. Let it be known that this opium will be sold to them and theirs. Let it be known that we will exist as long as they are on our soil and thereafter."

—◦—

Life in Tali continues. At dawn the roosters crow of a new morning and a new sun rising, and Mullah Sikhdad's *azan* inaugurates the day. Soon the doors open, and the men go to the mosque for ablution and morning prayer. The women say their prayers at home, roll up their sleeves and go to their kiln and kitchen. The shepherd boys come driving their herds. Their *hey-hey* is the start of commotion in the village. Next comes the chatter and laughter of the girls who appear with their buckets and containers and head for the streams and the mountain river.

It is summer. The village is lively and bustling. Everyone is hard at work to fill their grain vessels, hoard cured meat, and store firewood for the bitter cold that comes mid-autumn. Many have forgotten Farrokh and Geesu. Perhaps it is human nature. But there are those who will not forget. Day and night they wait and hope for news of them.

Fear of what has become of the two, fear of their capture by the Taliban has robbed Kowsar of sleep and spirit. The fire in her belly is extinguishing. Her joy of life with Farhad has made room for the pain in her heart.

❧

Autumn comes, the birds migrate, the trees stand naked, and a thin coat of snow settles on the peaks.

"It's enough," Kowsar says at breakfast one morning. "Enough sitting and waiting. I am going to find my brother. Farhad, I have frustrated you these past months, and Zubaideh has had enough of my crying. I want to go and find them. I want to tell them to come and live here. Hide out here and wait to see what God has in store for them. Perhaps that evil Obeid will die in battle. If he doesn't, come spring and poppy season, I will kill him myself. I will blow his head off with Zubaideh's gun. I will put the cowardly men of this village to shame. A bunch of ruffians sit in their schoolhouse and they all piss in their pants."

She stops and looks at Farhad. He says nothing, but there is angst in his eyes.

"You are afraid? Afraid of falling into Obeid's clutches? Afraid of leaving your warm home and wandering around villages and towns? Think of Farrokh and Geesu! Imagine what they are suffering. Think of when the snows come. In this land of hunger, no one will give them a bite to eat and a warm corner to sleep. Will you come with me or not?"

Farhad desperately turns to his mother.

"He will," Zubaideh says, looking him in the eye. "So will I."

Kowsar breathes with relief and reaches for the bread.

"You are right," Farhad finally says. "I may not be the Farhad of ancient epics, but I am the Farhad who would sacrifice his life for you."

With their winter supplies gathered and stored, Zubaideh leaves the farm and the herd in Golrokh and Mobin Khan's care, and they prepare to leave.

# 16

THERE ARE NO CLIFFS and valleys around Ab Kamari. The region is green and hilly, with rivers and meadows that are here and there interrupted by wastelands. I once came here with my parents when I was very young. I remember the mud houses. They all have domed roofs. Clustered together, they look like a congregation of hunchbacks. I remember there was a stream near my maternal uncle's house where shepherds brought their herds for water. A village boy shows us the way to the footpath that leads there. Time has left it and Uncle's house untouched. Everything is as it was a decade ago.

My knock starts their dog barking, and it comes running to the door. I remember it was white, with black ears and two black patches around its eyes. A few minutes later, the safety chain jangles, and the door opens. The first thing I see is the dog. Its ears are black, but there are no patches around its eyes. I think that dog gave its place to its offspring.

"Hello!"

I look up from the dog and see a ten- or twelve-year-old boy who resembles my uncle.

"Hello, Auntie's love," I say, smiling at him.

He frowns.

"Run and tell your father or mother that relatives have come from Tali."

His frown melts into a smile. He hushes the dog and the two disappear in the dark vestibule that leads to the yard. I look at Farhad and Zubaideh. I think they, too, are praying for our search to prove short-lived and come to an end here. A few minutes later, a bent white-haired man with a cane comes to the door. I immediately recognize him. At the time, his back was straight, and his hair was salt and pepper.

"Hello, Uncle!"

He stares intently at my face.

"Kowsar!?"

"Yes, Uncle, it's me."

I take his hand and kiss it.

"This is my husband, Farhad. And the lady is my mother-in-law, Bibi Zubaideh."

"Welcome to all of you," he says with a broad smile. "Welcome to our humble house. And this is my grandson, Rasoul."

"In the name of God, what a handsome young man!" Zubaideh says.

"Son, go chain the dog so it doesn't bother our guests," he says, patting the boy on the head.

We follow him through the vestibule. It smells of fodder and cow dung.

Uncle's wife is standing crooked on the veranda with one hand holding onto the column and the other shading her eyes as she peers at us.

"It's Kowsar," Uncle says. "My sister Golrokh's daughter."

"Farrokh's sister? How she has grown!"

"She has a husband and a mother-in-law, too," Uncle says, laughing.

I go to her and kiss her hand as well. She kisses me on the cheeks.

Their guestroom is unchanged. The same rugs and cushions, now discolored by the passage of time. The framed photograph of Uncle in army uniform on the wall at the head of the room and his muzzle-loading rifle and bag of gunpowder and pellets on display in the niche by the window.

We sit and Uncle's wife starts asking about every member of the family, one by one. Desperate for news of Farrokh and Geesu, but not wanting to break the rules of decorum, I offer quick and concise answers. I expect them to tell us what they know without me having to ask, but they don't.

"And what is going on in Tali these days?" Uncle asks.

"We have all been terribly worried about Farrokh and Geesu,"

I finally say. "Mother and Father have withered like hay. We have troubled you with our visit, hoping for news of them."

Uncle says nothing. He takes his prayer beads from his pocket and starts rolling them.

"Uncle, why are you silent? What has happened to them?"

"Wife, is anyone thinking about some tea for us?"

"Our daughter-in-law will bring it when it's ready," she says, tidying her headscarf.

"My dear girl," Uncle says, turning to me. "As they say, you can't go to battle not having had tea. Rest for a while. You've traveled far."

His poorly disguised effort at not answering my question makes me even more anxious. Something dreadful must have happened. I hug my knees and lean against the bolster. I sense that Uncle and his wife are not pleased with our visit. His wife keeps looking from me to Zubaideh and Farhad, and then turns and stares at her husband.

"Aunt, please. Tell me!" I plead. "Tell me what has happened to my brother."

"Speak!" she snaps at her husband. "The girl is beside herself with worry!"

Then she struggles to her feet and limps to the door.

Uncle waits for her to leave the room and says, "Farrokh brought the girl here. He said they've run away. He asked me to marry them."

I can guess the rest of the story.

"I sent the girl to our daughter-in-law, and I asked Farrokh whose daughter she is. He said Hashem Khan, your neighbor. I was up all night, thinking, worrying. In the morning, we said our prayer and I sat him down and asked him what he's going to do now that he has run off with her. He told me they were happy together and wanted to be husband and wife.

"I took a good look at him and said, 'Son, you're young. Your parents must give their permission. Without it, no one will issue a marriage license.' He argued that they are old enough, that they don't care about permissions. He said if a mullah won't marry them, then as a family elder, I have the right and the power to do so. It was only then that he told me about that Talib warlord wanting the girl. To be honest, I got scared. I'm an old man, I don't need some horned beast coming after me."

Uncle gets up and paces the room with his hands locked behind him, still rolling the prayer beads.

"I said, 'Son, marriage isn't simple. A wife costs money. A woman wants a home, a life. And how long do you think you can stay here? Nothing in this village stays hidden. People will find out. What will you tell the Talibs and mullahs? Punishment is severe. God forbid, you give them an excuse. They think long hair and a lungee makes them a Muslim and gives them license to enforce Sharia law any which way they like.'"

I don't want to hear anymore. I see his mouth open and close, and his white beard whisk up and down. Farrokh came to him for help, and he turned him away. Tears roll down my face. I look at Zubaideh and Farhad, pale and silent. I don't want to stay here a moment longer, but before I can say anything, Uncle's wife hobbles in with the tea tray.

"Uncle," Farhad says, speaking for the first time. "Then what? Where did they go?"

He sits down on his cushion, and says, "I don't know, son. When we woke up the next morning, they were gone."

"It's time for us to leave," Farhad says abruptly as he stands up.

"Yes, it is," I say. "We won't trouble you anymore."

I yank our burqas off the hook next to the door and turn to Zubaideh. She is slow to get up. I'm certain she dreads having to travel by night, and the sun is already setting.

"Have you lost your mind!?" Aunt says, picking up the teapot. "I won't let you leave. You haven't even had tea or a bite to eat!"

Words that should remain unspoken are choking me. I know if I don't give voice to them, they will gnaw at me for the rest of my life.

"Did you welcome Farrokh and Geesu so warmly that now you want to do the same for us?" I say, trying to hold back my tongue and temper. "I was the one who told Farrokh to come to you. I was the one who told him you were kind and compassionate kin and would help him. I told him you would give them shelter. Little did I know that you are more cowardly than a goat!"

I wonder where Farrokh could have gone. If his own blood didn't give him a safe haven, who would?

My aunt comes with us as far as the porch. She is talking, but I no longer care to listen. Out on the road, the wind is gusting in every direction.

"If no minibus comes to the stop," Farhad says, "we can walk to Qala-e Naw. It's not too long a distance for mountain dwellers."

To Zubaideh's profound relief, at the bazaar we see the same minibus that brought us here. It is now facing the opposite direction and the assistant driver is calling for passengers to Qala-e Naw to board.

"We will spend the night at Golab Inn," Farhad says as we settle in our seats. "We can leave for Bala Murghab in the morning. I pray we find a trace of them there."

❧

Despite its broad and rapid river, Bala Murghab is a barren region. I know Father's relatives live in a village called Juy Ganj. The driver knows it and drops us off nearby. I quickly sense something different about this place. The earth is of another color, of another smell, the people of another air. We have only walked a short distance when a squad of Talibs stop us. From the design of our burqas and Farhad's clothes, they know we are strangers. They take Farhad to the side and question him. Who are we, where are we from, where are we going.

"We are from a village outside Jawand," Farhad explains. "We've come to visit a relative we have here. Hayatullah Khan."

They must know him. Asking nothing more, they let us go on our way. We ask around in the village and find Hayatullah Khan's house. A middle-aged woman opens the door. There's a tattoo of a crescent moon on her chin, and her hair is slicked with oil and pinned back.

"Hello. My name is Kowsar," I say. "I'm Mobin Khan's daughter. We've come a long way from Tali to see you. My father and mother send their greetings."

"Welcome, welcome to our home!" she says warmly. "I'm Hayatullah Khan's wife."

"The lady is Bibi Zubaideh, my mother-in-law, and this is my husband, Farhad Khan," I say as we walk into the front yard.

The house is relatively large, and its layout makes it clear that here women and men live apart. At the far end of the structure is a smaller wing that belongs to the women. Farhad cannot come with us. Before leading Zubaideh and me to the women's quarters, Hayatullah's wife invites him to the guestroom and calls their attendant to bring him tea and refreshments.

"So, you must be Farrokh Khan's sister," she says, smiling at me as we follow her into a room that serves as the women's sitting room.

My heart leaps with joy. Farrokh is or has been here, and this woman realizes we've come searching for him. I desperately try to remember what Father said her name is, but I can't remember.

"I'm terribly sorry, but I can't recall—"

"My name is Palwasha, my dear," she says, laughing.

"Yes! Now I remember."

She takes our burqas and invites us to sit. As we settle down, a young woman walks in and eyes us with curiosity.

"This is Negin, my daughter-in-law. She came from Qorqoch four, five months ago. She has no family here but us. Praise to God, Bibi Zubaideh, what a lovely bride you found for your son. She is as beautiful as the moon of the fourteenth night. It's a shame that Hayat doesn't mix with his relatives, otherwise I wouldn't let you take her away anytime soon."

"You have brought a beautiful bride, too," Zubaideh says. "As delicate as a gazelle. You must burn wild rue to ward off ill will and jealous eyes."

I'm happy that the two women seem to have taken to each other, but I'm impatient for the requisite civilities to end so that I can ask about Farrokh and Geesu.

"Aunt Palwasha, what a valley you have here," I say, hoping to speed up the chitchat. "I had never seen a river this broad."

"I wish instead of the river we had a quiet and peaceful life. In this part of the province, there is war all around us. Battles rage every day. One day it's the government against the Taliban, the next day it's the Taliban against the Americans, and if it's neither, it's the villages along the river going at each other in defense of one side or the other. And it doesn't end there. When it's not the war and holy jihad, it's the locals fighting over some girl or grain or sheep and land. . . . Alas, as long as there are guns in men's hands and no law, this will be our life."

I want to tell her our lives are no better, but I don't. I look at the beautiful new kilim. Its design and colors are different from any other I have seen. Be quiet and patient Kowsar, I tell myself, wait for her to breech the subject.

"We baked bread earlier today. Shall I bring some with tea?"

I'm terribly hungry. I look at Zubaideh.

"If it's not too much trouble," she says. "The bumpy ride along these roads has made us a bit hungry."

Getting up, Palwasha nods to her daughter-in-law and she follows her out.

"What do you think?" Zubaideh whispers. "Are they, were they, here?"

"I can't tell. I hope she tells us soon."

I look around the room. It has only recently been added to the house. A hint of the smell of mud and straw lingers in the air. There is a window that opens to the back yard. The curtain is green with pomegranates and green leaves on it. Several neatly folded mattresses and quilts are stacked in the large alcove across from me, and behind Zubaideh, there is a white, richly embroidered sheet covering clothing hanging on wall hooks. The design is very different from the work of women and girls in Tali. The needlework on the four corners is more geometric and intricate with smaller stitches. In the middle there are large colorful flowers and the image of a leopard, an eagle, and four coiling snakes.

"Auntie, look at the sheet behind you," I say, breaking our silence. "It's so unusual. The design tells a story."

"It's probably the work of the daughter-in-law. She is obviously from a different tribe and people."

Palwasha walks in with a tray and dining cloth. Negin follows with a large teapot. They arrange the spread in front of Zubaideh.

"Come sit closer, dear Moon," Palwasha says as she serves the tea.

"Aunt, my name is Kowsar!"

"I know, but you remind me of the moon. And Bibi Zubaideh, it's interesting what you said about Negin looking like a gazelle. That's the nickname I gave Geesu. May God keep her."

My heart drops. My hope evaporates.

"So, they left? They're not here?" I ask desperately trying to remain calm.

"God willing, they have travelled safe," she sighs. "I will tell you all."

Negin offers me bread. I tear off a piece and stare at it. Palwasha takes it from me and smears some butter on it.

"Negin, my dear, run and fetch the quince jam," she says. "Farrokh liked it so much he finished an entire jar."

"Aunt Palwasha, you know we only came here looking for Farrokh and Geesu. We went to Ab Kenari, to my mother's relatives, but they weren't there. We thought they might have come to you. My father is grief-stricken and my mother cries day and night. Please, tell me!"

"I will, dear Moon. I will. But first you need to eat a bite or two and drink your tea."

Negin comes in with the jam. Palwasha opens the jar, patiently spreads some on the buttered bread and gives it to me.

"Eat, dear Moon. Everything will be all right."

I look at Negin, desperately hoping she will not make me wait. She remains silent. I force a few bites as Zubaideh patiently chats with Palwasha until our host motions for Negin to clear the dishes.

"Your brother and Geesu came here," she says as Negin leaves with the tray. "They stayed with us for about three months. When they arrived, Hayatullah Khan was at a warfront somewhere. I should tell you, my husband is a Talib. A prominent and powerful one. God knows where he is now, in Helmand or Farah or somewhere in Pakistan. In any case, Farrokh and Geesu told me everything. My heart broke for them. I gave them a room in this section of the house for them to hide out until we know what God has destined for them. No one comes to the women's quarters except my husband, and the yard and garden in the back are closed in by tall walls and can only be accessed from here. The two of them would go there when they couldn't tolerate being cooped up anymore.

"Geesu and Negin became dear friends, and Geesu kept herself busy helping her in the kitchen. I should tell you, I don't have a son for Negin to be my daughter-in-law. She is my husband's second wife. He brought her from Qorqoch a little over a year ago. Negin's father assassinated Hayat's nephew over some feud, and my husband took the man's daughter as blood money. She is forty years younger than him. When Negin heard Geesu's story, she threw herself in her arms and wept. The poor girl's heart is heavy. Who knows, perhaps she, too, was in love with some young man.

"After a while, there was some color back in Geesu's cheeks and Farrokh was in better spirits and hopeful. But hard as I tried to not let them find out about Hayatullah, they eventually figured it out. They were again despondent and terrified. There was no consoling Geesu. She cried and cried, sometimes sobbing so hard that she would start to pant and gasp for air. Only Farrokh could calm her down.

"My plan was to wait for Hayat to come back and to sit and talk to him. Every time he comes home, he is generous and kind to me for a while. When he returned, he spent the first night with Negin. He had asked her about Farrokh and Geesu. Who they are, why they're here. Negin pretended she doesn't know much. The next night he came to my room. I told him everything and asked him for help. At first, he was furious. 'Do you have any idea who Obeidullah is!?' he shouted. 'A serpent with seven heads. Where there's venom and enmity, Obeid is too.' I told him I don't care who that bastard is. I told him his flesh and blood has sought shelter in his home and asked for his help. It is his duty to save them from this mess. Thank God, he calmed down. He said Obeid was going to Bala Murghab in a few days. It's not far from here. Hayat said he would try to convince him to give up this vendetta.

"A week later, Obeidullah showed up in the village with a few of his jackals. Hayat had invited him to come for dinner. Geesu and Farrokh were as terrified as birds prey to a falcon. That night, Hayat filled the man's stomach and sitting with their tea, he opened the subject. I had told Shakur, Hayat's attendant, to let me know after he takes the tea tray to the guestroom. Negin and I snuck under the window and listened. Hayat explained that Farrokh is his brother's grandson. He said, 'The boy came to me with the girl, and he is waiting for me to marry them. But I wanted to have your permission first.' He went on to say that firing a few shots outside someone's home is meaningless and no one gives their daughter to a man for a few bullets. He told him to forget about Geesu and find another girl and properly ask her parents for her hand.

"I thought Obeid would raise hell and burn this house down to the ground, but he quietly listened to everything Hayat had to say. Then he said giving up would be an act of cowardice, a dishonor and disgrace, and he would not agree to it even at the cost of his life. Hayatullah's maniac side took over. He lost his temper and shouted, 'If you still want the wretch, empty your gun in my chest and then do whatever you want!'

"The two of them fought and argued, carrying on about their version and interpretation of Sharia law and the honor of a Talib. Obeid was adamant. He said, 'The girl ran away with a man who is not her husband. By law, she must be stoned.' Negin and I panicked. Hayat was in a jam. He went on arguing, but Obeid took out his telephone and called Mawlawi Khodadad as the voice of authority on the matter. I didn't know much about the man, only that he is now the governor of Badghis, blind and powerful, with a knack for issuing fatwas left and right. Once Obeid explained the circumstances, Khodadad told him to capture the two and hold them for now. We hurried back here and were thinking of what to do when Hayat came running and told me to get the two out of the house. We packed the few things they had and helped them over the garden wall.

"I loved them as though they were my own," she says, breaking into tears.

Zubaideh and Palwasha are watching over me when I come to. There is cold sweat on my face. I turn my eyes and see Negin sitting by the door with her legs folded and her chin resting on her knees. She is staring at me.

Palwasha brings a bolster and says, "Sit up and lean back, my girl."

"Farhad?"

"Don't worry. Shakur is taking care of him and keeping him company."

I stay there and rest for a while until I feel myself again.

"I need fresh air, I need to be outdoors," I tell Palwasha and Zubaideh. "I'd like to go for a walk if Negin would come with me. Perhaps by the river."

"My dear Moon, it rains terror here. Women and girls have been confined to their homes for a long time. The days when we could go for walks are long gone. We no longer dare. Go to the garden in the back. It's very pleasant there. Negin will come with you."

In the corner of the back yard, next to a shed, there is a small door with a tin plate nailed over it.

"Watch your head," Negin says as she unhooks the safety chain, bends down, and goes through.

On the other side, I find myself in a beautiful autumn garden carpeted with all shades of yellow, red, and orange leaves. A few shriveled pomegranates stubbornly clinging to naked branches, gently sway in the breeze. There is a narrow creek that flows the length of the garden. Negin follows it to the farthest of the four walls enclosing the garden.

"They climbed up here," she says, pointing to one side of the wall. "Farrokh went first and pulled Geesu up. He kissed her and told her they have to be brave, then he jumped down the other side. Geesu held onto the edge, swung her legs over, and Farrokh helped her down."

I look at the wall. There are faint vertical scrapes and scratches on it.

"I knew in my gut that Hayatullah's return would spell disaster for them," Negin says.

I imagine Farrokh and Geesu running from the house, wandering off into the wildernesses.

"Where could they have gone?" I ask her. "Farrokh had nowhere else to go, no other relatives to turn to."

"When Geesu rushed to their room to pack her clothes, I told her to go to Qorquch, in Moqur district. That's where I'm from. It's a Baluchi village with a handful of Tajik families. I told her to find a young woman called Mahakan. She was my best friend. Her father, Molda Khan, is the elder of the tribe. I told Geesu to memorize a verse by Hafiz, *Without lovers' fingers / For golden rings there is no demand*, and to repeat it to Mahakan. She would know I sent them to her. If Geesu and Farrokh make it there, she and her brother will shelter them for as long as they can."

"I am grateful to you," I say, clasping her hand. "You have given me back the hope I lost. God willing, you have saved them. But why didn't Palwasha tell us?"

"She doesn't know. I haven't told anyone but you. I don't trust anyone in this house."

Sitting on the ground with the creek between us, she says, "I forgot my sadness and loneliness while Geesu was here. She was a good friend. When they left, light and joy left with them. I lost my friend."

I look into her eyes. There's such sorrow in them.

"You are a victim of the sins of others," I say quietly. "Punished for a crime you didn't commit. That's how it always is in this country. They stopped burying women alive when they realized they can buy and sell us as brides, claim us as blood money, take us as slaves, offer us as gifts. They reckoned, why bury all this wealth?"

"Girls like me are alive but have no life. We are property," she says, running her fingertips over the water. "There is no cure for what we suffer. When I saw you and Farhad together, my heart broke for myself, and I thought, thank God at least one pair of young lovers managed to have each other."

"Was there someone you loved and left behind?"

"Yes. Seydou, a Baluch. He is Mahakan's brother. Intelligent and strong. So handsome. On horseback, he looks like a prince, a chieftain. We were so in love. He would hide behind our house just to see me for a moment, at night he'd sneak up to my window for a stolen kiss. He used to say, 'We will marry, and I will take you to Nariman mountain.' He said it's lush and green, with beautiful valleys blessed with wild fruit trees and hunting animals, pheasants and fowl. 'We will build a stone house and live far away from these barbarians. You will raise our children and I will hunt and farm,' he said. . . . We were afraid my father wouldn't allow us to marry. By then he was carrying a gun and spending time with an unsavory lot. One day he came home with a group of his Talib friends, mullahs, and village elders to sit and resolve a bitter enmity between him and Hayatullah over a murder. The two made peace in exchange for me as blood money. My father handed me to Hayatullah and said, 'Congratulations.'"

She breaks into tears and hides her face in her hands.

"Negin, don't cry! In these times, everyone grieves, no one lives the life they wish."

"My lips still remember his. Warm and sweet."

～

We leave the next morning. Walking along the roads and alleys of Juy Ganj to where the minibuses and cars for hire stop, Zubaideh and I tell Farhad all we have learned.

"We should go to Qorquch," I say, praying they will agree.

"My girl, we will go," Zubaideh says after a while. "But then I can go nowhere else but home. I'm tired, and I can't burden Mobin Khan with the care of the farm and herd much longer."

Farhad says nothing, though I sense he is of the same mind as his mother.

"Auntie, I promise. We will return home, whether we find them there or not."

Hard as it will be for me to give up my search, I know it cannot go on much longer. Apart from Zubaideh's exhaustion, I am certain whatever amount of money she and Farhad brought with them will soon run out.

We hire a car and leave Juy Ganj. The mountain road to Qorquch is more rugged than any we have so far traveled. And it is crowded with Taliban fighters in jeeps and trucks and on horseback. They have set up checkpoints at several passes in the mountains. The guards hail the driver to stop, and they question us. Where are we coming from? Where are we going to? Twice they search the car, and only once, a guard simply waves us through. I am now more apprehensive than ever. How could Farrokh and Geesu have made their way past them?

Several hours later, we arrive at a valley dense with autumn-stricken trees and fenced fallow lands lying naked under the feeble sun. The distant mountains are white with several coats of snow and the wind bears the smell of the coming winter. When we arrive in the village, Farhad asks a passerby where we can find Molda Khan's house. He directs us to an old stately home surrounded by tall walls.

Farhad sounds the knocker on the large wooden door and a minute or two later, an elderly hunchback pulls it open.

"Molda Khan is not in," he says.

"We are not here to see Molda Khan," Farhad replies. "We have come to call on Bibi Mahakan."

The old man turns his head sideways and peers up at him.

"Mahakan? How do you know her?"

I walk up to him and lift my face veil.

"Uncle, please tell Bibi Mahakan that Kowsar has come from Juy Ganj to see her."

The old man hesitates a moment then closes the door. A few minutes later he comes back and invites us in. The house is the most beautiful structure I have ever seen. It is built around a large meticulously planted garden courtyard. Each of the building's four wings, with ornate arches and shaded verandas, seem to be a separate residence. I am staring at everything around me when I hear Farhad greeting someone. Mahakan is a tall, fair-skinned young woman with long, wavy dark hair.

"Bibi Mahakan, my name is Kowsar," I say, walking over to them. "This lady is my mother-in-law, Bibi Zubaideh, and this is my husband, Farhad Khan. We are from Tali and were in Juy Ganj searching for loved ones who are missing. We met Negin at my relative's home. She sent us here with a request and a message for you that she entrusted to me. *Without lovers' fingers / For golden rings there is no demand.*"

Excited, she greets me as a friend and kisses me on the cheeks, welcomes Zubaideh, and says hello to Farhad.

"Uncle, hurry up and open the guesthouse," she says to the old man.

We follow him as he shuffles across the courtyard, opens a door, and stands aside.

"Bibi Mahakan," I say. "If you observe certain restrictions, Farhad can perhaps go to another room."

"No, my dear," she says, ushering us in. "We Baluch have different customs. We don't easily allow people into our sanctum, but when we do, we see no need to observe hijab."

She takes my burqa and waiting for Zubaideh to take hers off, she says, "Please, make yourselves comfortable. Bibi Kowsar, I'm impatient to hear about my dear Negin."

"She sends her greetings. Her heart is heavy and her eyes tearful. She misses her family, she misses Mahakan. She said she left behind her youth and love in this village."

"I know she has an unhappy life. When a father puts her young daughter's hand in the hand of a man four decades her senior, that girl's fate is plain as day. Still, coming from her and bringing her scent with you has brightened my heart. This is the first news I have of her since the day that man took her away."

Mahakan goes to the door and tells the old man sitting outside, "Uncle, tell Zari it's time for tea. Our guests are tired."

Returning to her seat, she says, "Alas, what Negin doesn't know is that her father has paid for his sins. He was killed a few weeks ago by one of his many enemies. A murderer is soon murdered. If not today, then tomorrow. How many daughters do they need to buy their life? In this land when a man is killed, he takes ten other lives with him. That's why the Baluch families here stay out of the others' wars and jihads, and we don't allow them into our lives and livelihood. If you stay here for a while, you will soon realize that all the corruption, thievery, and violence have their roots in families that are not of our tribe. As soon as one of their chiefs is killed, they seek the umbrella of some other lawless lout. As they say, we do onto ourselves... But you said you are searching for loved ones?"

My heart drops. Farrokh and Geesu never arrived here.

"So, they didn't reach you?" I ask, desperately hoping I'm wrong.

"Who, sister?"

Trying to remain calm, I tell Mahakan all that has happened as briefly as I can. She quickly gets up and calls the old man again. "Uncle, find Seydou and tell him to come at once."

Her brother arrives as the tea is being served. Seydou looks nothing like the man Negin described. I imagined her handsome hero to be as striking as the prophet Yusuf. He is not. He is of average height, has a hooked nose, small eyes, and a sullen expression. I tell myself, See him as Negin saw him. The handsome hero of her dreams.

"Seydou Khan," I say before Mahakan has a chance to speak. "Negin sends her greetings."

He is suddenly alert and his knotted brow softens.

"We were with her in Juy Ganj. She wanted me to tell you, it was God's will. She hopes you will soon wed and realize your dream of Nariman. 'The world is not worth its sorrow,' she said."

"'The lips say one thing, the heart another," he says quietly. "I no longer dream of Nariman. Can one throw away a gem set in one's heart?"

Mahakan looks troubled. I scold myself for being hasty and thoughtless again. Not only did I not give him Negin's message in private, I have managed to upset Mahakan.

"Seydou, our guests have loved ones who are missing," she says, changing the subject. "A young couple in love who fled from their homes in Tali for fear of a Talib warlord. They went to Juy Ganj, to Hayatullah, who is Bibi Kowsar's relative, and—"

"What a decent man they sought refuge with!" Seydou snickers.

"I know, brother. That's why they left his house and headed for Qorquch. Negin told them to come to us."

"Negin told them to memorize a verse as an assurance to you and Bibi Mahakan," I say. "*Without lovers' fingers / For golden rings there's no demand.*"

He rolls up his sleeve and shows me the verse tattooed on the inside of his forearm. My heart aches for him, and I think, why is this land of ours filled with lovers with broken hearts and singed wings.

"Seydou, have you heard any talk of a young couple on the run?" Mahakan asks. "Their names are Farrokh and Geesu. From Tali, in Jawand district."

Forgetting the verse on his arm, Seydou suddenly looks up.

"Yes! I have," he says, turning to me. "I fear to tell you, Bibi Kowsar. A young man and a girl who were not married were arrested by the Taliban a few days ago."

Farhad is standing in the middle of the room dressed in an unfamiliar looking long sheepskin coat and wool hat with long ear flaps. I think I'm hallucinating.

"Are you all right Kowsar?" he asks.

"Yes," I say, blinking my eyes. No, it's him standing there in that strange outfit.

"What are you wearing?" I say, slowly sitting up.

"Baluch clothes, I'm going to Tutak with Seydou. He thinks the Taliban took them there."

"I'm going with you. I won't let you go without me."

"No, sister," Seydou says, walking in with two pairs of knee-high boots. "There are no roads for cars from here to Tutak. We have to go on foot. You saw that high mountain? Tutak is on the other side."

"Farhad, how are you going to climb that mountain? It's covered with ice and snow!" I say in a panic.

"My girl," Zubaideh says. "I am fearful and troubled, too. But I cannot tell a man not to do what he believes he must. Praise God, they are both strong. I will pray for them."

"Don't worry," Seydou says, tossing a pair of boots to Farhad. "We will go discreetly to a friend to find out what has happened. Sitting here is useless. I know the way, and we have warm clothes. And your Farhad now passes as a true Baluch!"

# 17

SEYDOU THE SINCERE, Seydou the generous, Seydou the capable. The more time I spend with him, the more I admire and envy him.

"Farhad, live only two days, but live them like a man," he says as we climb the mountain. "I have not been defeated in love. I will wait for her. Hayatullah will die of old age or at the hands of some thug like himself, like Negin's father. Then I will take her to Nariman. That mountain knows that this Baluch will one day build a small house on its foothills, plow the land, and shepherd his herd ... I knew her father would not give his daughter to a Baluch, yet I harbored some hope. What I didn't know is that there are creatures like Hayatullah crawling this land ... Who knows, we might find a way to save your Farrokh and Geesu. If God so resolves, he will see them through fire unscathed."

As the slopes grow steeper, I find myself short of breath. Every few steps, I must stop for a moment or two.

"Aren't you the son of mountains?" Seydou says, looking back at me and laughing. "Don't worry. You will get used to it. After your first sweat dries, you'll be as agile as a mountain goat."

I can only nod.

"What about you?" he asks sometime later. "You fell in love and got married?"

"We told my mother, she asked for her hand, and we quickly got married," I say, panting. "For fear of the Talibs."

"You should thank God. Look at me and Negin. What a heartless louse her father was. He could snatch a bite of bread from an orphan. And in the end? Nothing. A few months after he gave Negin to Hayatullah, another brute shot him like a dog and took his young wife as his own."

We have come a long distance. Seydou seems to know the mountain like the back of his hand. Without looking around, he weaves his way upward, and he goes on talking without expecting any response. I'm grateful. I need every breath to keep up with him.

"Badghis has turned into a lawless land. On one side government crooks embezzle and defraud the people, on the other the Taliban extort and tyrannize them. And they all get away with it. No questions asked.

"We Baluch try to keep to ourselves. We want nothing to do with the government or the Taliban, but they want something to do with us. Every day they come up with some excuse to wrest money from us. We were a large tribe, but over time many of us migrated to Iran and Pakistan. And now, the forty or fifty Baluch families that remain are being crushed like grain between millstones.

"Back when the Taliban were first defeated and left, and a new government came into power, we thought Afghanistan was finally safe and ready for progress. We thought that the Westerners who came with their money had freed us from living in limbo. But that sweet nectar soon turned into bitter poison. . . . It was all lies. Ignorant thieves left, cunning pillagers replaced them. And life here remains what it was. Every day, we have less security than the day before."

Higher up, an icy wind whips at us. I feel it cutting into my bones. Seydou stops and looks back. His face is bright red and his eyes are tearing.

"Hey!" he shouts over the wind. "Don't catch cold and come down with pneumonia. Your wife will blame me, and my sister will have my head."

"Friend," I shout. "We have nasty winters, too."

We continue in silence until we reach a peak that overlooks a vast expanse of the province. The villages look like small oddly shaped patches and stripes.

"From up here it looks so peaceful and serene," Seydou says, absorbed by the scenery. "But a bowl of steaming *shurba* next to a heater would do better for me. What are you craving?"

"*Gurooti.*"

He shades his eyes with his hand and looks around.

"See that smoke?" he says, pointing to a small village at the foot of the mountain

"Yes, I see it."

"It's out of our way, but I'll have your wish realized. We'll go there and ask them to make *gurooti* for us."

"Do you know anyone there?"

"Of course, I do!"

"What a friend I have found!" I laugh, slapping him on the back. "He knows half the world."

Seydou leads the way to the left of the peak at a brisker pace. Heading down the mountain, with several boulders and ridges behind us, we are above the source of the smoke and not far from it. The scene is breathtaking. Two massive mountains part and as though regretting their separation, come together again in the distance, leaving a narrow valley nestled between them. There is a cluster of small stone houses in the middle.

"Seydou! It looks like a sliver of heaven."

"Come, let's rest for a while and enjoy the scenery," he says, sitting down on a rock.

I count the houses. There are nine. A few laughing and screaming children dressed in colorful clothes and vests made of pressed wool are chasing after a rooster with their white dog. Around the houses, snow covered farm patches bordered with rocks are deep in their winter sleep. In the distance, where the mountains reunite, a narrow waterfall feeds a river that flows the length of the valley.

"Seydou, perhaps the people living here have no notion of the reign of terror spreading in our towns and villages. I envy them their quiet paradise."

"Nariman mountain is even more peaceful. Years ago, in late summer when it was time to harvest the pistachio farms, me and the other village boys would go there for a few days of pistachio picking and hunting. At night we would start a bonfire, roast wild game, and have a feast. On moonlit nights, I would sit on a rock and stare at the pristine nature. One day I will take Negin's hand and go live there, away from guns and wars and Talibs.... Come now, it will be dark in an hour."

Following the trail of goat and sheep hoofprints in the snow, we make our way down to the valley. Near the foothills, the white dog picks up our scent and abandoning the children it comes barking toward us. Seeing strangers, the children run to the low hill where the houses are. By the time we reach the bottom, a man holding a hunting rifle is walking over to us.

"Don't worry, Farhad. They always carry their rifle for fear of wolves."

"Hey!" the man calls out. "Who are you?"

"Seydou from Qorquch. Son of Molda Khan."

The man slings the rifle over his shoulder and waits for us.

"We were on our way to Tutak," Seydou says. "By the time we reached the peak, we were cold and hungry, and saw the smoke down here. I told my friend, where there's fire, there's food."

"You are most welcome," the man says. "What God has given, I have to offer."

I was expecting Seydou to ask the man about his friend who lives here. But he doesn't. I realize there is no friend, and he probably doesn't know the way to Tutak.

Walking ahead, the man turns to the children standing with their dog watching us and says, "Shir Ahmad, run and tell your mother to go to her sister. We have guests."

A boy who looks to be eight- or nine-years-old runs off.

"I don't know Molda Khan," the man says. "We rarely go to that side of the mountain. I have never been to Qorquch."

"I'm from one of the Baluch families that live there," Seydou says. "If you ever come that way, please be our guest. It will be an honor to return your generosity."

The man carefully steps over the icy rocks around a farm patch and walks up the hill.

"You didn't tell us your name, man of God," Seydou says.

"Gol Ahmad."

"My friend's name is Farhad. He's from Tali. Have you ever heard of it?"

"No."

"How about Jawand?"

"Yes, Jawand, I've heard of."

"Tali is a valley nearby."

"So, you are the real guest, Farhad Khan," Gol Ahmad says, smiling at me.

"May God keep you," I reply.

The dog has stopped barking, but its ears are perked up and it's diligently keeping an eye on us. Gol Ahmad shoos it away, but the dog ignores him.

Gol Ahmad's son is waiting in front of one of the stone huts. His father asks if his wife has left. The boy nods and runs off to join the other children.

"If you would allow," Seydou says. "We should wash up."

"The river is over there," he says, pointing to the far side of the hill. "But if you wait, I'll heat up some water for you."

"We are mountain people and used to washing with cold water," Seydou responds as he walks away.

Behind the hill, we see the river we had seen from up high. The rushing water rolls and waves as though desperate to reach warmer climates. We squat down and wash our hands and face and drink a few handfuls. I've drank from many rivers and streams, but this water is strangely more satisfying. As we get up, Shir Ahmad hurries over with a cotton cloth for us to dry ourselves.

Inside his one-room hut, branches are already crackling in the heater and a kettle has been set on top of it to boil. With his right hand on his chest, Gol Ahmad welcomes us and invites us to sit close to the heater.

"I'll brew some tea as soon as the water is ready. We were going to have bread and sweetened tea for dinner, but I sent word to my wife to make *gurooti* for our guests."

Seydou smiles and winks at me.

"Thank you, man of God," I say. "You must have read my mind. I have been craving it all day."

"Well, when all you have is day-old bread, whey, and onion, put them all together and cook the poor man's dish."

"And a delicious one!"

"How many families live here, Gol Ahmad Khan?" Seydou asks.

"Nine huts, nine families. And we're all related."

As Seydou chats with our host, I look around the room. Other than the old kilim, the hut is bare of furnishings. Roughly cut wood beams secure the black rocks that make up the roof. To the left of the door, a bucket, a cooking pot, and a sieve holding plates and bowls sit neatly in a row. The family's bedding is stacked in a niche at the other end of the room, and there's a crate of branches and logs behind the heater.

"Do you raise livestock?" Seydou asks our host.

"Yes and no," he says. "Each family has a dozen or so goats and sheep, and a few acres of land. In the spring we plant peas, ervil, wheat, and the like. We sell the harvest and buy our basic needs. Some years pests ruin the crops. This was one of those years. A few days ago, we sold sheep and bought wheat and other necessities, otherwise we wouldn't make it through the winter. . . . That's our life here."

"It's no different in other villages," I say. "That's what my family's life is in Tali. We make do. But I envy you your peace and quiet. We lost ours the day the Taliban discovered our valley."

"They have done the same to other villages around these parts," Gol Ahmad says, preparing tea. "Praise God, Olang-Deraz is difficult to reach."

"Am I right in guessing that to go to Tutak all we have to do is follow the river?" Seydou asks.

"Yes, but at the end of the valley, it turns into a wide mountain river. Along the way you will see several streams feeding into it. Tutak is where we go to buy our tea, sugar, salt, and sulfur to fertilize the farms. It will take you about two and half hours to walk there."

"Don't worry, Seydou" I say sarcastically. "I know the way, and I have a good friend in Tutak we can stay with."

"We will leave after we've eaten," he says with a chuckle. "This time, you take the lead!"

We're sipping tea when there's a knock on the door.

"It seems dinner is ready," Gol Ahmad says.

He goes to the door and brings in the copper tray that his wife has left outside. He unfolds the dining cloth, sets aside the two loaves of bread tucked inside, and spreads it in the middle of the room. He puts a small plate with a whole onion within our reach and the steaming clay bowl of *gurooti* in the center.

"Enjoy!" he says with a broad smile.

The aroma of the food makes me even more famished. I reach for the large clay bowl and I'm chewing my first mouthful when I realize I haven't responded to his comment as tradition calls for.

"May you live long," I say with my mouth full. "Thank you for your troubles."

Gol Ahmad nods and smiles and starts to eat. With the large bowl empty, Seydou says a verse of thanks and sits back with a sigh of satisfaction. But I tear off another piece of bread and scoop up the last remnants of the sauce.

"I wiped the bowl clean, to spare your wife the trouble of washing it," I joke, pushing back the bowl. "Gol Ahmad Khan, may your spread always be so blessed."

"May yours be likewise," he replies with his hand on his chest.

"I ate without mercy. I better go wash my greasy fingers."

"There's warm water in the kettle."

"I need a good drink of water too," I say as I pull on my boots. Outside the door, I jolt at the sight of dark shadows huddled against the wall. I step closer and see Shir Ahmad and his sister squatting in the snow next to their mother.

"Shir Ahmad, what are you doing out in this cold?"

He doesn't answer me. But, his sister says, "We're waiting to see if there's any *gurooti* left for us to eat."

Pain stabs at my heart. The earth and sky whirl around me.

"Oh, God!" I groan. "There's nothing left. We ate it all."

"Sahib, I hope you enjoyed it," the children's mother says. "A guest is a friend of God."

"Come," she says to her children. "I'll get some bread from your aunt for you."

I lose sight of them in the dark. Walking to the river, I curse myself for my greed and thoughtlessness.

"Farhad, what's wrong? Did you take a fall?" Seydou asks when I return.

"I wish I had. I saw something that shook and unnerved me."

"What?" Seydou and Gol Ahmad ask looking alarmed.

"Gol Ahmad Khan, your children were sitting outside with their mother, waiting to see if there was any food left for them to eat. And I licked that bowl clean like a hungry dog!"

"And I'm happy it was to your liking," Gol Ahmad says. "Don't worry. They are young and don't know better. They will eat something at their aunt's house."

As Seydou and I get ready to leave, Gol Ahmad puts on his

frayed pressed wool coat, takes his kerosene lamp, and says, "I'll walk with you for a while. It will do me good."

At the end of the valley, where the two mountains meet, he tells us, "Stay on the trail bordering the river. Walk slowly and carefully. It's steep and rugged in some parts. Better to arrive late but safe."

We thank him and part ways. The moon is hiding and the terrain just as trying as he had forewarned. We walk in silence, our attention focused on the bumps and ditches that the white snow and the dark night have painted gray. My shame and anger at myself still weigh on my conscience. We walk a good distance before the trail becomes somewhat smoother.

"Farhad, why so gloomy?" Seydou asks.

"My heart broke for that kind man's wife and children. I haven't stopped cursing myself from the moment I saw them sitting in the snow."

He stops and turns to me.

"You saw with your own eyes that nobility and generosity have still not died in this land, you saw how big a heart this empty-handed man has. There was a time when this country was full of Gol Ahmads. With joy and kindness, they shared their child's bread with you. Gol Ahmad gives me hope. Hope that this land will one day be what its people deserve. I don't regret us eating all the food. His children will have some bread and go to bed. And

I am happy to have taken someone who has lost hope to a place where he saw honor, chivalry, and grit."

He looks at the trail ahead and walks on.

"Come," he says. "There is a spring after every winter, and a day after every night."

"And I'm worried that you don't know anyone in Tutak either."

"I actually do!"

We walk for close to two hours before we reach the point where the streams converge into a broad river. There is no snow on the ground, but an icy wind whistles in the air.

"Tutak is a large village with nasty dogs," Seydou says. "We should carry a stick in case one comes after us."

He takes his hunting knife from his belt and heads over to a stand of trees nearby. In the moonlight that now shines from behind a faraway peak, I gaze at the silhouette of the village. With its domed houses it resembles a watermelon field. Now and then a jackal howls or barks and the village dogs respond, letting it know that they are awake and standing guard over the chicken and sheep.

"If a dog comes running at you, beat it away," Seydou says, handing me a stick.

"I know mountain dogs. Grappling with them isn't that easy."

"Then I guess I'll have to come and drag you out from under it."

"Seydou, it's eleven o'clock," I say looking at my watch. "Everyone is sleeping by now."

"Don't worry."

As we enter the village dogs start barking from every corner. To my relief, Seydou knows his way around. Walking fast, we turn from one alley into another until he stops in front of a door and bangs on it with his stick, which sets off a dog.

"Who is it?" a man shouts.

"Anvar Khan, come leash your dog. It's me, Seydou from Qorqoch."

With the dog quiet and leashed, the man opens the door, holds up his lamp, and peers at Seydou.

"Welcome, young man! I hope Molda Khan is well," he says, and without waiting for an answer, he moves the lamp over to me. He is about fifty years old and starting to gray. He is handsome, with a high brow, strong cheekbones, large kind eyes.

"This is my friend, Farhad," Seydou says. "My good man, don't just stand there staring at us! Hurry up and open the guestroom, we are freezing."

"Come in, come in. I'll warm you up in no time."

He closes the door behind us and hurries to the guestroom. We leave our boots outside and follow him in. I sit close to the heater and watch him quickly take an armful of brushwood from a crate in the corner and start the heater. Then he leaves and returns with a kettle of water.

"Welcome, son," he says to me, putting it on top of the heater. "I woke my wife. She'll brew some tea once the water comes to a boil. No point starting the cookstove."

He exchanges pleasantries with us for a few minutes, then checks the kettle and adds more brushwood to the heater.

"Once the flames pick up, I'll throw in a log."

"Throw one in now," Seydou says. "We are chilled to the bone."

"I hope it's an auspicious matter that has you walking such a long distance at this hour and in this cold."

"We need your help, my friend," Seydou says. "Farhad's brother-in-law ran away with the girl he's in love with. They're from Tali, a village in Jawand district. I've heard the Taliban arrested the two and brought them here."

As Seydou talks, I see the expression on Anvar Khan's face change. He looks troubled. I'm suddenly afraid. I sense something dreadful has happened to Farrokh and Geesu.

He throws a couple of logs in the heater, takes the boiling kettle and says, "I'll take this to my wife and tell her to fry a few eggs and warm some bread, so you have something in your stomach."

"No, Anvar Khan," Seydou says. "We stopped in Olang-Deraz and ate. Don't trouble your wife. Tea is enough."

"Walking from there, your stomachs are empty by now. I'll tell her to fry the eggs anyway."

I can tell he is looking for an excuse to leave the room.

"No, please don't," Seydou insists, having also noticed the change in the man's disposition. "Just sit and put an end to our worries."

"You weren't as edgy as a saber before!" Anvar Khan says as he goes to the door, calls his wife, and gives her the kettle. "The sweat of your trip has yet to dry, and you want to know everything. Have your tea, then we'll talk."

I'm on tenterhooks, but there is nothing more we can say to press our host without being discourteous. The tea finally arrives, Seydou and I empty our bowls in one breath, and I say, "Well, Anvar Khan, we have warmed up, the sweat of the trip has dried, and we drank our tea."

He looks at me and without uttering a word leaves the room. A few minutes later, he comes back wearing a heavy coat and a wool hat and carrying a shepherd's stick.

"Put on your coats and come with me," he says.

Puzzled, Seydou and I both ask, "Where to?"

"Don't you want to know what has happened to them?"

He takes the lamp, we quickly get ready and follow him out. The wind is still furious, and the dogs again start barking. We walk the length of the village to a hill. Anvar Khan turns and looks at us, then starts up the hill.

"They are here," he says, stopping halfway up the slope. "Me and a few neighbors buried them."

My legs go numb. My knees buckle.

"Oh, God!"

# 18

WE LEAVE JUY GANJ by night, blindly running from Hayatullah's house down back alleys and dirt roads to some remote wasteland. We huddle behind the wall of a ruin with only my burqa to keep us warm. It is the end of September and the nights are windy and cold. I cry. Farrokh kisses me and holds my head against his chest. He tells me to be strong. I try to show him that I am, but I'm not.

He says we must wait for sunrise so we can find the main road and hail the minibuses until we find one heading to Qorquch or somewhere nearby. He says his heart tells him Negin's Baluch friend will give us safe haven. I tell him, as long as I have him, I have no fear and no sorrow.

We lie down and watch the star-filled sky. I rest my head on his shoulder and listen to his every breath.

"Farrokh, do you see God looking at us from behind the stars?"

He says nothing for a while, then quietly murmurs, "I see him, but he doesn't see us. His face is turned to the Obeidullahs and Kodadads of the world."

I silently pray. God, forgive us our sins and save us from this abyss. And I blow toward the stars. I look up at Farrokh. His eyes are brimming with tears. I see the sparkle of the stars in them.

"Geesu, I asked God for you," he says. "I asked him to at least cast a fleeting glance at you and me. I said, we are your subjects, too."

"I was always yours. Love for you was in my heart since childhood. The older I grew the deeper that love became, until one day I realized I couldn't be without you."

"I want us to be free," he dreams out loud. "To have a home, children, a few goats and sheep. To have no enemies and no enmity."

At the break of morning light, we leave. My feet are badly blistered from the night before and my plastic slippers cut into them. With every step I take, they chafe against the sores. I say nothing to Farrokh. The terrain is all thorn bushes, rocks, and clumps of dirt. We walk until I cannot tolerate the pain anymore. I take off the slippers and throw them aside. Farrokh looks at my feet and gasps.

"I'd rather die than see you so badly hurt."

He sits me down, cleans my feet with his shirt and kisses them. I want to tell him, Let's die here. Let's go to Murghab river and give ourselves to the waves. It is better than falling into the hands of the likes of Obeid.

"I'll carry you on my back to the main road," he says, getting up. "I won't let you walk another step."

But where is the main road? Neither one of us know. Now and then he stops and looks around, and without a word he turns and changes direction. He puts me down when he's exhausted and rests for a while. And we continue. The yearning to end our lives grows stronger in me.

"Farrokh," I say kissing his neck. "Let's go to the Murghab river."

He puts me down and grips my head between his hands.

"Geesu! Don't lose hope. Just pray that we make it to Qorquch.... I will take you away from here. I will take you where no jackal can get his hands on you. Don't speak of the river again."

"Perhaps there is another life for us after death. A good life. Without villains."

"Have courage, Geesu," he says, picking me up again. "We will have a different life. The life you want.... See that row of trees in the distance? That's the main road."

We stop for him to rest a few more times. I look at him and think, Farrokh, am I worth all this misery you're putting yourself through?

As though having read my mind, he says, "Geesu, I wouldn't trade you for a mountain of gold and lapis."

At the main road, he puts me down under a tree and says, "I'll stop the minibuses and tell the drivers you are my ailing mother, suffering and in need of a doctor."

I nod and lower my face veil. He walks to the edge of the road and looks in both directions.

Where will you take me, I think to myself. If our birthplace became our hell, where in this country can be our heaven? These men are everywhere. There is no escaping them. And the day we fall into their hands, they will tear us to pieces and roar in victory. To them we are precious prey. They believe punishing us will wash away their sins. They believe God will forgive their wrongdoings and reward them in the hereafter.

As the sun rises to brighten the sky, there are more cars on the road. Farrokh waves at a few station wagons and minivans, but they speed by. A cargo truck, rattling and spewing black fumes stops.

"Uncle, I have my sick mother with me," Farrokh says to the old driver. "If you take us as far as Qorquch, I'll pay you well."

The man says he can take us to the crossroads outside Qorquch, from there it's only a half-hour walk. Farrokh reaches into his pocket and gives the man two hundred afghanis.

"It's enough, son," he says. "You've overpaid. Bring your mother."

Farrokh picks me up and hurries to the truck. The driver's young assistant pulls up the hood of his jacket, ties the drawstrings under his chin, and goes to sit in the back. Farrokh puts me on the passenger seat, hides my feet under the hem of my Burqa, and climbs in between me and the driver.

"All clear," the assistant shouts from the back. "Go."

"If you don't mind me asking, where are you from?" the old man asks as he puts the truck in gear. "You don't look like you're from around here."

"You're right, Uncle, we're not," Farrokh tells him. "We were visiting family."

The old man says no more and focuses on the bumpy road. Some time later, after he has carefully steered the truck around a ridge and the road ahead is straight, he starts to talk.

"Who are you going to in Qorquch? The healer?"

"Yes," Farrokh says.

"The sahib really does have a healing hand. Many years ago, I had awful stomachaches. No doctor or medicine did any good. But he gave me incantations to soak in water and drink. It was like pouring water over fire. Never had a stomachache again. . . . What is troubling your mother?"

"Um, well . . .," Farhad stammers. "It's some women's problem. I don't know about these things."

And changing the subject, he asks, "Where are you from?"

"Bala Murghab. And all I own is this wreck. I've had it for twenty years. It has good bones. If it were one of those flimsy Japanese trucks, it would have been done for a long time ago. The damn thing is Russian. . . . I haul stone, brushwood, logs, sometimes sheep and goats. I stop in the winter. Death lurks on these mud and muck roads when they freeze and hides under the snow."

We pass several government and Taliban checkpoints in close proximity of each other. Despite the clang and clatter of the old truck, neither group stops us.

The driver carries on, but I no longer listen. My mind drifts to Tali. I long for my parents. I imagine Mother sitting in the kitchen, crying and talking to me. They uprooted you, she says, drove you away. My girl, I didn't know you had given your heart to Farrokh. Why didn't you tell me? I was deaf to his flute-playing, I didn't understand. If I knew a Talib was lying in wait for you, I would have put your hand in his, despite your father. And now, who can I turn to? There's no one and no place for someone like me to go to for help, for solace.

My heart breaks for her. I know that with me gone, the hardships of life have become even more unbearable for her. I fear for my father. I fear the harm Obeid could do to him. I imagine him wounded, bleeding. What happened to you, I ask him. He spits out blood and says, His father be damned, he beat me to near death. He broke me. Why did you go and leave me at the mercy of this ruthless creature?

"No!" I suddenly scream.

The truck screeches to a stop. Farrokh grabs me by the shoulders. "What is it? What's wrong?"

"I suddenly panicked," I whisper. "I'm sorry."

"My heart almost stopped!" the old man says, taking a deep breath. "When you see the healer, tell him that she is also possessed. . . . We don't have far to go now. The road to Qorquch is after the bend up ahead."

Farrokh nods and he drives on. At the crossroads, he pulls over to the side of the road.

"You can walk from here," he says.

Farrokh helps me out of the truck and carries me to a narrow creek near the road.

"God bless you, Uncle," he calls out to the old man. "May God keep you and your truck."

The old man smiles and drives off.

"Wait here, Geesu. I'll stop another car," Farrokh says, hurrying back to the road.

The sun is pleasant. I wish I could sit here until my bones warm up and the pain is gone. I raise my face veil. Even a few minutes is a blessing. I look at the creek. Farther away, it snakes its way to a treed area and the edge of a village, and then it disappears. I can see the domed roofs of a few mud houses. Flocks of birds are circling the sky, diving and soaring as one, never breaking formation. Qorquch is so close. I look at my feet. I wish I could walk. Farrokh wouldn't need to wait by that dangerous road, and we could take a shortcut through the trees and find Mahakan.

"Are you all right?" Farrokh asks, standing over me. "Are your feet any better?"

"I'm all right," I say quietly. "As long as your shadow is my shelter, I'm all right."

"We have to wait a while, at this hour of the morning all the cars, trucks, and minivans are full."

"Do you want some bread?" he says, remembering the loaf tucked under his belt.

I'm hungry, but I don't want to eat. Not here.

"No. When we reach the village."

We hear several cars screech to a stop one after the other. We turn to the road. Three pickup trucks crammed with armed Talibs. Paralyzed, we watch them jump out. Three of them run toward us with their machine guns at the ready and their fingers on the trigger. My heart hammers against my ribs, telling me we are caught, there is no escape.

One of the men steps forward and in an unfamiliar accent asks Farrokh, "Who are you? Where are you taking this woman?"

"She's my wife," Farrokh stutters. "We're going to Qorquch."

"Where are you from?"

Farrokh hesitates.

"I asked you a question," the Talib shouts and beats Farrokh on the chest with the butt of his machine gun. Farrokh falls back. The man kicks him in the face. Blood trickles from his nose.

"Stop!" I scream. "In the name of God, stop!"

The man ignores me, grabs Farrokh by the collar and pulls him up.

"What is your name and where are you from?" he shouts in his face. "Speak or I'll break every bone in your body. One by one."

Farrokh says nothing. The man lets go of him and kicks him in the stomach. Farrokh tumbles into a dry gutter and groans. The Talib stands over him and raises his machine gun again.

"Stop, you stinking filth!" I hysterically scream, leaping to my feet. "I'll tell you. His name is Farrokh. He's from Tali. So am I. You animal! Go ahead, beat us, shoot us, stone us, cut us into—"

The strike intended for Farrokh lands on my chest. I crumble to the ground. Spasms of pain dart through my ribcage. I turn to Farrokh. He is looking at me.

"Contact Obeidullah Khan. Tell him we found them," the man orders the other two Talibs standing a few steps back.

"Geesu," Farrokh moans. "This is the end. You were right. Murghab river was—"

"Farrokh *Khan*," the man snarls. "One more word and I will leave you no dignity in front of this wretch. Do you understand?"

A few minutes later, the two Talibs hurry back and say, "We are to take them to Tutak and hold them at the outpost as your guests until he comes."

They tie Farrokh's hands and feet and throw him in the back of one of the pickup trucks. They come back with a large burlap sack and shove me into it.

"This one is delicate," one of them says, laughing. "Put her on the passenger seat."

❧

My chest throbs. I think my ribcage is broken, but I no longer care. All I fear for is Farrokh. All I see is Farrokh falling and blood streaming from his nose. I pray. I pray these savages don't torture us. I pray they kill us quickly. Tears roll down my face.

Sometime later, the pickup truck stops. They carry me into a room, put me down on the floor, and untie the sack.

"Get out," one of them barks.

I try to crawl out, but my burqa is tangled around my legs. The man grabs the end of the sack, yanks it up and throws me out on my head. I'm instantly dizzy and disoriented. Their voices become hollow and protracted. I don't understand what they are saying. Then there's silence. They have left.

I hear the gentle voice of a woman.

"Girl, are you all right?"

For a moment, I imagine it's my mother.

"My girl, get up."

I don't want to. I want to lie here and wait for death. She takes my arms and pulls. Pain lashes inside me.

"Don't," I groan. "Leave me be."

She ignores me, sits me up, and folds back my face veil. The room smells of spat out dipping tobacco, urine, and mold. I feel nauseous. I look at her hands. They are dark, boney, and coarse. I look up at her face. It's as boney and wrinkled as her hands. A lock of gray hair has escaped her black chador.

"You are so beautiful!" she says.

I look down to avoid her eyes. Something about her makes me uneasy.

"I'm Nuroldin's mother. He told me to come take care of a woman prisoner."

I dislike her even more knowing she is mother to one of those brutes.

"Don't worry. They've brought other women here, but they have always resolved the matter quickly and let them go. When both sides sit and talk, they will find a solution."

I don't believe her.

"How is my Farrokh?" I ask without looking at her. "Have you seen him?"

"Who is Farrokh?"

"They brought us here together."

She goes behind me, holds me under my arms and drags me back onto a grimy mattress. Then she brings a pillow for me to lean on.

"Did they arrest you for adultery?"

"No, for being in love."

She stares at the rug, as though her mind has drifted to some distant time and place. Every woman has a secret in her heart that she will take to her grave. She is thinking of hers.

"Where are you from?" she asks.

"Tali."

"You ran away with him?"

"Yes. . . . Do you know when they will kill us?"

"Shame, shame," she sighs.

Perhaps she knows our fate, perhaps she has witnessed the fate of many who were brought here.

"What is your name?" I ask her.

"I don't have a name," she chuckles. "Everyone calls me Nurak's *naneh*."

"What did they call you before you became a mother?"

"I don't remember any more. I have even forgotten my mother's face. But once in a while I hear her voice. She sings, 'Senobarak a willow leaf, Senobarak an apple branch. . .'"

I reach into my pocket and take out Zubaideh's silver jewelry.

"Bibi Senobar, take these. I have no use for earrings and bangles anymore. All I want in return is news of Farrokh. And if you manage to see him, tell him Geesu said, I love you. Tell him she said, to reach the other world, we first have to die. There is no other way for us. Tell him to stand tall."

She snatches the jewelry from my hand, examines them, and stuffs them in her pocket.

"I had some like these," she says, satisfied that they are old and valuable. "I had a couple of old gold coins, too. I had saved them for my funeral and burial. I told my family to use whatever was left as alms. But Nurak sold them and bought guns."

"Never mind," she says, shaking her head. "I'll get your message to Farrokh. Now what can I bring you? Tea? Bread?"

"Nothing. I'm in too much pain to eat. My ribcage is broken and my feet are in a bad way. I pray they end my misery soon. I want to be with Farrokh."

She lifts the hem of my burqa and gapes at my feet, "What did they do to you?"

"That's from walking across the wastelands. They broke my ribs with the butt of a machine gun."

"Was it Nuroldin?"

"I don't know who Nuroldin is."

"Dark, skinny, tall."

"They all looked the same."

The door opens a crack and a man's hand holding two lengths of rope comes in.

"Mother, tie her hands and feet tight."

Senobar hurries to the door.

"Son, the poor girl can't run off anywhere. Her feet are covered with cuts and infected, her ribs are broken and she can barely breathe. If you are the one who beat her, I will never forgive you."

"It wasn't me, it was Mullah Ossman. Now take these and throw them in the corner. If you don't want to tie her up, then don't."

"Bibi Senobar," I say quietly. "Tell him to come in for a moment. I want to talk to him. I'll cover my face."

"Come in, son. The girl wants to tell you something. She is in her burqa."

He walks in and without looking at me, tosses the ropes in the corner, and squats down next to the door.

"Be quick!"

"I swear to God and to the holy Quran that we have committed no sin and no crime. We want to be husband and wife, properly, as Sharia and the law require. In what corner of this world do they arrest a couple in love and torture and murder them? We are pure, we have not committed adultery. Don't do this to us. This is savagery."

"Mother, tell her these things are not in our hands, they're in the hands of the powerful," he says as he gets up and hurries out.

Senobar closes the door and says, "My girl, he can't do anything. They're all errand boys."

I close my eyes. I'm tired of her. I want to be alone. I feel time stopped the moment the pickup trucks braked in front of us. I blame my body's clock for my agony, for stubbornly thinking I'm still alive. Senobar says something and then I hear the door open and close.

"God, why did you give us life in a land where love is a sin?"

—∽—

When I open my eyes, I see a lit kerosene lamp by the door.

"I brought you some rice," Senobar says. "Sit up and eat a little. It'll give you some strength."

I look at her. The shifting shadows from the flickering lamp distort her face. I'm burning with fever and my throat is so tight I can't utter a word.

"My girl, all this crying has left you as thin as a reed. It's enough. Pray instead. God is all-forgiving."

She holds the plate of rice closer to me.

"Now, sit up and eat. God is kind, a door may open to the good and decent, and all may be justly resolved. Do you want me to feed you?"

I shake my head.

"I cooked it myself, and I put some ghee on it. It tastes good."

She pinches a mouthful of rice with three fingers and holds it up to my mouth.

"Here. After you've eaten, I'll give you something for the pain. It will help you sleep through the night."

I push her hand away. She puts the rice back on the plate and with the same greasy fingers takes a small plastic bag from her pocket. There's a brown lump in it. She pinches off a small piece and says, "It will numb your pain and help you sleep."

I think it's barberry root extract, which I never liked. Mother used to force it in my mouth whenever I was sick. It was bitter and made me nauseous. I shake my head and turn away.

"It's opium. A tiny piece. The size of a mung bean. It's enough for you."

Opium. I wish she would give me the entire lump. I grab her hand holding the bag and point to the lump.

"No!" she says, shaking her head. "It will kill you!"

I try to say, I want to die, I want to die peacefully, with Farrokh. Give him some opium, too. No sound comes from my throat, but she reads it on my face, in my eyes.

"No. I'll have to answer to Mullah Ossman, and he has a heavy hand. What if he kills me and my son over you? Besides, it's expensive. I'm giving you this tiny bit because of the silver."

She knots the plastic bag and tucks it back in her pocket. Then she puts the opium in my mouth, brings the bowl of water, and holds up my head so I can drink. It's bitter, more bitter than barberry root extract. I swallow it and put my hand on her back as my thanks.

"I'll leave the tray in case you decide to eat. The opium will make you hungry," she says as she brings a blanket and throws it over me. Its stench churns my stomach.

Senobar pushes the tray aside and takes the lamp to leave.

No! Take the tray and leave the lamp, I need the kerosene to burn myself.

Perhaps I haven't spoken. She closes the door behind her.

My eyes are heavy. I am limp and numb. My throat is no longer tight, but my chest still hurts as I breathe.

I see light through my closed eyelids and reality returns.

"Farrokh," I moan.

Instead, Senobar answers.

"Wake up, it's past sun-up."

I slowly raise my head and force open my eyes. The tray is still there. Now there's a red watering can next to it.

"Do you have any news of Farrokh? Did you give him my message?

She doesn't answer.

"My girl, get up and do your ablutions. The leaders haven't changed their mind. Their chicken has one leg. Sharia law must be enforced. Obeidullah and Mawlawi Khodadad came last night. I've been told to have you ready before noon prayers. They will send for you. So get up, wash, say your prayers, and repent."

Then death is near and Farrokh is not far.

Then this misery will soon end.

"Bibi Senobar, I will wash and I will say my prayers, but I have nothing to repent. Let those two savages repent and beg God's forgiveness for murdering innocent people in his name. This is not God's will, this is not Sharia. . . . May God bless you, Bibi Senobar. Thank you for the opium. Now make me even more indebted to you and give me another piece. And don't worry, I'm already dead."

She shakes her head and helps me stand up.

"We will go slowly so your feet don't start to bleed again," she says, taking my arm.

At the door she picks up the watering can and calls out, "Open up. The girl is going for ablutions."

"Is she covered?"

Senobar sighs and leans me against the wall to go and bring my burqa.

"Open the door, she's covered now."

There are a few armed Talibs in the hallway. Nuroldin is among them. I wish he were alone so I could ask him about Farrokh.

"Mother," he says. "Take her to the back."

She walks me to the end of the hallway and opens a door to the outside.

"Walk slowly. Be careful," she says, holding my hand as we go down a few steps and around to the back of the building.

I take off my burqa and hand it to her.

As I rinse my face, I ask, "Where is my Farrokh?"

"On the other side. The men's section."

"I wish I could see him before I die."

Walking back to the room, I look down at my feet. They no longer ache and burn. I think my soul has accepted death and my demise has begun.

Nuroldin is waiting for us at the door. "Mother," he says. "Give her a prayer rug. When she's done praying, tie her hands and feet. I'll come for you."

Inside, Senobar takes a prayer rug from the alcove and spreads it on the floor facing Mecca.

"I'll give you a larger piece before he comes. It's best you don't feel anything. And if you pass out, they'll think you've fainted from fear."

I say my prayers sitting down. I pray for Farrokh and myself. In the end, I murmur, "God, bless us with an easy death. Don't let us suffer more than we have."

I get up and go to Senobar. She gives me a larger piece of opium and brings the bowl of water.

"Quickly. The cretins will be here any minute."

I put it in my mouth. I welcome its bitterness. I drink the water and sit on the mattress for Senobar to bind my wrists and ankles. When she's done, she helps me to my feet. I try to shuffle to the door, but it's impossible. I stop and look down at my feet. They are already turning blue.

"I think I made it too tight," Senobar says.

"I think you did," I say, smiling at her.

She kneels down and loosens the rope, then goes to the door and calls her son. A man says he is not there, that Obeidullah sent for him. A few minutes later, Nuroldin returns.

"Mother, is she in hijab? I need to come in."

Senobar pulls down my face veil and calls him. Nuroldin sits in the same spot he sat the day before. He looks pale and agitated.

"Your mother has talked of your pure heart," I tell him. "Say what you came to say."

"I don't know the Talibs who have come from other places," he says. "But I pleaded with Mullah Ossman to find a solution, to come up with some sort of settlement. He said, 'The problem these two are facing has deep roots and I'm not powerful enough.'"

"Thank you, but your mother has already told me their decision. What did you really come here to say?"

"Well," he says hesitantly, "Obeidullah has asked me to give you a message."

"Then speak."

"He said it's not too late. He said if you repent and say that the boy led you astray and deceived you into running away with him, he will ask Khodadad to issue a fatwa of absolution for you."

"Interesting!" I chuckle. "What a curious version of Sharia law that can be changed with a lie. Please tell him, my answer is no. Tell him I said I will not sell myself, nor will I disgrace my love."

"So," Nuroldin says, looking up at me, "you won't agree."

"No."

"They will stone you."

"I understand."

He sighs and gets up.

"Mother, has she said her prayers?"

"Yes," Senobar says, staggering to her feet.

"Did you take opium again?"

"I needed it. I needed to dull my anguish, feel unburdened. My heart has been a bowl of blood ever since I realized they're going to take this girl's life."

Nuroldin shakes his head and turns to me. "Are you sure?" he asks again.

"Yes. I am."

The opium is seeping into my veins. I understand what Senobar means by feeling unburdened. I am calm, at peace. I sit quietly awakening memories of Farrokh, of life in Tali. I find myself smiling. I don't know how much time has passed when Nuroldin knocks on the door again.

"Mother, it's time."

"Her feet are still tied."

"Untie them. But not her hands."

Senobar frees my ankles and helps me up. I feel light. The pain is gone. My chest no longer hurts when I breathe. A few armed guards follow us as we walk down the hallway and exit the building.

The scene outside is surreal. Several hundred Talibs, all dressed in white, have gathered to watch and celebrate Sharia law being enforced. Their appearance and clothes are strangely clean. The moment they catch sight of me and Senobar, cries of "*Allah o Akbar*" rise and they make way for us. In a clearing further ahead, a few pickup trucks packed with armed Talibs in their usual bedraggled guise are parked alongside each other. I sigh and think, if only they had bathed for the occasion. I giggle.

Senobar squeezes my arm. "Girl, have you lost your mind? Stop it! There's still time. Tell Obeid you were deceived, led astray."

"Mother Senobar, God bless you for the opium."

I see Obeidullah and Mawlawi Khodadad sitting together on a carpet not far from the pickup trucks. There's a white shawl draped over Khodadad's head and he's wearing his usual dark glasses.

"They've brought her?" Khodadad asks as we approach them.

"Yes," Obeidullah says, staring at me. "She's here."

"Has she performed ablution and prayed?"

"Yes, Mawlawi Sahib, she has," Senobar replies.

"Is she penitent?"

"No, I am not," I say loudly. "What should I repent? The fact that I did not want to be forced into marrying this man and escaped with the one I love? Where in Sharia law does it say that two people who want to be husband and wife should be put to death? Where does it say that firing a few bullets makes a girl your property? Mawlawi, you are the one who should repent, who should beg forgiveness. God didn't blind you! Simin—"

Khodadad starts shouting out suras as loudly as he can and Obeidullah quickly waves for Senobar to take me away. The crowd jeers and hoots as she pulls me in another direction. I suddenly find myself in an open area encircled by the crowd. I see Farrokh. He is standing shoulder deep in a narrow pit. His eyes are on me, but they are stripped of their soul. I quicken my steps, pulling Senobar along.

"Farrokh!" I scream. "My love, hold your head high. Don't be afraid. We will soon be together."

"Shut her up!" a man yells over the uproar.

"Throw the wretch in!" another hollers.

Senobar stops. We are in front of the pit dug for me. I look at her. She is frozen, her eyes fixed on the hollow at our feet.

"Push the hussy in!"

Senobar is clutching my arm, unable to move. I see a man separate from the crowd and race toward us. In a split second he shoves Senobar aside and kicks me in the back. I fall in.

Shouts of "Allah o Akbar" rise and rocks hail down on us. I am strangely calm, unafraid. I turn to where Senobar fell. I see her running away with her arms shielding her head. My torso jerks with every rock that strikes me. I look at Farrokh and groan at the sight of his body lurching. I hear his screams through the roar of the crowd.

"Farrokh!" I cry out as loudly as I can. "I leave you in God's hands. Never forget that I love you."

He shows no reaction. Perhaps my voice was lost in the mayhem. Perhaps those words never left my lips. His skull is cracked. Blood is streaming down his temples and forehead.

"Farrokh, no rock can separate our hearts. Die in peace, my love."

And I pray. God, take back the life you gave me and don't let me see Farrokh tortured. Don't let me see my beloved broken. Don't let me hear my heart wail.

A rock strikes my temple. Salty blood fills my mouth and throat. My body shakes. My vision blurs.

I think God heard me.

# 19

MAHAKAN SETS DOWN the tray laden with a bowl of watermelon, a plate of pumpkin seeds, a large teapot, and tea bowls. She hands a soft pillow to Kowsar and sits, cracking seeds between her teeth and talking about anything and everything. Zubaideh has drifted to sleep, and Mahakan wants to while away the night with Kowsar, waiting for Farhad and Seydou to return. She talks about herself, about Negin and her brother's love for her. Kowsar tells her about Tali and its people, about the school, Teacher Sadeq, Nadim Khan and his books. She talks about Khodadad, Obeidullah, and the plague of opium in the valley. All the while, Farrokh and Geesu are ever present in her mind. Sometimes she stops midsentence staring at some unknown spot.

As dawn breaks, Farhad and Seydou arrive. As gently as they can, they share the news they bear. Kowsar wails and plunges into that gray abyss. Zubaideh rubs her feet, Farhad lays her head on his lap and strokes her hair, caresses her face. Mahakan makes sweet sherbet and spoons it into her mouth. But Kowsar has no desire to waken to reality.

It is early evening when she regains consciousness. She opens her eyes and looks at Farhad sitting beside her.

"Let's leave," she quietly says. "It's over. Our search is over."

A few minutes later, she slowly sits up. She feels lightheaded and her vision is still slightly blurred. A painful lump throbs in her throat.

"Without my brother and Geesu, this world is not worth a grain," she says. "Farrokh was of my being, Geesu was of my soul. How easily they killed them."

Zubaideh and Farhad silently cry, knowing that the news has broken Kowsar. Sensing that the ants, the ashes, and the gray are now ingrained deep inside her and will never leave. Mahakan blankly stares at a flower on the carpet. Seydou stands in the corner.

Kowsar's thoughts turn to her parents, to Geesu's parents. How is she to take the news to them? With what words is she to tell them of how their son and daughter died? How can she and they live with this pain? Life has lost meaning. Everything seems hollow and empty. She knows she must return home.

"Farhad, we should leave," she says. "Mahakan, Seydou Khan, I am grateful to you. I will never forget your kindness. I hope someday I can repay the compassion and generosity you have extended to us."

Mahakan gets up and draws open the curtains. The sun is slowly setting.

"May God rest their souls in peace," she says, looking up at the sky. "It will soon be dark. I won't let you leave tonight. I will not allow you to travel these roads in the dark. Stay the night, and in the morning I will wish you safe travels."

Kowsar looks at Farhad and Zubaideh. They nod, knowing Mahakan is right.

The beautiful Baluch girl kisses Kowsar and says, "Let me be your hostess one more night. You and I may never see each other again. Stay the night and go in the morning with no regrets in our hearts."

She gets up to leave for the kitchen when there's a knock on the door.

"My girl, if no one is observing hijab, I would like to come in."

"It's my father," Mahakan says. "He wants to see you."

Kowsar quickly dries her tears and tidies herself, Zubaideh straightens her scarf, and they all stand up.

"You are welcome, Father," Mahakan says, opening the door. "We have no one observing hijab."

"*Ya Allah*," Molda Khan says as she takes his cane and leans it against the wall.

"Hold my hand, my dear. I'm afraid of this door saddle. It has tripped me to the floor several times."

She helps her father through the door and to a floor cushion. Kowsar looks at him with curiosity. His thick hair and long beard are the color of snow, and his moustache curls up from where it meets his beard. The years have left his face wrinkled and his cheeks hollowed. Yet, his eyes are as piercing as the eyes of an eagle.

"Father, our guests are in mourning," Mahakan says, tucking a bolster behind him. "The God-unfearing took the lives of their loved ones."

"Yes, I know, my girl. Seydou has told me everything. Shame, shame. Who should I complain about to God? For forty years now, all there is, is news of death, violence, and war. May God have mercy on us."

He sighs and grows quiet. Only now he realizes that everyone is still standing.

"Forgive me! Please sit," he says, holding out his hands, palms up. "May you live long, may God will this to be your last sorrow. Seydou said the two were coming to us for shelter when they were captured. The poor innocents! And now, all we can do is mourn."

He holds up his hands in prayer and recites verses of Quran for the deceased, and adds, "God, rest the souls of our departed. Guide the misguided down the right and righteous path. Amen."

"More lives laid to waste, youth squandered," he says, shaking his head. "Alas, I don't know why and how our world so suddenly changed. In the old days, people were kind, decent. There was no bedlam the likes of which we see. . . . I told Seydou to have sheep slaughtered and distributed to the needy. May God forgive them."

Bracing his hands on the cushion, Molda Khan pushes himself up to his feet, and says, "My girl, hand me my cane. I should go help Seydou."

"He doesn't need your help, Father!" Mahakan says as Kowsar, Farhad, and Zubaideh come to their feet.

"He does all the work. But to be honest, if I don't hover over him and pester him to do this and that and to make sure the meat is equally portioned, I will be in a fluster and unable to sit still."

"Father, our guests wanted to leave, but I have asked them to stay another night."

"It is not our custom to allow guests to travel by night," he says. "I will send you off with my prayers tomorrow morning."

Halfway to the door, he turns back and says, "If you believe there is danger awaiting you in Tali, you mustn't go. You should stay here. We Baluch would lose our heads before we let a guest lose a single strand of hair."

As Mahakan helps her father out the door, Kowsar sits, closes her eyes, and thinks about Farrokh and Geesu. The melancholy music of a flute resonates in her mind, she sees the long-tailed black nightingales and starlings circle above the trees, but shrouded in ice and icicles they have no perch to offer them.

During the night, the clouds snowed heavily for the wind to toy with, sweeping the flakes into the air and blowing them at the windshield. Leaning over the steering wheel, the minibus driver curses under his breath.

"This isn't Badghis, it's Windghis," he says, as though talking only to console himself. "Snow came long before winter is due, making life miserable for the poor. Much of what they planted is now buried under snow and their sheep have no water or food in the mountains."

Farhad holds Kowsar's hand as she stares out the window, her spirit drained, her drive and desires extinguished. The minibus crawls ahead, taking her to where she imagines is a tortured valley, where living will be a sharp-toothed file grating away at life.

Farhad wants to speak, to say something, but no words come to him. Now and then he turns and looks at her, knowing that the shadow of the devastating blow will never leave her. Still, he puts his faith and trust in time to return his passionate and ambitious Kowsar to him.

"Uncle, after you've dropped off the other passengers, take us as far as Tali," he says as they approach Jawand. "I have my mother with me. She can't walk through all this snow."

"It'll be two hundred afghanis," the driver says, looking at him in the rearview mirror.

"The snow turned you into a cutthroat?" Zubaideh snaps.

The other passengers get off at the stop in Jawand, and the driver heads for the valley. As the plain spreads before them, Kowsar imagines Farrokh and Geesu running across it in the dark of night. Terrified, they fall and rise, and gasp for air. They run but arrive nowhere.

"Come, Kowsar," Farhad says. "We've arrived."

Kowsar jolts out of her thoughts and looks at him and Zubaideh. She has neither the will nor the power to climb out of the minibus. Farhad pulls her to her feet, straightens her burqa, and lowers her face veil.

"Come, my girl, we're home," Zubaideh says. "There's a lot of ice. Farhad will hold our hands and we'll slowly go down the trail."

A few steps away from the minibus, they can see Tali under a blanket of snow below them. A graveyard swathed in a shroud, Kowsar thinks. She stops, suddenly afraid of going there.

"Farhad!"

"What is it?"

"Remember you said you will take me to Herat or Kabul after we're married?"

"Yes, I remember."

"I know you don't have the energy or the means to take me to either right now. But take me to Qala-e Naw, to Wasima, instead."

"What are you talking about? We just got home! Who's Wasima!?"

376

"She's a writer from Badghis. Remember, I bought her book at Haji Zaman's bookstore when we went there for my wedding dress."

"Why do you want to see her? Kowsar, I don't understand!"

"I want her to write the story of the girls from Tali. We are all from Tali, all of us alike, cut from the same cloth. . . . Farhad, I'm afraid of this village. Please, don't ask me to go back! I will die in that place of gloom and sorrow."

Lost and perplexed, Farhad looks at his mother and again at Kowsar. He feels his life is about to crumble around him. Forever the one to free him from uncertainty, Zubaideh takes what's left of her money and puts it in his hand.

"Go, Farhad. Go be a man for your wife. Go and make this one wish of hers come true. . . . Hurry before the minibus leaves."

❧

"Let's take a room at Golab Inn before we go looking for Wasima."

"No, Farhad. Let's go to Teacher Sadeq's house first. Hopefully we'll be lucky this time and find him there. He might even know Wasima."

Teacher Sadeq is shocked and delighted to see them. Sitting in his guestroom Farhad and Kowsar tell him about all the people he once lived among and all that has happened since the Taliban expelled him from Tali. Kowsar tells him of her hope to go to Wasima and for her to agree to write the story of the girls of their valley.

"I know what you have suffered," he says, with tears in his eyes. "The village of Murghab, where I went to teach, suffered the same destiny as Tali. The school closed, the children were sacrificed. I went to a school in Qadis, only to see the same happen again. It has been sometime since I last taught. With my father now old and frail, I sit behind the counter at his shop, doing something that is not to my liking. But I have no other options.

"My dear Kowsar, I do know Bibi Wasima. But she moved to Kabul some years ago. If you decide to go there, my neighbor, Shir Mohammad, has a car and makes a living taking on passengers. He's a good man. I can ask him to drive you there."

"Yes, we will go there," Farhad quickly says. "It will be good for Kowsar to have a change of scenery, to be away for a while."

Surprised by Farhad's sudden eagerness, Kowsar smiles and thinks, it must be the sting of Zubaideh's words, telling him to go be a man for his wife.

❦

They spend the night at the Golab Inn and leave the next morning. Shir Mohammad is an interesting man of many stories. He has memories to share of every bend in the road, every bluff and cliff they pass.

He drives and reminisces, but Kowsar is rapt by the scenery around them. It is the first time she's traveled outside of Badghis. She sighs and thinks, if only I had seen all this beauty when my heart was not broken and filled with pain.

As they drive down from the Kotal-e Sabzak pass, the weather changes. Herat is warm and sunny, and defying autumn, the trees have kept their leaves.

"Strange country we have," Shir Mohammad chuckles. "Winter in Badghis, autumn in Herat, steamy summer in Helmand and Kandahar. And just like their weather, each has its own wars and turmoil. Just pray that we don't get trapped in the middle of some battle. A few times I got stuck in a mess of cars waiting for hours for the road to open."

For a while, there is quiet in the car. But as though disturbed by it, Shir Mohammad says, "Farhad Khan, I hope you don't mind me asking, why are you going to Kabul? Taking your wife for treatment?"

"Yes," Farhad laughs. "Taking my wife for treatment."

"You didn't take her to Mawlawi Khodadad for healing prayers?"

"No, who's Mawlawi Khodadad?"

"You mean you haven't even heard of him!?"

"No. We're from a small village far away."

"He's blind. He wasn't at first. Worked at the Department of Education in Badghis. Suffering for the sons of this land, he sat in abstinence and mortification of the flesh for so long that he went blind. He lost sight of his left eye on Qadr Night. A few years later, his right eye. . . . People even come from other countries and wait for weeks to see him. His disciples leave him no time. One day he's in Murghab, the next he's in Maghar or some other town or village. Just a few days ago he had two lawless people from Jawand stoned. Believe me, his hand is firm in upholding Sharia. If we had ten of him, this country would turn into paradise. . . ."

Kowsar no longer hears him. Her tears flow under her face veil.

"Are you all right?" Farhad whispers, worried that the driver's words will trigger another attack.

"Yes. My mouth and throat are dry. Find someplace to stop and get some water."

"We're heading into Bakwa desert," Shir Mohammad says. "There's nowhere to buy water. You should have told me to stop earlier."

"Here," he says, giving Farhad a half-empty bottle. "There's some left. Give it to your wife. And next time, remember to bring water."

"Thank you. I'm not that thirsty," Kowsar says, pushing Farhad's hand away.

"If I didn't know better, I would have thought your wife is from the city," Shir Mohammad says, laughing. "She doesn't drink from a bottle someone else has drank from. You should— Damn Satan! Just what I was afraid of. They've again barricaded the road to stop the foreigners."

There's a long line of cars up ahead and the sound of explosions in the distance. Shir Mohammad pulls over to the side of the road and thinks for a moment.

"Let them riddle each other with bullets. We'll just detour through the desert."